"Who are you?" Maggie demanded. "And what are you doing on my land?"

"I'm the new handyman. Hired on last night." His warm brown eyes would have melted butter.

"Well, I sure didn't hire you. Who did?"

"A couple of cute little girls. Your daughters, I presume?"

Maggie couldn't believe what the twins had gotten her into. Still, she couldn't help asking, "And what made you stop here?"

"Why not? This is a pretty place. You certainly need a handyman. I need a job." He smiled and leaned a bit toward her.

Maggie really wished he hadn't done that. For one thing, he was too close. His wasn't exactly a handsome face, more rugged looking. Full of personality, his brown eyes stared back at her with discernment. As if he, too, had seen the rough side of life.

Books by Lois Richer

Love Inspired

A Will and a Wedding #8
†*Faithfully Yours* #15
†*A Hopeful Heart* #23
†*Sweet Charity* #32
A Home, a Heart, a Husband #50

† Faith, Hope & Charity

LOIS RICHER

credits her love of writing to a childhood spent in a Sunday school where the King James Version of the Bible was taught. The majesty and clarity of the language in the Old Testament stories allowed her to create pictures in her own mind while growing up in a tiny prairie village where everyone strove to make ends meet. During her school years she continued to find great solace in those words and in the church family that supported her in local speech festivals, Christmas concerts and little theater productions. Later, in college, her ability with language stood her in good stead as she majored in linguistics, studied the work of William Shakespeare and participated in a small drama group.

Today Lois lives in another tiny Canadian town with her husband, Barry, and two very vocal sons. And still her belief in a strong, vibrant God who cares more than we know dominates her life. "My writing," she says, "allows me to express just a few of the words God sends bubbling around in my brain. If I convey some of the wonder and amazement I feel when I think of God and His love, I've used my words to good effect."

A HOME,
A HEART,
A HUSBAND
Lois Richer

❤ *Love Inspired*®

Published by Steeple Hill Books™

STEEPLE HILL BOOKS

Steeple
Hill™

ISBN 0-373-87050-7

A HOME, A HEART, A HUSBAND

Copyright © 1999 by Lois Richer

This edition published by arrangement with Steeple Hill Books.

® and TM are trademarks of Steeple Hill Books, used under license.
Trademarks indicated with ® are registered in the United States Patent
and Trademark Office, the Canadian Trade Marks Office and in other
countries.

Printed in U.S.A.

Trust in the Lord with all your heart and lean not on your own understanding. In all your ways acknowledge Him and He will make your paths straight.

—*Proverbs* 3:5-6

To Connie,
who persists in following her own path despite
the barriers life and other stubborn people present.
Live long and prosper!

Chapter One

"**S**he's doing it again!" Katy McCarthy whistled.

"Who's doing what?" Her nine-year-old twin sister refused to move her eyes from the computer screen.

"Mom. Getting all gussied up. That's what Grandpa calls it."

"Hmm." Keeley kept her eyes glued to the monitor and refused to be drawn by her sister's ramblings.

"I don't know why anybody would wear such an outfit," Katy muttered, peering through the grate once more. "Dresses are silly."

With a sigh of resignation, Keeley left her computer and knelt on the floor beside her sister to peer through the old-fashioned floor grate into their mother's bedroom below.

"It's that Brian guy again," Keeley whispered knowingly as she watched her mother spritz on a bit of perfume and fluff her hair around her shoulders. "She always dresses fancy whenever she goes out with him. She says she feels special then. They're in love."

Katy jumped to her feet. "Are not," she yelled, her

face red with anger. Her hands were clenched on her hips. "He's...old. She wouldn't be in love with somebody that old."

"She is," Keeley assured her with the knowledge that came from being born eight minutes earlier than her sister. "Our mother is looking for a husband, and Grandma and I think Brian is the one." She flicked her blond curls behind her shoulders just like she'd seen the stars do on TV.

"But he lives in Calgary," Katy protested, moving to sit on the bed. "He wouldn't want to drive this far every day."

"Well, duh!" Keeley grimaced at the dirt Katy had just deposited on her bedspread. "Get your feet off, Katy. You're wrecking my bed!"

Obediently Katy swung her sneakers to the floor, her mouth puffed out as she considered her sister's words. "Well, how could he live here then, Keeley, huh?" she demanded in a superior tone of voice. "Married people live together, in case you didn't know."

She watched Keeley rearrange her "cosmetics" on the little table their grandfather had made for Christmas last year. Katy knew that Keeley was waiting for her to ask the question again. Well, she wasn't going to do it! She'd sit here until her sister answered, and if that wasn't pretty soon, she was going to mess up this bed *really* good.

"I think," Keeley began quietly, twirling a shiny fat curl around one finger. "I think that if they got married, we would all live with Brian."

"In the city?" Katy shrieked, pink gum dropping out of her mouth, which now hung open. "But what about the farm? We can't leave it!" She stared out the window, aghast at this possibility.

"They'll probably sell it," Keeley said. She swallowed

the lump in her throat. She didn't want to leave, either, but not for anything would she let Katy see that. Someone had to be the grown-up around here and think of her mother's feelings.

"No!" Katy's wail and stamping feet penetrated to their mother's room below and seconds later Keeley groaned as she heard the warning knock on the wall.

"Now you've done it," she rasped angrily. "And just when Mom is all set to go out, too."

"Girls! I don't want to hear any of that going on to-night. You know that Mrs. Pettigrew has very bad nerves. She simply can't take all the bickering that the two of you indulge in," Maggie McCarthy called as she left her room to climb the stairs to her daughter's room.

Both girls knew their mother had put in a grueling day today, especially when Billy Wolf, their always-dependable farmhand, hadn't shown up for work.

In fact, it had been a hard week. Seeding time was always tough when you lived on a farm. That was partly why Keeley wanted her mother to go out tonight. Maybe then she'd feel better, laugh more. Mom never laughed much anymore. And she never seemed to have time to dress up really pretty, not unless Brian was coming.

"Wow! You look beautiful, Mom." Katy raced over, baseball glove dangling from one hand, to give their mother a hug. "Where are you going?"

"Brian has invited me to dinner and the opera," Maggie told her daughter. "And for once I'm going to accept the invitation. That section by the bay is too wet to work tonight anyway. It needs a little longer to dry."

"What's the op-era?"

Keeley groaned. Katy was always full of questions.

"Singing. There's a story and the singers tell it in music." Maggie brushed the golden tumble of curls off

Katy's red face and shook her head at the pink bubble. "Get rid of the gum, Katy. You know it's hard on your braces."

"I hate braces," Katy complained as she tossed the wad into a nearby garbage can. "But I like music. Still, it's a funny name. Sounds like operate." She considered that for a moment and then whirled around. "Hey, maybe I could go with you guys to this op-era?"

"Uh, I don't think so, Katy." Keeley grinned at her mother. "You wouldn't like it. It sounds like screeching and screaming to me. Worse than cows bawling."

"Yes, but *I* might like it." Katy sniffed haughtily.

Keeley felt like bopping her sister on the head. Couldn't the child see that her mother and Brian needed time together? Just then the doorbell rang. That would be Brian, and Keeley knew he hated waiting.

"Go and have a good time, Mom. Just relax and enjoy yourself." Keeley could see the questions forming on Katy's face and decided to get her mother out of there. Quick. Before her sister blew it. "Forget about the farm tonight and enjoy the opera. We'll be fine, won't we, Katy?" She hustled her mother toward the stairs.

"Yes, well, all right. Thank you, dear. Good night, girls." Maggie looked a little puzzled but she paused just long enough to kiss each of them tenderly. "Get to sleep early, will you, Keeley? And you too, Twenty Questions. We've got lots to do tomorrow."

"Aw, Mom. It's Friday night!" Katy groaned.

"We'll go straight to bed, Mom. Don't worry. Just have fun." Keeley motioned for her sister to be quiet as they waited for their mother to leave.

Shaking her head, Maggie finally slipped downstairs to greet her date. Keeley managed to keep Katy quiet until they heard Brian's low voice reply and the sound of the front door closing.

"Come on," Keeley ordered, heaving a sigh of relief. She dragged Katy over to the window and told her to wave as Maggie looked up. At last the couple drove away in Brian's brand-new silver-gray Mercedes and Keeley could relax. Only then did she meet her sister's frown with a smile.

"Maybe he'll propose tonight," Keeley whispered softly. "If they got married, Mom could take it easy for a while. Brian's got lots of money and a nice place in Calgary."

"So what?" Katy yelled, fists clenching by her side. "I don't care what you say—I am not leaving this farm. Ever!" She hiccuped down a sob. "Somehow we've got to come up with a way for us all to stay here." With an angry glare at everything in the frilly pink-and-white bedroom, Katy stomped out and raced across the hall to her own sanctuary, loud sobs punctuating her flight.

Keeley ignored it. She had to. There were important things to focus on right now. Later on, when her twin had calmed down, she'd collect Katy and go to the barn with her. A few minutes among the horses and her sister would listen to reason. They needed to stick together now more than ever if they were going to find a way to make her mother happy.

Of course, staying on the farm *would* be nice, but it wasn't necessary. Not if leaving meant that Mom could smile more often and worry less. She and Katy could manage—they'd have to!

"But, oh God, please don't make us have *him* for our daddy," Keeley prayed. "In fact, we don't even really need a daddy. Maybe you could just get my mom a big strong man who could be our new farmhand? That would be good enough.''

Grady O'Toole steered carefully around the series of potholes that littered the gravel road. Two flats on the camper in one afternoon and now a cracked windshield. What next?

"Why did I ask that?" he groaned, slamming on his brakes as he rounded the bend. Big, friendly, black-and-white cows stood placidly here and there, munching on the fresh spring grass.

He tried to shoo them off the road, but evidently the juicy green shoots were just too good to give up because the animals completely ignored both him *and* the truck horn.

A rambling old farmhouse sat shining in the twilight of the evening. Grady figured that decrepit monstrosity was about a quarter of a mile away and since it looked like his only option, he decided to go for it. Grabbing his jacket and locking the truck, he headed off down the rough road, his snakeskin-booted feet protesting at yet another trek into the unknown.

A little girl answered the door. She was a bit of a thing with ruffled blond hair and the biggest blue eyes Grady had ever seen.

"Is your daddy home?" he asked, smiling even as he wondered who such a dirty kid belonged to. She didn't look unkempt, just as if no one bothered to wash her face lately. Surely she couldn't be alone.

Of course, Grady reminded himself dourly, he was in the boonies. It was likely that no one in this backwoods ever locked their door, and it would be easy to let a kid run free and wild instead of fencing everything in.

"My dad?" She shook her head decisively. "No. He's gone."

"Well, how about your mother?" Grady sincerely hoped the mother was one of those big, capable types who would take five minutes to corral the animals and let him get on his way to the nearest campsite. He was beat.

"Mom's out. On a date with Brian."

Grady jerked backward, staring at the child in stunned amazement. "I beg your pardon?"

"She went on a date," the little girl enunciated. "In Calgary. Someplace where they do lots of singing—really loud singing. Mom had on her special clothes, you know?"

Grady grasped at straws, wondering vaguely if he should have stayed with the cows. "Uh, maybe I—I could talk to someone else at home?" he stammered.

"My sister's home. Yeah, I guess you can talk to her. I have to get her though. She's on the Internet. Again. Keeley!"

The sudden bellow nearly deafened him and Grady stepped backward only to find the little girl's fingers clutching his sleeve.

"Come on," she invited. "Don't let the mosquitoes in. Hey, do you know where mosquitoes go when it rains?" She was studying him seriously.

Grady frowned and then shook his head stupidly. "Sorry."

"I didn't think so," the little girl muttered in disgust. "Nobody knows that one." She sighed heavily. "Wait here. I'll have to go upstairs and get her. When she gets on that computer, Keeley doesn't hear *anything*."

She whirled away and was gone in a flash, leaving Grady standing there wishing he'd taken the four-lane highway back to Calgary instead of rambling down some back road. The whole scene reminded him too much of a future he'd never have, and memories of that loss were the last thing he needed today.

"Did you want to see me?"

He glanced down to find the little girl back in front of him, with a carbon copy standing curiously beside her. So much for the older sister. Grady glanced from one to the other in amazement.

"Boy, you two really look alike. Hi, Keeley, I'm Grady." He held out his hand and engulfed hers in it. "And your name is?"

"Katy," muttered the one who had opened the door. "But how could you tell us apart? No one ever can."

"Really?" Grady said, raising his eyebrows. "It's quite easy, actually. You're not really alike at all."

"Of course we are." Katy frowned. "We're identical twins."

"Yes, of course." He grinned. "But I meant that inside you're different. For instance, Keeley likes computers but you like baseball, right?" Katy stared at him in amazement and Grady smiled. "And I'll bet that Keeley likes blue ribbons in her hair and you don't like any."

"How did you know that?" Keeley asked open-mouthed, twirling a blond curl with one finger as she studied him.

"Oh, I just know. Are you two here alone?" He glanced behind them searching for an adult. Surely no one would leave two small children alone at night, in the country.

"Just for a few minutes," Keeley told him solemnly. "Our grandmother is on her way over. Mrs. Pettigrew had to leave. Her husband was hurt on the tractor. Farm accidents take a high toll on those who make their liveli…on people who live on 'em," she told him in a rush, clearly relieved at remembering most of the phrase. "They always say that on TV. Do you like TV, Mr....what was your name?"

"Grady," he reminded her, smiling and holding out one big paw. "Grady Shawn O'Toole, at your service."

"Wow!" Keeley breathed in a sigh, her eyes huge. "I never thought you'd get here so fast."

"Pardon me?" Grady frowned. He'd been on the road for weeks, eating his own cooking and bathing whenever he'd been close to water. No one knew where he was or how to find him, let alone expected him, so just what was going on here?

"You were expecting me?" he asked in a strangled tone.

"It's a miracle," she told him solemnly. "God sure does work fast."

"Uh, nobody sent me," Grady told her, flushing at the intense scrutiny of those big eyes. "Not exactly. I'm just passing through. Or I was." He shook his head, trying to remember what had brought him to the door of this strange house. Oh, yeah.

"There are cows blocking the road over there," he informed her sternly, pointing to the west where his truck and camper sat waiting. "I couldn't get through."

To his amazement, the two little girls merely nodded.

"Walton's," the tomboy said. "They're always having problems." Again the girls looked at each other and shrugged, as if he should have known.

"I'll phone them right away," Keeley told him. Clearly she was the one in charge. "Come on in. You don't have to stand in the porch."

Grady had to admit it was nice to step inside a place where his head didn't bang on the ceiling and he could stretch out on a chair without hitting something on the other side. The trailer was great but it wasn't home. Of course, he didn't have a home anymore, did he?

He scraped his boots on the braided mat, sniffed the scent of fresh-cut lilacs mixed with furniture polish and followed them through to the kitchen.

"Walton's number is busy. Have a seat."

He sank down onto the kitchen chair with relief and took a cookie from each of the blue-eyed sprites hovering on either side of him.

"So how long till your grandparents get here?" he asked, munching on the homemade chocolate-chip cookie. "Where do they live?"

"In Willow Bunch," Keeley told him, grinning. "That's about five miles away. They used to live here when my mom was a little girl. Katy's got Mom's old room."

"Didn't you come here on purpose then?" That was Katy, snapping her suspender to a beat he couldn't hear. "It's kind of far away from everything."

Grady smiled. No kidding, he felt like crowing. Just one short year ago this would have been the back of beyond.

"Actually, I left my truck and camper on that road over there." He jerked his thumb over his shoulder. "Just until the cows decide to move on. Then I can get going."

"Going? Going where?" Keeley asked anxiously. Grady felt a twinge of discomfort as her clear-eyed glance studied him. "I thought you were looking for work?"

His eyes opened wide and he stared at the two elfin-featured girls. He was prevented from answering by the rush of activity at the door. A tiny woman with bluish tinted hair cut in a fashionable chin-length bob swept through, her arms wide in welcome.

"Hello, darlings! I've come as quickly as I could.

There's someone camping on the old Kelsey trail, did you know?" She embraced the girls in a hearty hug and then turned to face him.

Grady shifted to his feet with alacrity, noticing the piercing quality of deep blue eyes that exactly matched those of the girls.

"I'm Kayleen Davis," she told him, firmly squeezing his hand with her tiny fingers. "My, you're tall. Who are you?"

"I'm Grady O'Toole...."

"He's the new handyman, Gran. And he's not camping there. He had to stop because the cows were out again." Keeley kept her hand folded in her grandmother's, as if she expected the older woman to flit away somewhere at any moment.

Mrs. Davis waved them back to their seats and dropped into one herself. "Those Waltons," she muttered, picking up a cookie from the plate and dunking it in the huge glass of milk Katy poured for her. "Thirty years I lived here and never a week went by that somebody didn't have to round up those cows."

"Uh, I'm not really..." Grady gave up trying to break into the fast-paced conversation between the children and their grandparent.

"Mom's gone with Brian, Gran. Again. Keeley says they're gonna get married and then we'll have to sell the farm," Katy accused, tears rolling down her cheeks as she clung to her grandmother's blue-veined hand.

"Well, they are," Keeley began self-righteously. "Mom's working herself to death out here. I heard Mrs. Enns say so at church last Sunday. And Mom's always tired. Mrs. Enns said if we moved to the city, our mother would have all the pretty clothes and fun times that other young women have." Grady hid a smile. She was clearly quoting the conversation verbatim. Grady watched as Mrs. Davis tenderly brushed the tomboy's disheveled curls off her tear-stained face and patted Keeley's rigid shoulder comfortingly.

"Your mother does work hard," she murmured. "Very hard. And she does need a little fun in her life. Now that Grady is here, perhaps she'll have more time to spend with you two." She smiled a warm, endearing smile that stopped Katy's weeping. "Now, then, Mr. O'Toole."

The miniature whirl of energy turned that electric blue gaze on him and Grady straightened self-consciously from his slouching position.

"We rise early around here, but I'm sure you're well used to that being a handyman and all. If you want to drive your rig over by that weeping birch, you can park there and we'll run a cord out to it. Maggie, my daughter, will fill you in on the particulars in the morning." She waved her arm and the children pushed away from the table obediently, brushing her cheek with a kiss.

"Right now, however, my granddaughters need to get their sleep. I know Maggie has a list of chores planned out for them tomorrow. Away you go, girls."

And they did, Grady noticed in surprise. In about twenty seconds, they had pressed smothering kisses on their grandmother's porcelain skin and flown up the stairs.

"Mrs. Davis, I really don't think…"

"No, young man." She smiled. "You probably don't. I've noticed that about a lot of young men these days. But there is no point discussing this any further tonight. It's almost time for the news and I always watch that at ten." She waved her tiny birdlike hands toward the door.

"Away with you now. I'll try the Waltons' again. We'll have those cows moved in a jiffy. Get your rig into position and get yourself bedded down for the night. Maggie will deal with you in the morning.''

Shrugging, Grady did exactly as he was told, amused at the way everyone assumed he was here looking for work. Well, it wouldn't hurt to camp here for one night, although he couldn't help thinking that Maggie would probably be less than interested in taking on a hired hand after her evening on the town. He doubted she'd be much of a boss anyway. Too interested in having fun, no doubt.

Which was a good thing, he decided later, lying in his trailer and staring out into the barely dark sky. He wasn't looking for a job anyway. Not now. What he really wanted to do was get back to Calgary and find out what was happening with his company. But of course, that was impossible. He was going to have to do as old Reverend Holden had advised him and wait on God to show him the next step.

''Stand on the promises of God, son,'' the older gent had advised, his hand firm on Grady's shoulder. ''You've had a tough time of it but there is a reason behind it all. You've got to steer a steady course now and concentrate on letting go of the stress. Worry never produces anything but fear.''

The advice was sound and Grady had been glad of the past few months and the income that had let him travel where and when he wanted. How many times had he sat beside an isolated brook or mountain stream and reveled in the wonder of God's creation? But lately he'd chafed at the long hours of being alone. Maybe God wanted to use him in this little backwater. Who knew? He'd just have to trust that, sooner or later, the plan would become clear.

''It would sure be nice if it was sooner,'' he muttered,

grinning to himself. He needed to set his mind on something, to get involved in a project. Was this it?

A little after one-thirty, Grady's wide-open eyes riveted
on the expensive gray car as it rolled into the yard. A man
got out and moved out around to the other side to escort
a slim, light-haired woman in a fitted blue dress to the
door. In the yellow glow of the yard light, Grady watched
unashamedly as the man tugged the woman into his arms.

She seemed to teeter for a few seconds on ridiculously
high heels before falling forward. Grady could see the
man's large hands slide down the woman's back and stop
at her waist.

Grady grimaced as he watched her press her hands
against the man's chest and pull back from the embrace.
The guy really must be a creep if he could stand there, in
front of the kids' windows, acting like some lovesick teenager.

And what kind of a woman would allow a man to touch
her in view of her children? So what if they were asleep?
They might wake up. Where was the woman's discretion?
He turned on his side in disgust and ignored the pair. It
reminded him too much of a past he only wanted to forget
and of the woman who had taken everything he had to
give and left him with nothing.

This might be a good place to camp out after all. He
could check on things in Calgary. There was no point in
showing up too soon and tipping his hand. Not when he
was this close to getting back what Fiona had so nearly
destroyed.

Okay, maybe he'd wait it out and play the part of farmhand. For now.

Chapter Two

"Remember, kiddo? It's supposed to be *heavenly* sunshine," Maggie McCarthy muttered softly to herself as she forced her eyes open in the bright sunlight. She made her bed, hung up her one and only good dress and tiptoed into the kitchen to make a pot of coffee. While it dripped she popped two pieces of bread into the toaster and got out the cream.

Her eyes fell on the note her mother had left taped to the cupboard, and she grimaced as she reread the word *accident*. Kayleen was even now in the spare room upstairs and Maggie rolled her eyes as she envisioned the grilling ahead of her.

Snatching up her toast and coffee, Maggie headed out to sit on the porch and enjoy the cool breeze of the morning. Her favorite willow chair was there, right where it had been ever since her father had given it to her almost eleven years ago on her wedding day.

"What could be better than sipping your coffee on a sunny spring morning with the birds singing in the bushes?'' she asked herself, drawing a breath of fresh spring air into her lungs.

A thousand answers popped into her mind, but she ignored them all. She wasn't going to think about seed bills or broken machinery right now. She sure wasn't going to think about the bank and mortgage payments that were due and past due, let alone dwell on her hope for a bumper crop. She wasn't even going to think about Brian's proposal last night. She was just going to enjoy this brand-new day and concentrate on God's promise from Psalms.

''I will bless her with abundant provisions; her poor will I satisfy with food.'' Maggie closed her eyes, allowing the words to sink in to her brain.

''Good morning.''

''Aaagh.'' Maggie swallowed the burning hot liquid and felt the stinging tears fill her eyes, obscuring the design of gray snakeskin boots standing on the porch in front of her. She let her eyes slide up blue-jean-clad calves and thighs to a wide leather belt. Then, more slowly now, over the wrinkled chambray shirt to the lean craggy good looks of a perfect stranger who stood leaning against her peeling white balustrade.

''Good morning,'' she croaked, staring.

''I don't suppose you'd be willing to share some of that coffee?'' he asked, tilting one eyebrow questioningly. ''I forgot to buy some fresh beans yesterday and I'm all out.''

''I…I suppose.'' For the life of her, Maggie couldn't think of a word to say. She watched his dark brown head tilt to one side as he grinned at her mockingly.

''Not a morning person, huh? That's okay. Of course, it might be easier if you quit partying all night and got to bed a little earlier, Mrs. McCarthy.''

She sat openmouthed as he breezed into her kitchen, poured himself a coffee and returned, carrying it in her very favorite black whale mug. Nobody used that mug but her, and then only on special occasions. When he folded himself onto the porch swing, Maggie could restrain herself no longer.

"Who are you?" she demanded furiously, glaring at him as he swung his feet up on the railing. Her railing. "And what are you doing on my land?"

"I'm the new handyman. Hired on last night." His warm brown eyes would have melted butter. "I can start anytime now, ma'am. I've been up since five."

"Five? As in a.m.?" She groaned, sinking her head into her hands and letting the heavy curtain of hair obscure her face. "Don't tell me about it. Seven-thirty is quite early enough."

Wait a minute! Handyman, she asked herself, frowning. What handyman? "Who hired you?" she demanded, wishing she could go back to the night before and refuse that last cup of cappuccino Brian had ordered for her. What imp of perversity had made her drink even more coffee?

Of course, she hadn't been able to sleep after *that*, which made getting up more difficult than it usually was, and let's face it, morning was *not* her finest hour. Maybe her mind would clear a little faster with a plain old regular-type coffee fix, she reasoned, swallowing another mouthful and wincing as it burned down her throat.

"Three little ladies who figured you were too busy partying to spend much time running this place." He tapped at a loose spindle with one foot as if for emphasis. "Appears to me they were right."

"Partying?" Maggie gave a derisive hoot of laughter at his description of the previous evening, and then grabbed her aching head as pain shafted through it. "I hardly think you can call the opera 'partying.'" She straightened and took another sip of coffee with the faint hope that it would help her withstand the scrutiny from his melting chocolate eyes.

"Opera? Yeah, right." He sounded like her father, pandering to her irrationality, Maggie fumed.

"Yes," she retorted. "The opera. A Verdi one. I can't remember which. I do remember that it was long. And it was loud. Very, *very* loud."

"Not an aficionado, then, I take it." His tone was openly mocking.

"I really don't care if you take it or leave it," she muttered angrily.

"But you would like to leave the opera behind?" he questioned. His husky voice was rich with laughter as she shook her head slightly to clear it.

"That and the cappuccinos I drank when I knew I'd already had enough of them," she grated. "My head feels like little lead bullets are pounding into it." She rubbed her thumbs against her forehead. "I can't afford to be sick," she whispered in despair. "There's too much to do."

"Like what?" he asked, leaning forward, elbows on his knees.

Maggie really wished he hadn't done that. For one thing, he was too close. For another, those crinkling brown eyes were right in front of her face and she could see the tiny lines radiating from his eyes and mouth. It wasn't exactly a handsome face, more like rugged looking. Full of personality. His eyes stared back at her with discernment. As if he, too, had seen the rough sides of life, Maggie decided.

Maggie jerked her head back and straightened the slipping line of her housecoat. "Who, exactly, are you?" she demanded huskily, and wished her foolish voice would act its age. "Why are you here looking for work?"

"Why not?" He smiled lazily, sipping his coffee. "This is a pretty place. You certainly need a handyman. I need a job."

"Sure you do," Maggie agreed, glancing across the yard at the shiny black truck and fairly new-looking trailer. "I can see that you haven't got a dime. Must have blown it all on the club cab over there. Or maybe the trailer. Those things don't come cheap. Self-contained, isn't it?"

"You're right," he agreed, brown eyes narrowing assessingly. "I saved up for a long time for that rig. And I've toured it around the southern states for the past few months. It's been a good investment."

Maggie stood up. There was no point in looking a gift horse in the mouth. If he wanted to work, she'd work him. He'd probably leave after the first hour. But that was okay, wasn't it? Then maybe she could get some peace and quiet to decide about Brian, the farm, the twins and her future. Or the lack of it!

"Fine," she told him abruptly, tightening her belt. "You can start with the horses. They need to be let out and their stalls cleaned." She filled him in on the going rate, days off and his job description. "If that's agreeable to you, you can start right away."

He nodded. "It's fine. There's just one thing. I need to take next Friday off. Personal reasons. I'll work Sunday if you want."

Personal reasons, she mused, staring at his implacable face once more. He was hiding something, something important. But what?

"I suppose that's okay, but we don't work Sundays. That's the Lord's day, and we go to church in the morning. The rest of the day is your own. If you need more time, just let me know.'' Maggie studied his lean body with a frown. ''There's a lot to do around here, you know. It won't be easy work.'' As she turned to move into the house, Maggie barely caught the softly breathed words.

''Maybe if you pitched in,'' he muttered, ''things would get done a little faster around here.''

She threw him a frosty look and kept moving, swallowing the short succinct phrases that would have explained exactly how long she had pitched in and how tired she was of being the one responsible for everyone and everything.

Maggie showered and dressed while her mind roved over the newcomer once more. Where had he come from? she asked herself again. No farmhand she had ever known wore snakeskin boots. And his hands were clean and well cared for, as if he'd had more than one manicure in his lifetime.

Hours later Maggie had more questions than answers about one Grady O'Toole. She snuck a look over her shoulder, watching as he patiently showed another knot to Katy. He was good with kids, that's for sure!

And not bad with barns, either. The horses had been curried as if by a professional, and their stables were fresh and clean. He'd repaired two fence posts and moved some bales into the barn. Maggie had also noticed the filled water troughs for the chickens and seed scattered in their yard.

Katy's high-pitched giggles forced Maggie's stare away from Grady and toward the front of the house where Kayleen sat sipping ice tea in the shade. Her mother had a smug look of satisfaction on her face that sent prickles of worry up Maggie's backbone.

''Bother,'' she muttered, rubbing her grazed knuckles

as she tossed the wrench to the ground where it couldn't do any more damage. "Why won't the thing start?"

"Problems?"

She jumped, banging her head on the metal hood as she whirled around to glare at Grady, who stood grinning behind her.

"I wish you wouldn't creep up behind people," she gritted, sucking on her throbbing, grease-stained knuckle. "And yes, you could say there's trouble. I need to finish seeding and this stupid tractor refuses to move."

"Let me look," he said, smiling, edging her aside.

"Why?" Maggie demanded. "Do you know something about farm machinery that I don't?"

He grinned that breathtaking smile that made her knees weak. "Oh, is that what this is? Farm machinery." He flicked a strand of hair out of her eyes. "I thought it was something off the ark. Like maybe an ossified woolly mammoth." He took another look at the decrepit piece of metal. "Or maybe a dinosaur."

Maggie slapped her hands on her hips, rapidly losing patience with his amused derision. "Which only goes to prove you know nothing, absolutely nothing about farming," she grated. "It isn't that old."

"Listen, lady—" he grinned, bending to pick up the wrench "—I grew up on a farm and I've fixed more machinery than you've ever seen. And nothing—" his brown eyes flicked derisively over the tractor "—nothing was ever this antiquated."

"Well, it's all I can afford right now," she told him defensively, hunching down on the grass to wait as he tinkered. "New tractors are expensive. They don't grow on trees."

"There are all kinds of programs available for farming operations to purchase equipment," Grady informed her softly. He half turned to peer down at her quizzically. "Why don't you apply for one?"

Maggie snorted. Ha! A lot he knew. "Don't think I haven't," she muttered, thumping her sneaker against the ground with force. "I've filled out more forms than I ever want to see again in this lifetime. Even the tax department doesn't have that much information on this place."

"And?" He crooked one eyebrow at her. "Where's the new tractor?"

She hung her head, resting it on her knees as the sun beamed down on them. Maggie hated telling him. Hated saying the words that denigrated her and her family, especially after she'd spent the last five years slaving over this farm.

"We're too debt heavy," she murmured. "I'm carrying some pretty big loans already."

She didn't mention that most of those loans stemmed from her husband's last purchase before his death. If they had a good year, Roger spent every dime. And the last dime he'd spent had been a doozy. All to acquire a piece of land that she didn't want, couldn't sell and hadn't the resources to farm. Inevitably she had ended up digging in deeper and deeper to cover more and more debts.

"If you factor in the transient nature of my staff and the accidents they've had around here lately…" She tilted her mouth down in wry self-mocking. "Well, I suppose no one in their right mind would lend money to this operation. I'm just not a very good risk."

"But surely your parents…"

"They help as much as they can," she told him quietly. "But my dad had triple bypass surgery in February. He's still recovering and in no condition to come back to the farm. Even if the doctors would okay it. Which they won't." She shrugged, glaring at him angrily. "Anyway, this is my job and my problem—not theirs."

He studied her intensely for several long, drawn-out moments before turning away. "We'll just have to pray that this thing works then," he murmured.

"It needs more than prayer," she told him.

"There *is* nothing more than prayer," he answered quietly, and then buried himself under the hood.

Maggie thought about that bit of theological wisdom while Grady worked silently for the next few minutes, grunting as he twisted the wrench several more turns. His hands flew over the engine, touching this and tapping that until everything seemed to meet his approval.

"You broke off some wires," he said, grinning from ear to ear. "I think I've got it. At least for now. Go ahead and try."

Maggie raised her eyebrows, well aware that no two-minute diddling with this engine was going to start it. Shaking her head, she jumped up into the seat anyway and turned the ignition. To her surprise, it coughed wildly for a moment and then caught, sputtering away. Loudly, it was true. But still running.

"I don't believe it." She exhaled, swiping a hand across her cheek to push away the strand of hair that clung. "Bessie's almost purring."

"'You will pray to Him and He will hear you,'" Grady quoted, winking. "You just need a little faith, Mrs. McCarthy."

"Faith. Right." Maggie didn't want to think about faith right now. Faith was the evidence of things hoped for. She wanted to see a little evidence that her faith was working! "Yes, well," she mumbled as she put the machinery into gear and eased up on the clutch, checking once over her shoulder to make sure the seeder was following properly behind, "I'll remember that. You can tackle some of the odd jobs around here. I'm going to do some more seeding," she called. "See you later."

"Yeah, later," Grady muttered, watching as she bounced along in the old metal seat. He rubbed his hands on the oily rag with little success. "Bessie? Whoever would call that hunk of junk a pet name?"

"My daughter would," Kayleen answered, chuckling behind him. He turned to find those intense blue eyes fixed on him. "Maggie is usually able to find joy in the smallest thing. Which is good, I suppose, given that she hasn't had much happiness lately." Her eyes brightened. "I'm just so thankful that you came along, Grady. You picked the best possible time."

"I didn't exactly plan to come out here," Grady muttered, staring down at the tiny woman.

"Of course you didn't." She chuckled again, wrapping her arm in his and leading him toward the house. "But God works in mysterious ways, don't you think?"

"Yes, ma'am, I guess He does," Grady agreed dazedly, wondering if he should blame God for his stupid decision to hang around this run-down, dilapidated place.

"Now, you've just time for a cup of coffee and some of my fresh blueberry pie before you'll need to gas up the truck and drive it out to the field," Kayleen told him briskly. "Maggie will need more seed by then. Nobody's idle when it's seeding time. Come and sit down, boy."

Grady sat, although he couldn't remember the last time someone had called him "boy". Not that it mattered; he rather liked it. Made him feel as if he belonged. He glanced around, wondering suddenly what the twins were up to.

Keeley was busy vacuuming; he could see her pushing

the machine back and forth across the worn living room carpet. But Katy wasn't anywhere nearby.

"You'll be needing to take the old three-quarter-ton out to Maggie," Mrs. Davis informed him, one finger tapping against her chin as she considered that. "It's already loaded, I think. Probably yesterday. Katy'll go with you and show the way. I'll send a bite along for Maggie. And her sun hat." She shook her now-silver head. "She won't stop till the field's done. Not if she can help it. And she'll be burned to a crisp by noon. She has the fairest skin of all my children."

Grady politely inquired after the rest of the family and learned that the Davis family had four daughters. The rest seemed to have left home for high-powered careers well away from the bucolic life of the farm.

"Maggie never went to college. She married Roger two days after she graduated from high school. And when Roger wanted to farm, Dad and I decided it was time to let the younguns take over. They got a loan and bought us out and we moved to town. Roger's parents died three years ago. Car accident."

"What happened to Roger?" Grady mumbled, his mouth full of pie.

"He's gone now."

That was the second time someone had spoken of Mr. McCarthy as missing, Grady noted. Curiosity tweaked his tongue.

"Gone where?" His eyes widened. "Do you mean he ran off and left a woman with two daughters to run the place?"

"Didn't exactly run off." Kayleen smiled sadly. "He died. Five years ago. Heart attack." She carefully pleated the red-checked cotton of her skirt with fingers that were rough and worn from hard work.

"Sorry." Grady murmured the word perfunctorily as the pieces of the story fell into place.

"Yes, it was a sorry situation. Particularly when Maggie found out he'd cashed in his life-insurance policy. There was no money. Nothing. She scraped herself up and moved on, just as we knew she would." Kayleen's eyes were filled with tears. "She hugged and kissed her babies and then got on with her life, but it's been rough."

"But what did he do with the money?" Grady asked softly as he patted her thin shoulder awkwardly. "Whatever he bought, couldn't she return it?"

Kayleen jumped to her feet and dashed the tears from her eyes, shaking her head while her eyes avoided his. "Here I am gabbing, and Maggie is probably waiting for you to bring some more seed. She'd be furious if she knew I'd told you all this. She likes to keep her affairs private." Kayleen's voice dropped to a whisper Grady could barely hear. "Only, lately, I think it's gotten to be just a little too much. She's young and pretty and this place is wearing her into the ground. She's almost desperate to get away. Oh, I'm so afraid she'll make another mistake."

The tiny woman was lost in her private thoughts, her mind miles away, and Grady left the kitchen without speaking. It wasn't that he didn't want to know about Maggie McCarthy's personal life; he did. But some things were too private to share with another. If anyone could understand that, it was Grady.

He spent the next thirty minutes finding the truck and making sure it was loaded and ready to go. If he was lucky, the clutch would hold until he got it back here.

"Katy! Come and help me out." He stood in the yard and bellowed for all he was worth. A few seconds later the little girl appeared in the door of the barn.

"Come on," Grady called out. "You're going to show me the way to the field your mother's working in."

Katy dusted off her hands agreeably and climbed in to the rickety old truck. "What's she seeding?" Katy asked, her chin jutting out as she studied him.

"Canola. At least, I think it is." When he'd checked inside the seeder earlier today, Grady had recognized the tiny black seeds that were crushed to make margarine and oil. The same stuff was in the back of this truck. "Ready?"

"Uh-huh." Katy peered out the window like a wise little man until they came to the first corner. "Turn right here. We go about a mile west."

Grady nodded, shifting the noisy gear into third as they bounced along the rutted track. "What were you doing in the barn?" he asked, risking a look away from the road to her shining face.

"Cleaning the sheep's pen. I think the babies are coming pretty soon. The mother is huge. Her name is Bettina." She grinned happily, one arm wrapped around her middle. "I love animals. You can always ask them all the questions you want and they don't care. Not like adults."

Grady smiled at the sourness she inflected on the word *adults*. "What do you want to ask adults?" He kept his eyes on the road ahead and let her think it over.

"Tons of stuff. Like, do viruses get sick?" She twisted her fingers together and stared at the configuration. "And why is it called a paramecium if there's only a single organism? It shouldn't be a *pair* of anything."

"Okay." Grady nodded, hiding his smile. "That's logical, I suppose. What else?"

"Well, I was wondering…" Katy murmured, frowning as she tilted her mussed blond head upward. "If you turn the monitor off on the computer, does the screen saver still work?"

Grady couldn't help it; he burst out laughing. "I'm sorry, Katy. I don't know. But I think so. It's a program built into the computer that tells it if the keyboard has been inactive for a certain time. If it has, it signals the screen saver to come on. Even if you turned it off, the keyboard would still be inactive, so it should still work." Grady puffed up his shoulders, proud of his response. "I think," he muttered after several minutes of intense scrutiny from those deep blue eyes.

"I have so many questions." Katy sighed. "Keeley says I drive everyone crazy with them and Mom calls me 'Twenty Questions' when I ask too many. But sometimes I just hafta know. Ya know?" She peered up at him questioningly.

"Well, why don't you ask your mom? I'm sure she could help." Grady decided the second thing he'd repair on this truck would be the shocks, if vehicles had shocks back when they made this wreck. His backside ached something furious.

"Mom's usually too tired when she gets done working on the farm. Once she fell asleep when I was reading to her about El Salvador." Katy grinned, her happy state restored once more.

"That was my social project at school," she told him seriously, her eyes glittering with excitement. Grady watched the way her head tipped back proudly. "I got an A."

"Wow!" He gave her a thumbs-up with a grin. "A's are pretty cool. I don't know anything about your dad, and not much about El Salvador, either, but you can still talk to me." In fact, Grady told himself, he enjoyed his discussions with the girls very much. They were articulate and very well informed, but like all kids, they had boundless curiosity.

"My dad's been gone for a while. I don't remember him very well, but I bet he loved us." Katy's voice was tiny, her face begging him for reassurance.

"Of course he loved you," Grady replied, wondering why he'd started this. "Fathers are like our Heavenly Father. They always love their daughters. That's because girls are made of sugar and spice and everything nice."

Katy stuck out her tongue. "Yuck! That's Keeley. I'd much rather be made of snips and snails and puppy dog tails," she told him. "That's more interesting. And babies. I like to learn about babies of all kinds. Don't you? Hey, we're going in the ditch!"

Grady straightened the wheel with difficulty as he tried to quiet his ragged breathing and pounding heart.

"Er, where do you learn about babies, Katy?" Grady asked the question, thinking of Keeley's hours on the computer and the various information that was available on the Internet.

"In the barn, of course." She sounded disgusted. "You can't believe the storks bring babies if you live on a farm. Besides, we don't have any storks in Alberta! I've already seen two calves and eight kittens being born this year. And Nettie—that's Keeley's horse—is going to have a foal pretty soon." She peered up at him in concern. "You see, what happens is…"

"Uh, Katy, we're here." Grady heaved a sigh of relief, praying that she'd abandon the topic now.

His relief was short-lived as the little girl bounded from the truck and raced over to her mother who sat in the tall grass at the edge of the field, a long green stem between her teeth.

"About time you got here," Maggie muttered, getting

up to dust off her jeans. "I called Mom on the radio ten minutes ago. I want to get back to work."

Grady saw the tiredness etch her pretty face and tugged out Kayleen's care package. "Here. This is lunch from your mom. Why don't you relax with it and your coffee while I fill the seeder?" When she would have objected, he held up one hand. "I've done it before. Don't worry."

"Mom, Grady and I were talking about where babies come from."

Grady heard a startled cough from Maggie interrupt Katy's high-pitched voice. He wheeled to find Maggie's bright eyes staring right at him. He could feel the heat rising to his cheeks and would have looked away but she wouldn't release his gaze.

"You talked about what?" Maggie asked, her voice husky from the coughing. She took another sip of the steaming coffee.

"Babies. I 'splained it all to him," Katy told her mother.

"I see," she murmured. As he watched, Grady saw a wicked gleam of teasing fill her eyes. "Didn't he know about babies, then?"

"Nope." Katy fiddled with her mother's hair for a moment. "Why don't you have more babies, Mom?" Katy stopped suddenly, her eyes narrowing speculatively. "Unless you're too old?" she quizzed.

"Katy," her mother protested, face bright with color.

Maggie continued in a soft tone. "Honey, I have two daughters and I'm very happy with them. If that's all God gives me, then I'm thankful." She hugged her daughter tightly, brushed a kiss against the dirt-smudged cheek.

"I'll load the seeder," Grady muttered, turning away. "You can finish lunch."

She jumped up the moment he shut off the auger, and

shoved the containers back into the bag her mother had sent.

"I've got to get back to work now." Maggie dragged herself back up on the seat of the tractor and shifted gears with only a slight grinding. "Tell Granny I'll be done about six," she yelled, gathering her hair in a bunch and stuffing it under the hat he had given her. "You could fix up that broken screen on the back door, couldn't you, Grady? And the gate by the back pasture?" Her eyes were cool and formal as she gave him a list of chores for the afternoon.

Grady could see where the sun had burned the tip of her nose. At least she'd had sense enough to wear long sleeves. As he watched her drive away, Grady felt a sadness creep up on him. Maggie McCarthy was earthy and natural and very, very beautiful. In addition to her physical attributes, she was warm and caring. Exactly what he'd hoped for when... He cut the thought off before it could go any further. There wasn't much point dwelling on a future that would never be.

Grady wheeled around to pick up the sack and thermos of half-drunk coffee that Maggie had left behind. She'd eaten the pie voraciously, he remembered. As if she hadn't had breakfast.

"Come on, Katy, me girl," he called in his best Irish accent. "Time to get home. We're going to fix those front steps this afternoon."

"Can I help?" The child gazed up at him eagerly, her fingers slipping into his. "I like building things."

"Good." He grinned, holding her door open. "You can measure for me. I can't see a thing without my glasses."

"Why don't you wear them, then?" she demanded, frowning.

He grinned, enjoying the child and her quick repartee.

"Because I hate glasses," he told her succinctly. "Probably the same way you hate braces."

She quirked an eyebrow at him, studying his face for a while as she snapped her bubble gum in loud annoying clicks.

"Maybe," she agreed, nodding. "But at least you can take them off. I'll never get rid of these things!"

"Never is a long time," he murmured, trying to remember back to his own childhood. "It only seems like things will never end, Katy. But everything does." He should know. Not that long ago his life had come to a complete and utter standstill, and he didn't know yet if he would ever get it back.

"Granny told me the Bible says there's a time for everything." Katy sighed, slipping off the seat as he pulled to a stop by the side of the house. "I wish the time would come when we'd stop being poor." Her voice dropped to a murmur as she bent to pet the big collie nudging at her leg. "Then maybe I could stop worrying."

Grady stopped and waited for her to continue. But when Katy kept her eyes downcast, staring at the ground, he brushed a hand over her mussed-up hair and asked the question straight out.

"What have you got to worry about, Katy McCarthy?" he whispered gently as she kicked the hard dry ground with one foot. "Can't you tell me?"

She looked up at him and Grady was astonished to see huge tears in her eyes, poised at the ends of her golden lashes. "If I tell you, you can't say anything. Not to anybody. Promise?"

Grady held his hand over his heart and nodded.

"My mom's gonna sell our farm," Katy whispered loudly. "And when we move to Calgary, I won't be able to have my horse or Bettina and her babies or even Laddie." She threw her arms around the dog and hugged it desperately. "And I don't *want* Brian for my new daddy. I don't want a new daddy. I just want to stay here forever and ever."

"I know it's hard, little one," he murmured, brushing the tears off her freckled cheeks. "But whenever I get really scared and I don't know where to turn next, do you know what I do?"

Katy shook her head, blond strands flying everywhere.

"I pray about it," he told her quietly. "The Bible says that God cares even about those little brown sparrows over there and that He knows just when they need something. So I figure, if He knows what they need, He must know what I need, too. And if He knows, He'll figure out how to get it to me at just the right time. So I ask Him to help me not worry about it anymore.

"Do you think you can do that, sweetie?" He watched the bright blue eyes start to glow.

"Yes." She nodded at last. "I think so. And my Sunday school teacher said that if we really believe in something and ask God for it, and work as hard as we can, God will help us get our heart's desire." She suddenly bounded up the stairs. "I gotta go do somethin', Grady. I'll be back to help you in a while." And with one final bound through the door, Katy had gone.

Chapter Three

Tired and sore, Maggie stood in the doorway and marveled at the two children seated on the living room floor. The two best things in her life sat watching the television. They were identical twins, the doctors had assured her nine years ago. Alike in every way.

Huh! A lot they knew. Keeley and Katy were as different as night and day. Always had been. Keeley was quiet, thoughtful; slow to react and very stubborn. She liked to spend time thinking about things. Katy, on the other hand, favored her father. Roger had never been one to stifle his opinion, and Maggie had learned early on in their marriage to do things his way first, regardless of her own opinions.

"Now that was a nasty thought," she chided herself. "'Love hopeth all things, believeth all things, endureth all things.' Remember that." She slipped her shoes off and started up the stairs to take a shower, ignoring the stiffness in her arms and legs just as she ignored the grumbling complaints and hissed warnings coming from the two on the floor.

"Girls," she murmured, peering over the balustrade. "No arguing. Not tonight. I'm just too tired."

"Yes, Mother," they recited together, and Maggie smiled as she moved upstairs, knowing that Keeley would soon have Katy involved in some computer project. Either that, or they would both end up out in the barn, waiting for the new little lamb to appear. "And peace will reign," she told herself. "For a little while, at least."

"Did you get finished?" Kayleen asked from the bedroom after Maggie had showered.

"Yes, it's done at last," she muttered, entering her room and towel-drying her wet hair. "Now maybe we'll get a little break before we have to start the spraying. If I can find the money for it."

"You've still got some of that flax to sell," her mother reminded her, sorting out the piles of laundry onto the bed.

"Yes, but that's about all that's left. Then I'm tapped." Maggie changed into a cotton chambray sundress that was faded and worn but extremely comfortable. Then she gathered her hair into two tortoiseshell combs, letting the thick strands curve and coil as they wanted. "And it isn't going to be long before we have to start haying." She groaned, slipping one hand to her back at the thought of it.

"Count your blessings, dear. At least you've got Grady. By the way, Glynis Logan called this afternoon from Banff. She's sold two more of your quilts." Kayleen's eyes were sparkling with some pent-up secret and Maggie's eyes widened at her excitement.

"Okay, give," she demanded. "How much?"

"She sold the one you did of the mountains for fourteen hundred dollars," Kayleen said jubilantly. "*And* they've commissioned a smaller one, too."

"Fourteen...oh, my word," Maggie breathed, grabbing her mother's hands and squeezing. "Maybe the kids can go to camp this summer, after all. Of course, I have to pay for those parts first, and then there's the feed store bill. Where in the world...?" Her voice trailed away and she wiped away a tear of relief. "I'm just glad the Lord found a buyer. That store has been a godsend for me."

"Do you have anything else that could go? Glynis said she's had a real run on your quilts with the big influx of tourists this year." Kayleen studied the pair of well-mended cutoffs in her hand. "Which one owns these?"

"Katy." Maggie grinned, whisking her own underthings into a drawer and smoothing the quilt she'd fashioned for herself years ago. "The knees were gone anyway, so I cut them off. That child goes through clothes faster than I use sunscreen."

"Mom! Grady's here," Katy bellowed up the stairs.

Maggie rolled her eyes expressively at her mother before slipping on her sandals, walking out of the room and downstairs. "You don't have to bawl like a calf, Katy. I have perfectly sound hearing. Besides, it's not polite." She smiled guardedly, her eyes whisking over Grady's dusty clothes. "Nice job of the steps," she murmured. "I'd been meaning to get to them."

"I thought somebody already had." He grinned mischievously. "There were about five pounds of nails in those short stubby pieces. And every one of them was bent."

"Yes, well—" Maggie strode toward the kitchen to hide her red face "—I'm afraid carpentry is not my forte." She heard him mutter something. "I beg your pardon?"

"He said 'That's for sure,'" Katy told her innocently,

glancing up from the television show she and her sister were watching.

Maggie glared at her tall and lean hired help and watched his teeth flash in a grin that wasn't in the least apologetic.

"Sorry." He shrugged. "Did you get the seeding finished?"

"Yes." She sighed, pouring out two cups of coffee and cutting two huge wedges of the triple-layer chocolate cake her mother had baked that afternoon. "Finally." She motioned him to a chair and sank into one across from him, slicing into her cake with abandon. "Man, I'm hungry."

"You missed supper," he murmured, sipping his coffee as he watched her. "I could have done the seeding, you know. You're not all that strong. Missing meals probably isn't a good idea."

"I'm a lot tougher than I look," she told him defensively. Her shoulders lifted proudly. "I have to be. Besides, I like to finish what I start."

Maggie saw the frown that marred his craggy good looks and stopped eating her cake.

"Why don't you let me carry some of the harder jobs for a while?" he asked, his voice low and thoughtful. "I think you and your kids need to spend some time together, too."

"I spend as much time with them as I can." Maggie glared at him. "It isn't enough but it's the best I can do right now." She snapped the fork onto the plate with a decisive click.

"I'm not criticizing, Mrs. McCarthy. I just thought since school would be out soon, maybe you could ease up a bit. I'm perfectly willing to take on the heavier stuff as part of my duties."

Maggie automatically picked up one of his hands and

noticed the blisters and welt that screamed redly across his palms. Regret twigged at her conscience.

"I don't know if that's such a good idea," she murmured, brushing a thumb across the largest blister. "You're obviously not used to this kind of work."

His eyes were glowing with a kind of inner light that she didn't understand. When he finally pulled his hand away, Maggie could feel the loss right down to her toes. Silly to feel so strongly about him injuring himself, she told herself. She paid him to work.

"I haven't done it for a while," he agreed softly. "But I'll toughen up fast. I don't have this delicate white skin to watch out for." Seconds later his hand touched her arm. "What have you done to yourself?"

"Oh, that." Maggie shrugged, looking down at the long angry welt on her upper arm. "I scraped myself on something a couple of days ago. It's fine now."

"It doesn't look *fine*," he spat out harshly. "It looks like it could have used some stitches."

Maggie felt funny, watching the way his eyes flashed when he looked at her like that. Quickly she moved to the sink and rinsed out her cup before placing it and the other dishes in the dishwasher.

"It's fine," she told him hurriedly. "I'm no beauty anyway, so what's another little scratch? We farm girls get used to that stuff." She turned back to the table, striving to look him in the eye.

"You're kidding, right? You could give several well-known movie stars a pretty good run for their money."

Maggie shifted uncomfortably under his intense scrutiny. "I'm sure," she mocked, her face heating. "Anyway, I appreciate all the repairs you've made around here, Grady. It's nice to have the screen door fixed at last, and Mom said you managed to get the stove working again."

She wiped off the table and flung the dishcloth into the sink.

"Tomorrow's Sunday so we'll all be going to church. We'd like you to join us, if you want. We usually leave around nine."

Grady nodded and Maggie took the matter as settled. She opened the door to her workroom and switched on the lights then turned back as she suddenly remembered something.

"Oh, by the way," she added, stopping when she realized that he'd followed her, had almost run into her from behind. "Sorry." She stepped backward automatically and kept going when she realized how close he was. "Uh, Grady?" His big brown eyes flew from the quilting frame to her face. "This is my private work area." She waited until he absorbed that. "I don't let anybody else in here."

"I want to check out the window," he told her quietly, staring with interest at the bright array of colors laid out on the makeshift cutting table. "What do you do in here?" he asked, staring at the clutter that covered every available surface.

"Oh, I do a little quilting," she told him offhandedly. "Right now I'm doing a seascape in various colors and textures." She frowned, laying a bit of rippled, sand-colored cotton against the pale aqua, lost in the colors. "It's not quite right yet."

The tension grew between her shoulder blades as Grady stared at the finished works that lay against the wall. She felt open, exposed. As if he had seen right inside her to her most private thoughts.

"I know it doesn't seem like me." She made a face. "No one, least of all me, expected that someone as clumsy as I could actually make something turn out. But they sell and that's what counts."

"Stop doing that!" His order was quiet but fierce, and Maggie's eyes opened wide.

"I beg your pardon?"

"You're always denigrating yourself. As if you're some kind of country bumpkin instead of a beautiful woman who has managed to provide for her family as best she can. There's nothing wrong with being a farmer, for heaven's sake!"

He sounded exasperated, Maggie thought privately. Couldn't he see that this kind of a life didn't begin to compare with what could have been?

"This is beautiful work and it shows a very powerful creative spirit." His brown eyes blazed into hers. "I strongly suspect that it's that same spirit that's gotten you through the past few years after your husband's death."

"Well, I couldn't very well give up, now could I?" she spat out furiously. "I had the girls to think of." She dared him to comment on that.

"Yes, you did," he answered right back, his eyes shaded by the shadows in the room. It was clear Maggie's position as his boss didn't intimidate him in the least. "But a lot of women would have refused to break their nails on a relic like that tractor, never mind muck out animals and repair broken steps." He looked up then and Maggie could see the admiration on his face. For some reason it angered her and she slapped her hands on her hips in a snit of fury.

"Don't make me out to be a saint just yet, Grady," she told him harshly. "I hate grunging around on this farm, looking like a beggar and owing every shop in town. I like silk as much as the next woman you know," she answered snippily, watching his face. "If someone offered to buy this place and give me a job in the city that would provide for my kids and their needs, I'd jump so fast you wouldn't see me for the dust.''

Maggie knew her face was red and she couldn't help the sharp tone of her voice. ''You come here in your fancy clothes and brand-new vehicles offering to do a bit of charity work for us, and then you think you have permission to draw conclusions about our lives. Well, you don't,'' she snapped, angrily dashing away the tears that welled up in her eyes. ''You don't know how much I'd love to work in a nice quiet office where you put everything away at five and don't worry about it again till the next morning.'' She sucked in a breath and continued.

''Just once I'd like to be able to buy myself some decent clothes instead of having to sew up my own stuff. I'd like to take the girls on a real vacation and let them see how the other half lives. And once, just once,'' she retorted on the last breath of air still pent up inside, ''I'd like to have long smooth nails that weren't torn down to the quick or blackened and filthy from greasy, dirty old farm machinery!''

She turned her back on him as the whole miserable weight forced her shoulders to droop in despair. It was hopeless; she should know that by now. She would never climb out from the mountain of debt that had accumulated around her.

''I'm sorry,'' she murmured at last, keeping her hands up by her face as she sat at the old oak desk. ''I'm just tired. I shouldn't have dumped all that on you.''

''You're probably very hot, too,'' Grady muttered, striding over to push and shove at the window with several loud grunts of exertion, until it finally flew open and a fresh evening breeze wafted in. In just a few minutes the room temperature had dropped several degrees.

''Thanks,'' she whispered, ashamed of her outburst.

"I suppose it must be difficult to keep it all together," he mused, running one fingertip along the edge of her cutting table. "And then to have to work on these, too." His eyebrows met in a grimace. "That's a lot of pressure."

"Oh, this isn't work," Maggie assured him, brightening as she gazed at the arrangement of fabric before her. "This is what I look forward to at the end of the day. I guess I should be thankful that I have a paying hobby." She glanced up apologetically and found his eyes strangely glittering as they focused on her face.

"You should be thankful for a lot more than that," he growled, moving toward the door. He stopped a moment and then turned toward her as if he just had to say the words that were bottled up inside. "You should be very thankful, Maggie McCarthy. You have a place to call your own. A place full of memories and history. You have your parents to lend a hand when you need it." His almost black gaze bored straight into hers.

"You've known the love of a man and you have two wonderful daughters who think you're the best mother around. They are happy, well-adjusted girls who live comfortably. That's far more than most people ever get in this lifetime." A second later Grady had disappeared through the door and Maggie was left wondering what was behind the stark raw pain she'd seen in those eyes.

"I'm sorry, Father," she whispered, getting up to stare out the window at the lowering gloom. "All I really need is You and You are always there. Help me to keep on keeping on. Amen."

Then with a resolute determination, Maggie picked up her large shears and began cutting out the pieces she intended to use for seashells, completely losing herself in her work until the old cuckoo clock chimed nine and she rushed out to send the girls to bed.

Grady O'Toole perched on a folding chair on a patch of lush green lawn and stared at the big old farmhouse.

"Why me, God?" he demanded. "Why did You give me everything I thought I wanted and then yank it all away? What have I done wrong?"

The girlish giggles coming from inside the house pricked at his mind until he could tolerate it no more. With a grunt of dismay he stood and began walking toward the thick grove of trees behind the house.

In his mind's eye he could see Fiona—beautiful, elegant Fiona who thought you could deal with the problems life handed you by buying someone off. He remembered the night he'd proposed and the way she'd cooly accepted his kiss on her cheek.

Funny, he thought to himself. *I hadn't remembered that cool, chilly kiss until today.* He sifted through the memories and his mind zeroed in on another. *She hated the ring I chose.* The thought was traitorous, but try as he would, he couldn't ignore it. *She wanted something more showy, something that would be suited to her position in the firm. She hadn't cared that his diamond had been nearly flawless. Size and one-upmanship, that's what Fiona was all about.*

"I shall expect to travel, Gradin," she'd told him that evening, straightening the red silk dress with her polished fingernails after he'd tried to hug her. "And I think we'd better start looking at houses soon. You can afford better than this." Her piercing glance tore apart the small apartment and its understated furnishings. "After all, we shall want to entertain."

Grady approved wholeheartedly of entertaining. He'd

gone along with her plans quite happily until he'd discovered that Fiona had no intention of including anyone in the invitation who didn't have substantial power or influence in the business community. Her choice of guests was strictly limited to those people she could use to get ahead.

And still he hadn't seen through her.

Grady walked slowly through the bush, only half hearing the twitter of birds in the treetops. The land sloped down here and he followed it gladly, thankful for the energy it required to find a way through the thick undergrowth. If only it were so easy to take away the words in his head.

The engagement party had been a disaster that no one could have predicted.

"We want only those people who are really glad for us." Fiona's voice had been harsh. "I don't think that includes every little secretary and typist from your company, Grady."

"You don't understand, dear," he'd told her, half smiling at her wish to have everything just so. "A lot of these folks helped get the company where it is now. I *want* them to share in our happiness."

She had shaken her head with determination. Her hazel eyes had flashed daggers at him. "This event will be reported in the society columns," she hissed. "I will not be embarrassed by some snippy little underling trying to ingratiate herself into our lives."

There should have been misgivings then. Especially when his parents had shown up. His mother had never been one for society events and she'd stayed glued to her husband's side all night, afraid to say anything that might reflect badly on him. His father, Grady remembered, had been much the same. Only later had he found out Fiona's part in their discomfort.

The gloom of the thicket suddenly gave way and Grady realized that he was at the edge of the river. A small one, it was true. Still, it gurgled and ran along at a good speed. Crouching at the side, he stuck one hand in and smiled at the chilly temperature. Just what he needed to take his mind off the past.

A minute later he was fully immersed in the cool water. Its revitalizing freshness washed over every part of him better than the dinky shower in his camper ever could. He swam around for several minutes, letting the chilly temperature lower both his temper and his body heat. When at last he emerged, Grady grinned at the feel of the breeze caressing his skin.

"What can compare with Your creation, Lord?" he asked, staring at the huge moon overhead. He donned his clothes quickly and then found a huge warm stone to sit on as he stared out at the lush valley around him.

There was no doubt that Maggie's farm was demanding and she wore herself out trying to cover all the bases, but it was a lovely area and he couldn't imagine that she would ever really want to leave such peace.

"I don't know why I'm here, Lord," he mused, chewing on a stem of wild oats. "I should be at home, trying to save what little there is left of my business." But the words rang hollow. Now wasn't the time. Hadn't Harvey told him that over and over again only this morning on the phone?

"You can't come back, Grady, old pal. We haven't got things in place yet. I'll let you know when. Just relax and get yourself healthy. There's always another empire to be built, you know." Grady remembered grumbling about the slow hand of justice and Harvey's laugh of derision.

"For some people there is no justice," he said with a snort. "And I'm very much afraid that your ex-wife falls into that category, my man. The best we can do is salvage what we can and move on."

Grady had hung up, fury making it impossible to speak. But the words rang round and round his head like a bell that wouldn't stop bonging.

"Nothing can salvage my child. Nothing."

With a sigh of despair for a past that was too painful to dwell on, Grady clambered back up the hill, thankful for hard work and early mornings that made it nearly impossible not to sleep at night. He needed sleep. It was the only way he could forget.

Chapter Four

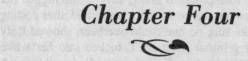

"**W**hy, Margaret Mary McCarthy! My word, girl! I haven't seen such a handsome man in a month of Sundays! Wherever did you find him?" Minnie Hugenot flapped her two-inch, black, paste-on spider lashes provocatively at Grady, who was standing some distance away. "And such muscles, too. Oh, my!"

The obvious stare at Grady's biceps made Maggie blush. She'd never been so happy to have church over.

"Oh, for Pete's sake," Katy muttered, kicking her toe against the carpet of the church's foyer. "What a lot of fuss!"

Keeley elbowed her. "Hush up, Katy. Maybe Mom'll take the hint and see how cute Grady is."

"I thought you said she was going to marry Brian?" Katy glared at her sister in frustration. "Why does it matter what she thinks of Grady?"

"It just does, that's all. Anyway, Brian's away right now and Grady's here!" Keeley's voice dropped. "But we've got to get them together. I told you. That's how they do it in all the best love stories." Her smooth forehead wrinkled in thought. "I've got it! Let's ask Mom if we can go for a picnic when we get home. Then you can ask if Grady can come. You and I'll go butterfly hunting and they'll be left alone. Grown-ups like that."

"I don't know," Katy began, and stopped when she had to move out of the way of Minnie's burgeoning hips. "I don't think Mom would like it much."

"Mom isn't supposed to know, silly." She tugged her twin over between the now-empty pews, and after casting a look to make sure no one could overhear, showed Katy the computer printout sheet she'd tucked into her white patent purse. "I got this off the Internet," she whispered, grinning. "I asked a question on this romance bulletin board and got a whole bunch of answers from a bunch of different people. I picked the ones I wanted."

"Keeley! If Mom knew, she'd…" Katy's voice died away from sheer shock.

"Well, she's not going to know unless you tell her." Keeley glared, advancing forward menacingly. "And you're not telling. Are you?"

"N-n-no. That is, not unless it doesn't work."

"If it doesn't work, we move on to step two." Keeley refolded the sheet and tucked it away again. "Let's face it. We have to do something. Otherwise our mother is going to make us move to Calgary!"

"Good! When are you leaving?" Johnny Applebaum's dirty face peered up at them from under the edge of the pew. "I can hardly wait!" He burst out laughing at their furious looks and dashed underneath the bench and out the other side. "I'm going to tell everybody you're going," he called.

"Come on, Keeley," Katy urged, ducking between Mrs. Simpson and Mrs. Anderson. "We've got to catch him before he squeals!"

"And then what?" Keeley gasped, lunging down the stairs. "You're not going to beat him up again, are you? Katy, you've got your best dress on!" In a desperate attempt to avert tragedy, Keeley followed her sister across the churchyard and into the Caragana hedge.

Maggie's anxious gaze followed her daughters out the door. She turned back to find Minnie watching her speculatively. "I expect Grady will be leaving before too much longer."

"You do rather seem to have a problem hanging on to the male of the species, don't you, dear? I hear Brian Dalgleish is away now, too." Minnie's voice was soft but the meaning was there, and Maggie felt herself flushing. "Now tell me, Maggie. Is my suit finished?"

"Yes, nearly," Maggie murmured, watching as the steady stream out the door lessened. "I wouldn't mind one more fitting before I do the finishing though. Just to make sure."

"I've never had a dressmaker who had to have so many fittings," Minnie said, looking down her long knobby nose at Maggie. "Perhaps when you get some more experience, you'll be a bit quicker at it."

Maggie stifled the words that rose in her throat, trying to remember that she was in the house of God and this was no place to make snappy replies. "It's only been two weeks, Minnie. And I did have some seeding to do."

"Yes, well—" Minnie searched through the crowd and began moving past Maggie "—just make sure I get *all* the remnants back. I don't want to find my suit as part of one of your little projects."

As her best paying customer sidled down the stairs, Maggie gritted her teeth. "One of my *little* projects indeed," she muttered angrily.

"Are you talking to yourself now, too?" Grady stood behind her, grinning like a Cheshire cat.

"No! I was just..." Maggie searched for the right words as she gathered up the girls' Sunday school papers and her Bible. "Never mind." She sighed and then peered around, remembering. "Minnie Hugenot went looking for you."

"Yeah, well fortunately for me, she's hard to miss and I avoided her." He looked very satisfied with himself. "Are you ready to go? I told the girls I was going to ask you if we could have a picnic. Since it's such a nice day and all."

Maggie searched his features, wondering what had prompted this sudden invitation.

"I could pick up a barrel of chicken. You wouldn't have to do anything. They come with plates, cutlery—everything."

He sounded almost desperate, Maggie thought. Maybe he was lonely. And the girls would love to have a picnic. Anything to get out of clearing the table and loading the dishwasher.

"All right," she agreed finally. "I was going to go to my parents', but I'll bet they'd enjoy the rest just as much, Mom's been out at my place so often lately, I'm sure she'd like to relax in her own garden." She felt his arm go under her elbow as they walked down the steep stairs. It had been a long time since she felt so protected. "I'll pay for half."

His hand fell away immediately once they reached the sidewalk and he whirled to face her.

"No, this is my treat." Maggie started to argue, but he stopped her with an upheld hand. "Please? Let me do this."

There was no time to say anything for Minnie bore

down upon them like a two-ton truck, removing all obstacles in her way. Maggie nodded at Grady and turned her glance away as the other woman spoke.

"Mr. O'Toole," she cried in a loud, peremptory voice. "Welcome to our little church! As head deaconess, I would be delighted to welcome you to my home for lunch."

Maggie watched as Minnie waited breathlessly for Grady's answer.

"Thank you very much," he replied solemnly, although Maggie could see the glint of merriment dancing in his eyes. "But Mrs. McCarthy and her daughters have agreed to a picnic lunch with me."

"A picnic, eh?" Minnie's eyes were speculative. "It's too bad that I've already been asked to practice with the choir this afternoon," she murmured thoughtfully. "Otherwise I might have tagged along."

Maggie had to hide her grin at the obvious relief covering Grady's handsome face.

"Oh, that is too bad. Are you and the girls ready, Mrs. McCarthy? We should be on our way."

Maggie felt the warmth of his palm cup her elbow again and moved along at his bidding.

"I wish you'd stop Mrs. McCarthy-ing me," she grated when they reached his truck. "My name is Maggie to everyone around here. It has been since the day I was born, and I don't like to answer to anything else."

She stepped up awkwardly, hiking her slim straight skirt up in order to reach the high step of the truck. She'd had to beg a ride because the car had a flat this morning and she had no time to change it. Maggie just caught his assessing look at her bare brown legs and hastily smoothed the navy fabric over them.

"I know," she muttered defensively when he got into

the cab of his truck. "I should have worn hose. But it's so hot! I don't think God cares about that stuff anyway. Especially not way out here in Willow Bunch!" She stopped the torrent of words just in time to notice the tic at the corner of Grady's mouth as he turned his dark head toward her and smiled politely.

"No," he agreed mildly. "I don't suppose it matters to God what's on your legs."

"Believe me," she mumbled, searching her purse for a tissue and mopping the moisture from her face, "if Nettie Fitzgibbons had noticed, I'd have had to listen to a decorum lecture. She used to measure my skirts when I was in fifth grade. I had to kneel on the floor, and if the fabric didn't graze the tiles, I was in big trouble."

"Such as?"

He actually sounded interested in her small-town history, Maggie noticed. She took another breath of the air-conditioned breeze shooting out the vents.

"Her favorite punishment was writing lines. I think she picked it because I had such terrible handwriting. Still do." She grinned, noticing the tiny flecks of silver that hid themselves in the rich chestnut darkness of Grady's hair.

He sat staring at her, his eyes full of something—longing? Maggie told herself not to be foolish. Nobody in their right mind would envy her dull, boring life!

"You must have had a wonderful childhood," he said, tilting his head to stare at the groups of people who still stood laughing and chatting on the lawn. "Everyone knows everyone else. There aren't any terrible secrets you have to hide." His voice dropped to a quiet hush. "I envy you your life, Mrs. McCarthy."

"Maggie," she corrected automatically, frowning up at him across the small space. "Why would you envy me?"

She held up one hand and counted off each finger as she spoke. "I'm up to my ears in debt, doing something that is dirty and thankless and has a very poor return. My best horse has gone lame. It doesn't look like the wheat will be doing much unless we get some rain, and I can't sell what little I've got in the bins because I didn't get enough quotas last year."

"Still," he murmured, staring at the lush greenness around him with that starry-eyed gaze Maggie had seen before. "Just look around."

"I did," she told him succinctly. "Last night." She shook her head in disgust. "The pressure system is broken again, which means it's going to be another long, dry summer. The crops need to be sprayed within the week or there won't be any point and Buster McLean is all booked up. And the only thing that's doing really well in the garden is zucchini. Do you know how sick I am of eating zucchini?" Maggie lowered her brows and visually dared him to comment on how wonderfully versatile the vegetable was.

"Oh." He changed tactics. "Think of yourself then. Think of how…"

"What? Think of what? My fingernails, which are chipped and broken all the time, no matter what I do," she added in frustration. "That I haven't had a professional haircut in years? Or maybe I should remind myself of how wonderful it is to have clothes I've made myself. I mean, who wants to wear those designer silks and cashmeres anyway!" She felt the heat warming her cheeks but ignored it to focus on Grady and her pent-up wrath.

"As for a nice steady paying job in clean surroundings, doing something other than fighting the land or making pretty *useless* things for other people—well, how utterly boring!" The silence yawned between them as Maggie realized exactly how self-pitying she had sounded. "I'm sorry," she whispered, staring at her rough, reddened fingers. "I shouldn't have said all that."

"Why not, if it's the truth?"

Her head jerked up of its own volition and Maggie stared at him in surprise. "Of course it's true," she told him. "But it's not your problem."

"Is it that Brian fellow's?"

His question was impertinent and Maggie should have told him to mind his own business. Instead, she let him in on the truth.

"It could be. He's asked me to marry him. Brian even *wants* the girls. There are a lot of men who wouldn't be interested in a ready-made family."

"And there are a lot of men who would kill for one," she heard Grady mutter under his breath. But when he lifted his head, his face was free of any emotion.

"You must think I'm a terrible mother," she murmured, staring through the windshield at the children still racing around the lawns. "I love my daughters. But I want more for them than a meager, hand-to-mouth existence on that farm." She heard her own voice harden and felt the anger once more.

"I want Keeley to have the facilities available where she can learn all she wants about the latest in computers, not just play on a used one I bought from a friend. I want her to have a top-notch teacher who will help her with her piano. Mildred Springs does her best, but she hasn't had the training. Besides, Keeley's learned all she can from Mildred."

He listened, Maggie had to admit. Unlike her parents, Grady actually seemed to hear what she was saying.

"And Katy?" His voice was low and concerned. "What about Katy? Her whole world revolves around the farm and her animals. Would you ask her to give it all up?"

"No, of course not!" Maggie glared at him angrily as the prick of conscience nagged at her deep inside. "But Katy hasn't known anything else. Once she saw the sports that were available to her—the swimming and track and volleyball that she could participate in, year-round—the farm would soon lose its attraction."

"Are you sure, Maggie?" He pointed to the little girl who sat sprawled on the church lawn, playing with five tiny kittens. "Are you sure that what Katy *really* needs is to move away from her friends and people she's known all her life into a nameless, faceless city?" He nodded toward Keeley, standing nearby, giggling with a group of girls.

The words cut at her, eating away the little bit of resolve that she'd gathered over months of soul searching.

"I don't know why I even told you," she told him. "You can't possibly understand what it's like. The eighteen-hour days, the unending bills, the tasks that really need doing but have to wait because you just don't have the energy or the strength or the resources to do it all alone." Tears welled in her eyes. "Alone—that's the worst part. Without anyone to talk it over with or discuss options, knowing the whole world rests on your shoulders."

"But you have your parents."

"Yes," she agreed tiredly, leaning her head back against the smooth leather rest. "They are wonderful. They help me out far more than I could have ever asked, and I love them dearly, but can't you see? They're getting older. They're tired. They need a break even more than I do, and I hate," she ground out viciously, "*hate* always dumping my problems on them when they've got their own lives to lead. They should be traveling south in the winter, like other retired couples." A tear dropped onto her open palm and she closed her fist around it in frustration.

When Grady finally spoke, his words were slow, as if he'd thought about them carefully first. "I know you don't think I understand. And I probably don't," he admitted quietly. "I cannot imagine how you've managed with small children and the farm and everything these past few years." He stopped and then went on more slowly. "But you have everything here. A family, a home, neighbors and friends you care about, a little bit of heaven carved out of this impersonal, industrialized, polluted earth." Grady's voice dropped to a whisper, as if he were speaking to himself. "I just don't understand how you can even think of giving it all up."

Maggie laughed mirthlessly, gathering her sweater around her. Suddenly the cab seemed cold. It mirrored her insides perfectly.

"I'd give it up in a minute," she whispered raggedly. "I'd gladly leave this place right now if I could be assured of a little peace and security in my future."

Grady shook his head. "There's no such guarantee in this life," he told her harshly. "And I, of all people, know what I'm talking about."

Maggie stared at him, stunned by the anger and pain in his voice. But she was prevented from asking him about it by the simple reason that he opened his window and called to the girls.

"We want to get on the way for our picnic," he told them, smiling as if nothing mattered more than getting them a bucket of chicken and basking in the sun. "I think we should go down by your creek." He smiled as he helped each child into her seat. "That way we could swim if we get too hot."

Maggie took the high-pitched squeals of excitement in the back seat as agreement with this plan, but she couldn't forget the look of agony on Grady's face the moment before. Nor could she help noticing the way his features softened when he spoke to her daughters, or miss his tender touch on each blond head.

What is in Grady O'Toole's past that caused such terrible pain that only my life seems able to assuage?

It was a good question. Unfortunately, the answer eluded her.

Chapter Five

"Maggie McCarthy, I'm going to skin you alive!" Grady glared at the local crop duster as the words rolled through his brain. He was furious with her. "When did Mrs. McCarthy tell you not to do her fields?" he demanded with his lips pursed.

Buster McLean shifted from one filthy booted foot to the other, his gaze downcast. Not that it mattered, Grady decided grimly. The man wore a greasy cap pulled low on his forehead and it was difficult to even *find* his eyes, let alone read them.

"Well, like I said, it was right after I told her the cost. I do this to support my own farming operation, you see. I know Maggie needs the work done all right," he apologized, shoving his hands even deeper into jeans that seemed destined to pool around his size-sixteen feet. "But I gotta pay for the stuff out of my own pocket. That's why I need to be paid up front. If she can't pay, I can't spray." He grinned stupidly at the little rhyme and then shrugged as Grady lowered his eyebrows menacingly.

"How much?" Grady kept his tones low. When the

answer came, he merely stared, eyes widening expectantly. "No," he said quietly, flicking the bug off his arm as if to emphasize his point. "I meant what is your best price on this particular job? And don't expect anyone to barter you down. Either you want the job or you don't."

Buster tugged off his hat and scratched his forehead with fingers that hadn't seen water in a while. He had beady little eyes, Grady noticed. They seemed to shift back and forth and around, everywhere but on him.

"You don't want terms?" he asked querulously.

"No terms," Grady agreed. "Mrs. McCarthy pays cash on the barrel head."

"Oh. Well, see, cash is a different matter altogether. Why didn't you say so in the first place?" And Buster named a figure that was considerably below his first one.

"Fine." Grady pulled out a check, filled it out and signed it with a flourish. "You'd better make sure it's a good job," he told the other man. "And she wants an early-morning spray, when it's calm and the kids are still inside."

"Doesn't everyone?" Buster slapped his filthy cap back on his balding head and stuffed the check into his pocket. "I suppose I could come over tomorrow about six," he offered, hitching up his pants.

"Make it five," Grady told him smoothly. "And I want a bill for that check. Marked 'Paid in full.'" He waited while Buster dug around in his truck for a pad and wrote out the receipt. "I'd appreciate it if you could go through me in any future dealings," he murmured, folding the paper and tucking it into his shirt pocket. "Mrs. McCarthy is pretty stressed-out these days."

"Ain't much of a wonder." Buster grunted, heaving his girth up into the seat. "Truth to tell, most of us figured she would have bailed out long ago."

"And as long as she was around and still kicking, I guess you just thought maybe you could keep skimming, is that it?" Grady nailed the guy with his sternest look. "The way I figure it, you've been making things tougher for her instead of easier. So maybe, as a helpful *friendly* gesture, you can come by on Saturday. She could use your help at fixing up the barn."

Buster had the grace to turn red as a beet under such straight talk. "I never tried to take her," he blustered loudly. "It's just that with her having so many bills and all, I thought it would be best to add some interest and sorta make sure of things. It's just business." He blabbered on for several minutes before promising he'd be there.

"Well, thank you, Buster. That's right neighborly of you." Grady smiled in his best down-home fashion. "You might mention it to Burt Copperfield, too. I'm sure he'd want to help out. Say!" Grady opened his eyes up wide and innocent. "Isn't he the guy that did some plumbing work on the McCarthy house last fall?" He pretended to think for a minute and then shook his head ruefully.

"On second thought, don't ask him, Buster," he pleaded sadly. "The guy's useless. Why, I was down checking over the pressure system for Mrs. McCarthy late last night, and I have to say I never saw such a mess of a job in my life. And the price he charged!"

Grady suddenly slapped a hand over his mouth in embarrassment. "Oh, brother," he gasped in pretended chagrin, averting his eyes, "I hope I didn't say anything out of turn. You're not, er, friends, or anything, are you?"

"He's my brother-in-law," Buster told him, lifting his head a fraction to study Grady's face. "And he usually does very good work!"

"He is? He does?" Grady kept his face straight. "Oh.

Maybe this was just a rare occurrence then." He tried to look apologetic. "Don't mention it, will you? I don't want to get anyone in trouble, although with that soldering, I don't know how he makes a living." He shrugged and let that sink in a little longer before turning away. "See you Saturday, Buster."

"Yeah." Buster's voice was thoughtful. "I'll be there." And he drove away at about half the speed he'd driven up.

"You do that," Grady muttered to himself as he watched the brand-new four-by-four pass through the gates. He pulled on the leather gloves Maggie had insisted he wear. He just bet Buster would be bringing along Burt, the plumber, as well. Grady grinned at the dog and tugged the roto tiller on once more.

Grady ploughed through the dark black topsoil around the spruce trees that framed the yard site. It would be interesting to see just what happened on Saturday, and he was looking forward to watching Maggie's face when it did.

That was, if he got back in time.

"I'm coming in on Friday, Harvey," he informed his lawyer minutes later on the cell phone he always carried. "I have to know how things stand, if I have a future."

"Don't be ridiculous, Grady." Harvey snorted. "Of course you have a future. Your trust is as secure as it ever was. She can't touch that at least."

"You hope! And my reputation? My business? My friends?" Grady said the words, knowing that it was fruitless to ask. Nothing could undo the damage Fiona had done.

"Your real friends are still here, waiting for you to call. Is it worth worrying about the others?"

"And Shaughnessy's? Is it going to fold?" Grady held

his breath, his heart aching for the people who had worked so hard to help him build his company up from nothing.

"I closed it down, Grady. I handed out notices and laid everyone off so that they could at least collect employment insurance."

"You what?" Grady glanced toward the house to make sure no one noticed him.

"I had to, old son. They've tied us up for so long that business has really dropped, and no one was bringing in any new accounts. This way, your staff can at least try to get work somewhere else until you start up again. I sold all the equipment and furniture and used it to pay bonuses. Grady? Are you there?"

Grady sank down onto the ground, his heart racing a mile a minute. Gone. It was all gone. Without any pomp and circumstance. Without him even knowing it. Fiona had taken away his precious company without even really trying.

Harvey was shouting his name and Grady could hear the fear in his voice.

"I'm here," he whispered at last. "Just thinking."

"You scared me out of my tree," Harvey said. Grady could imagine his lawyer flopping into his black leather chair and grinned tiredly when a squeak of protest signaled just such an action over the phone line.

"Did Fiona say anything?" It galled him to ask it, but Grady swallowed his pride and waited for some indication that his ex-wife cared that his company was now defunct. Harvey's nasty little laugh made him suddenly feel better.

"Well, now there's the rub," Harvey muttered. "Her lawyers didn't even know till I'd cleaned the place out. Your staff was very good about keeping everything hush-hush. Everyone and everything was long gone by the time I got there to lock the door. Except for one thing."

Harvey paused expectantly and Grady knew he was supposed to ask the next question. Swallowing thickly, he held the receiver tightly and said it in a choked voice that gave away his inner agitation. "What was left?"

"The welcome mat!" Harvey chortled heartily at his own joke, making Grady's mouth tip in amusement. He could just imagine Fiona's lawyers in their three-piece pin-striped suits, outraged at letting the not-inconsiderable tangible assets of Shaughnessy's evade their greedy grasp.

"I told them they were welcome to it. With your compliments." Harvey's voice hardened. "I've filed petitions against your ex-wife and her legal eagles to hold them at bay while the board investigates your supposed crime. Just got the decision this morning. The judge agrees that they will have to wait a while until he can hear their case."

"And what do we do until then?" Grady noticed the school bus pulling up, and suddenly wondered to himself why this phone call had seemed so urgent as two excited little girls tumbled down the steps.

"Grady, my friend, we send dear Fiona her monthly installment on the settlement she was promised until such time as she marries again as per the agreement. And nothing else. Not a dime. You don't see her, you don't talk to her. You stay safely where you are until I get this straightened out."

Grady sighed, watching Katy throw herself into her mother's arms and the laughing embrace Maggie gave her that ended in both of them flopping on the lawn. Seconds later Keeley had joined in and they were madly tickling each other.

"I want it over, Harvey," he muttered, raking a hand through his hair. "I just want it finished. I want my life to begin again. If I have to pay her off to be free, then let's just do it.''

"Not yet. First we'll see what they've got," Harvey suggested. "I have several investigators checking things out right now and I don't want you jeopardizing my work at this delicate stage. Just stay where you are and relax. I'll handle it for now."

There was a pause and Grady could hear the rustle of papers being shuffled. He was ready to sign off when Harvey's voice came back on the line. "By the way, where are you, anyway?"

Grady told him a little about the farm and Willow Bunch but he didn't mention Maggie and her daughters He wasn't sure why, except that it was none of Harvey's business. Not yet anyway.

"It sounds wonderful," Harvey agreed. "Enjoy it while you can. And stay away from here."

Grady hung up after promising to do just that. He spent a long time watching the tall willowy woman chasing and tagging her giggling daughters.

Grimly he shook off the thought of the family he would never have, and yanked on the cord to start the tiller— Work, that was the only panacea. Work until he was too numb to feel the pain.

It might have been five minutes or an hour later that he became aware of the child on his right side, marching along as she kept step with him.

"Hi, Katy." He switched off the motor reluctantly. "How was school?"

"Boring. We had that stupid social test today." She kicked at a clump of dirt and then scrunched down to peer at the earthworm wiggling in the light. "Melinda Fairchild made fun of my braces again." Her voice was soft but full of defiance.

"And?" He frowned down at Katy's wide, easy smile. "What did you do?"

"Nothing!"

"Katy," he warned in a low menacing voice.

"I didn't!" Katy shrugged and stood, dusting her hands on her jeans. "Of course, she did get my gum stuck in her hair at recess, but that wasn't *my* fault. She shouldn't have leaned back when I was blowing bubbles. They had to cut it out and she has *very* long hair. Some of it's a little shorter now."

"Katy!" He tried to stifle the burst of laughter that rose in his throat at her innocent look and self-righteous tones. "That's terrible."

"So's she," Katy told him, snapping her gum with satisfaction. "She has more brand-name clothes than anyone and she still isn't happy."

"Things don't make people happy, Katy. You can have all the *things* in the world and still be sadder than a beggar." *If anybody knows that,* he thought, *I do.*

"I know," Katy mumbled, pushing her hair out of her eyes. "But sometimes it would be nice if stuff was spread around a little more, don't you think?" She pulled out a blade of grass and chewed on it thoughtfully. "Like if you took all the rich people and made them only half as rich, then there would be more for poor people like us."

"We are not poor, Katy McCarthy!"

Grady and Katy straightened guiltily, wheeling round to see Maggie standing behind them, hands on her hips as she surveyed her daughter with a frown.

"We have food and clothes. Warm beds to sleep in and Granny and Grandpa nearby. That's being pretty rich."

"I know, Mom." Katy hugged her mother's waist in apology. "And I'm not complaining. Honest. It's just that

Melinda makes me so mad sometimes. She has so many toys and she won't ever share!''

"Yes, well, you remember that when Keeley wants to borrow something of yours," Maggie chided with a gentle smile, brushing the blond mess off her daughter's face. "Now go and do your chores and then you can play a bit before supper. *If* your homework is done."

"Okay." Katy went racing off toward the house, her voice carrying on the breeze back toward them. "See you later, Grady."

"I guess all my bellyaching has rubbed off on my girls," Maggie murmured, stubbing her toe in the ground. The action was identical to Katy's and Grady couldn't help but smile.

"It's not funny." She glared at him. "And just a few minutes ago, when I asked Keeley how school was today she began weeping on my shoulder because Becky Snodgrass told her she knew her jeans were Elissa's old ones from last year and that they were supposed to go to the Goodwill pile at church." She glanced up at Grady, a tear poised on each long thick lash. "Why are kids so mean?"

The pain in her voice stung him and Grady could see that she barely had herself under control. He reached out and took her hand, patting it gently.

"Don't worry about it," he advised softly. "All kids go through this, but they survive. Yours will, too. Probably better than most because they already know what's really important in life."

"Is it so wrong to want them to have nice things?" Maggie's voice was ragged. "A few really nice clothes that they can take pleasure in, that would make their lives a little less dreary?"

"Maggie, Katy and Keeley take pleasure in every day. Look at them." He pointed at the pair gently petting the new foal. "What toy would you buy them that could ever replace that in their lives?"

"Yes, it's nice." She sniffed, leaving her hand wrapped in his. "But the other kids get to go to Calaway Park for their birthdays. Or they rent the laser tag place, or the water slides." Fresh tears rolled down her cheeks as she watched the girls carrying buckets of feed for the animals.

"All I can give them is a little party here on the farm with a cake and a dress I made myself. It's not fair," she railed in a tortured voice, her face an agony of pain. "I just want them to be happy."

Without a thought, Grady pulled her into his arms, pressing her head against his shoulder as her tears soaked his shirt.

"Of course it's not fair," he said gently, feeling her hands grasp at him. "Life never is. But we take what God gives us and we make the very best of it that we can. And hope that someday things will be better."

"I'm sick of waiting for someday," she mumbled against his neck. "I want them to remember their childhood as a happy time, blissfully carefree. Not an era when they had to watch and scrimp and save for every dime that came their way."

"Is that why Brian was out here again yesterday?" Grady had to ask the question. It had bothered him for hours. "Are you thinking of exchanging one set of problems for another?"

She pulled away at that, back as far as his arm let her, her blue eyes chilly in the extreme. "Brian's not a problem," she told him coldly. "He's a solution. He thinks he loves me. He and I and the girls could live quite happily together. We'd have everything we need. I could sell the farm and pay off the money I borrowed from Mom and Dad last year. Life would be so much easier."

"He only *thinks* he loves you?" Grady rolled his eyes. "But you don't love him. Do you?" For some reason he needed to hear her answer to that question. Badly.

"Brian is a wonderful man. So good and kind. He respects me and he wants to make a home for the girls. He has everything I could possibly want in a husband." She tilted her head back, defiance in her eyes.

"But do you love him?" Grady held her gaze, refusing to give up even when she pressed away from him and stood churning her fingers together. "Do you?"

"I can't let emotion sway me again, Grady." She shuffled her feet. "I did that when I was eighteen, and look what happened."

"So what happened? You were happily married and became a mother to two wonderful daughters, Maggie! Are you sorry?"

"No." She glared at him in frustration. "But now I'm alone and I have to make some decisions about our future. I'm not sure I can last another year on this farm, living the way we have been." She met his gaze straight on. "I'm out of money, out of energy and out of patience. It's time for a change."

"And the biggest change would be for you, wouldn't it, Maggie?" he murmured, meeting her gaze. "You'd be free of this place and the memories it holds for you."

"Is that so wrong?" she demanded, head tilted back. "To start a new life for my family?"

"No, of course not. It's just that I think you're going to be disappointed. You can't run away from life, Maggie. You have to face it head-on."

"Is that what you're doing out on this farm looking like your world has fallen apart? Are you facing life head-on when you make those secretive calls on your telephone?" Her eyes slashed at him like cold hard steel and her words bit into him. "Practice what you preach, Grady."

He stared down into her beautiful face and wondered for the tenth time exactly why he was here. He was staying put as Harvey had demanded, but the longer he stayed, the more involved he became with this intriguing woman and her two delightful daughters.

"Well?" She was standing there, hands on her hips, demanding his response with that stubborn glint in her eye.

"You don't understand," he told her quietly, turning away to pull the tiller out of the soft loam. "And I can't explain. It's too personal."

"Too personal?" She laughed mockingly. "And you think delving into my life and telling me who not to marry and when and where I should live isn't? Oh, brother!"

Grady looked back at her, letting his eyes rove across her smooth clear forehead, the blond brows and glittering blue eyes. There was a smattering of very pale freckles on her nose just where that snobbish tilt began. Her wide laughing mouth was turned down in a frown and Grady could feel the sparks emanating from the silver glints in her hair. Maggie McCarthy was furious. And very lovely.

"I'm sorry," he said stiffly, turning away. "It's none of my business. Forgive me for interfering." With one motion he had pushed the tiller back and begun rolling it toward the shed.

"That's it? That's all you're going to say?" She stood in front of him now, anger bringing two pink spots to her cheeks.

Grady nodded. "Yes. That's it."

Her glistening hair spun round her shoulders in a cloud of gold as she whirled away. She'd gone only a short distance before she turned back. "I *am* going to have my life, you know. I *will not* grow old and withered and bitter, worn down by years of trying to make this place a go.'' She glared at him, hands clenched at her sides. ''Maybe I was a fool to get married so young. And maybe I didn't know what I was getting into when I tried to keep this place going. But, believe me, I certainly know now and I no more want it for my daughters than I do for myself.''

Grady forced his lips to remain shut, standing solemnly as she finished her tirade. He could see the tears trembling at the corners of her eyes and knew that at this particular moment she was at the end of her tether. She needed a break.

''I've tried,'' Maggie whispered brokenly. ''I've tried so hard! But I just can't do it anymore. I'm worn-out trying to keep everything together. Is it so wrong to want a little space and time for me?''

The words were soft, not meant for his ears, Grady knew. And yet he couldn't let them go. Not without trying to make her see the whole picture.

''Maybe…'' he murmured, keeping his eyes averted as she struggled to regain her composure, and then meeting those deep blue eyes with his own. ''Just maybe this is your time. Maybe this is your shining moment.''

Maggie laughed bitterly, glancing down at her torn shirt, faded dirty denims and ragged sneakers.

''There is nothing even remotely shining about me right now, Grady O'Toole.'' She exhaled in defeat. ''And certainly nothing the least bit glamorous about farming. Don't make this into a Norman Rockwell painting, okay?'' she warned sourly. ''There is no intrinsic merit in driving yourself into the ground trying to make something out of nothing.'' She turned and began walking back to the house. He just caught her last words. "Believe me, I ought to know."

"Mom!" Keeley's voice carried across the yard and Grady watched as Maggie's proud head lifted. "It's Brian. He wants to know if we're free tonight. There's something he wants us to go to."

Maggie twisted her head around, her eyes meeting Grady's without flinching. There was something cold and hard in them that reminded him of Fiona, some determination that he knew he could not shake.

"Yes, I'm free," she called out. "We all are. It's time we had a little fun in our lives."

And as he stood watching, Maggie broke into a quick sprint that took her to the steps of her home. It was the first time, he reminded himself, that he'd seen her run for the sheer pleasure and abandonment of it.

"Help her, Lord," he murmured. "Keep her on your path. Whatever that is." Then he turned and headed back to the camper for a lonely supper on his own.

"What is going on?" Maggie stared at the crowd of men who were parking their trucks in her front yard. "What is everyone doing here?" she called loudly, drawing their attention to her. "Don't you know it's Saturday?"

"Of course we know. We thought we'd help out with that work on the barn," Chester Bird told her, buckling his tool belt around his skinny hips. "Been meaning to get here for a while. Today seems a good time."

"But…"

"And we thought we'd come along and help with any spring cleaning you want done," Minnie Hugenot added, wheezing out of her small car. "We've done everyone else's but we wanted to wait until you were finished seeding."

"But…"

"I reckon Grady could show us what needs doing on the barn," Slim Tattersall mumbled, his hat pulled low over his eyes. "The women brought lunch so we'll get to work right away. Gabby, you need anything for the house?" He watched impatiently, Maggie noted, not even offering to help as his tiny wife stumbled up to the step with several buckets and mops, a bag of cloths and several cleaners.

"No, thanks, Slim," she puffed, careening through the door with difficulty. Maggie moved to take the buckets and bags from her. "You fellows get to work. We'll call you when it's coffee time."

Maggie watched as Grady led the group of men toward the barn. Embarrassed, she noted the worn boards, rotting roof and wildly hanging doors. The barn was a wreck.

"Speaking of coffee," Nettie murmured, fanning herself, "why don't we start with a cup? That'll give Maggie and the girls time to get dressed. Had a late night, did you, dear?" Nettie winked in a totally unteacherlike fashion as her eyes roved over Maggie's tattered chenille housecoat.

"Can't really blame her, can you?" Minnie demanded, staring out across the yard. "Not with a hunk like that hanging around."

The rest of the group giggled and twittered, their glances openly curious as they went from Maggie to Grady and back again.

"Actually, the girls and I were out with Brian last night," she told them, trying to ignore the blush she could feel heating her cheeks at their knowing looks. "We went to the circus."

There was a long pause in the conversation then as the ladies digested this bit of information. Maggie waited for someone to ask when she was getting married, but to her surprise, no one did. Perhaps because of the warning glint in Henrietta Higglesby's dark brown glare. Of all the local ladies, Henny seemed to best understand how much Maggie needed to feel feminine and beautiful. It was Henny who gave Maggie the trial samples from her makeup selection at the drugstore.

"I think that's wonderful," Henny enthused, patting Maggie's shoulder gently. "You're just wearing yourself out on this farm. It's time you had a break. You take some time for yourself and the girls to enjoy."

"Thank you, Henrietta," Maggie said softly. "That's just what I plan to do more of this summer. We need a break."

"I don't know how on earth you do it all," Bonnie Copperfield muttered, urging everyone inside. "No wonder you're so thin. Come on, ladies, let's get to work."

In a daze Maggie got the girls up, had a shower, dressed and went down to her kitchen. Everything was out of the cupboards and Gloria Stampford was reaching from her perch atop the ladder to wipe out the highest shelf.

"I haven't done that in ages," Maggie warned. "It's probably filthy." It was embarrassing to have people see what a poor housekeeper she was, but there simply was no time to dust and clean with the animals and the children and homework and final exams.

"This is nothing," Gloria told her, grinning. "With my four, I barely have time to load the dishwasher. When Henny was cleaning out Jared's room, she found a frog under the bed! That was in March, so you know the thing had been there all winter."

"Yeow!" The screech came from downstairs and seconds later Bonnie Copperfield came racing up. "I've gotta get Burt," she called as she hurried out the door. "There's a leak down there!"

"It's been there for ages," Maggie tried to tell her, but Bonnie was halfway across the lawn.

"Let her go," Nettie advised, emptying her bucket of dirty brown water into the sink. "Bonnie will have Burt over here in a minute and he'll get it straightened out."

Maggie watched as they all went back to their jobs and decided it wasn't worth explaining that the leak had appeared *after* Burt's last visit. True to her word, Bonnie dispatched Burt and another man to the bowels of the basement and ten minutes later both men carried out several parts.

"These are defective," Burt told her, two red spots of color on his cheeks. "But don't worry. They're under warranty. The company will pay for the repairs. I think I've got some in my truck."

Relieved that for once there would be no extra expense, Maggie took her bucket outside to start on the windows and found two men on ladders painting the exterior of the house.

"No," she called out, hurriedly setting her pail on the railing. "I didn't order any paint."

"I did!" Elmer Palen peered down over the edge of the roof where he seemed to be replacing some shingles. "It's demo stuff that we're supposed to try out and report on. Grady thought this house might be a good test case since it's so old and weathered."

"Oh." Maggie frowned. *Grady thought that, did he,* she muttered to herself. "Thank you," she called a minute later, but Elmer just waved the hand holding his hammer.

"You can't get the woodwork wet if they're going to paint," Grady said from behind her. He was studying the workers around the barn with an absent air. "Maybe there's something inside that needs doing."

"You know very well that there's something *everywhere* on this farm that needs doing," she told him with a huff. "Did you call all these people? I will not be an object of charity with everyone feeling sorry for me!"

"I hardly think that's the case," he murmured mildly, his eyes meeting hers. "They're your friends and they want to help. Why don't you just relax and accept it?"

"Because it's denigrating!" She frowned fiercely. "Everything is run-down and shabby, as if I don't care how things look."

"Maggie?" Grady had his hand on her arm, warm and comforting. His eyes glowed with something that made her feel special and cared for. "Can't friends help friends without you taking it the wrong way?" His tone was softly chastising. "They've seen you slaving away here. They know how hard it's been, and they want to help. Try and graciously accept it in the same manner that it's given, will you?"

"Hey, Grady! Mac says the chicken coop needs some strengthening. Mind if I do that?" Buster McLean's voice broke into their conversation, his eyes watching as Grady's hand slowly fell away from Maggie's arm.

"That would be very nice of you, Buster," he agreed absently, but his dark caressing gaze stayed on Maggie.

"Okay, I'll do that, then." Buster hurried away as if he'd been bitten and Maggie could only stare.

"Buster? Donating labor? I don't believe it!"

"Well, believe it." Grady laughed. "And enjoy it. It may not happen again in this lifetime."

Maggie studied her new hired hand for several minutes, noting the way his hands were stuffed into his pockets, the way his shirt opened at the throat, showing the tanned skin there.

"Thank you," she murmured at last, leaning forward to press her lips against his cheek. "I don't know how you did this, but thanks." She turned away lest he see more of her tears.

"You're welcome." Grady sounded pleased and something else. It was that which made Maggie turn back and study his handsome face once more.

"Proud," she whispered to herself as she dusted the curio cabinet in the living room. "He looked as if he had some interest in this place and was proud it was getting fixed up."

And that was strange, wasn't it? Grady O'Toole had only shown up a few short weeks ago and she doubted he'd be staying on much longer.

"So why should he feel proud?" There wasn't any answer to the question that rolled round and round her head.

"Maggie? Can you come here a moment?" Henny called from Katy's room. "There's the strangest thing on this shelf."

Maggie climbed the stairs with a grimace on her face. She could only imagine what had made the woman's normally strong tones weak and breathless. Seconds later she understood completely. In fact, she felt a little weak herself!

"Back out and shut the door, Henny. Just go slowly. That's the way. There!" Maggie snapped Katy's door closed with a quick flip of her wrist and sagged against the wall. "No more pets, I told her. Not one more. And she promised she wouldn't bring anything else into the house. She promised!" Maggie let her weak-kneed body slide down the wall until she was sitting on the floor.

Seconds later Henny was there, too, white-faced and shaking.

"I'm sorry, Maggie. I'm not usually so lily livered. But that…thing scared the wits out of me."

"Don't worry, Henny." Maggie patted the clenched hand. "I felt pretty scared myself." She stood up carefully. "I'll go get her," she murmured, praying her legs would carry her down the stairs. "Katy got it here. She can get rid of it."

"I'll go with you," Henny blurted, scurrying behind. "The girls probably need help downstairs anyway."

Maggie let her go, knowing the woman needed to calm down. She needed that herself, but first she needed to talk to Katy. She found her daughter behind the barn with Grady, cutting up some of the dead trees they had removed from around the garden.

"But why does the Bible say God is jealous?" the chirpy voice demanded. "God has everything, and if He hasn't got it, He can just make it, can't He? It doesn't make any sense."

"Neither does having a six-foot-long snake in your bedroom," Maggie murmured, her jaw tense. "But you've got one, Katy. *And* after I told you no more pets in the house."

"A snake?" Grady glanced from mother to child. "What kind of a snake?"

"A very long, fat, slithery one," Maggie informed him. "It nearly gave Henrietta Higglesby a heart attack, not to mention me."

"Oh, that's Bowie," Katy exclaimed, as if that told them everything they needed to know. She glanced at her mother and hastily added some more information. "You know, our classroom pet. It's a boa constrictor, Mom. I have to look after him this weekend. It's my turn."

"It was here last night? Uncaged?" Maggie sat down on the nearby bale before she fell down. "But I was walking around barefoot!"

"It's not poisonous, Mom!" Katy sounded aggrieved. "It gets things by squeezing them. Bowie caught a rabbit once and swallowed it whole."

Maggie shuddered, glancing up at Grady with her best pleading expression. "Please go with Katy and get that *thing* out of my house, Grady," she whispered. "Now!"

Maggie could see Grady's mouth twitch and guessed that he probably found the whole thing hilarious. But the thought of that slithering, slippery skin wiggling around through her home gave Maggie the creeps. She lowered her eyebrows and frowned. "Now, please!"

"But Mom!" Katy launched into her attack. "Bowie doesn't like it outside. He gets cold."

"Too bad. I want that reptile out of my home. Now."

They all turned as a series of shocked screams issued forth from the big old farmhouse. Seconds later a group of excited women poured out of the doors, pushing and shoving their way down the steps.

Grady and Katy headed toward the house at a fast clip, gathering male helpers as they went. Heaving a sigh of resignation, Maggie headed for the madly chattering ladies' group standing on her lawn.

"Slid right through the grate it did," Gloria Stampford gasped, her face white with fear. "I was just dusting Maggie's dresser when it slithered down in front of me."

"It's okay, Gloria. It's relatively harmless. Grady and Katy are going to get rid of it."

"Do you *like* snakes in the house?" Bonnie stared at her strangely, eyes wide and accusing. "I mean, how can you sleep, knowing that thing could slide up beside you and squeeze you to death?"

"Believe me," Maggie muttered, closing her eyes to relieve the throb at her temples, "if I'd known that snake was there, no one would have slept for a thirty-mile radius."

They all stood silent, watching as Katy emerged from the house with Bowie calmly curling over her shoulders and down her arms.

"We'll put Bowie in my truck until I can get a cage," Grady called. "Then I'll keep the snake in the trailer until Katy takes him back to school on Monday."

They watched as Grady tried to close the door of the truck. But the snake kept slithering out one crack or the other, obviously not thrilled with Grady's accommodations.

"If that isn't just like the tempter," Minnie declared, wiping her hands on her big checked apron. "Sneaking in when folks aren't looking. Just like a nasty thought or a hasty word." She beckoned to the others and stepped gingerly up the stairs. "I'm going to use that for my lesson on Sunday morning."

"See," Grady murmured in Maggie's ear as the rest of the ladies went slowly back to work. "There's some good to come out of even this."

"Yeah." Maggie rolled her eyes. "Now the entire congregation will be talking about the McCarthy snake house. Just what I need!" She stalked back up the stairs, conscious of the group of men who stood nearby, huge grins splitting their faces as they joked with Grady about women's squeamishness when it came to snakes.

"Why me, Lord?" she asked for the hundredth time.

"'This is the assurance we have in approaching God,'" she repeated to herself. "'That if we ask anything according to His will, He hears us.'

"Okay, Lord. I'm asking. Please don't let that snake

escape," she begged, fervently scrubbing the bathroom floor. "You promised that if I'd ask, You'd hear me, and I'm really asking You now. I'm holding You to Your promise."

It wasn't that she didn't trust God, Maggie told herself later that afternoon as she peeked inside Grady's truck. It was just that she couldn't help checking to make sure that repulsive reptile hadn't somehow slid out. Satisfied that Bowie was still trapped inside the vehicle with the window open just a crack, she tried to slip away, only to find Grady planted in her path, grinning for all he was worth. She ignored his knowing grin and stepped around him.

"You have to have faith, Maggie," he chided quietly. "When you ask for something, you have to trust that it will be done."

Chastened, Maggie went back to work. "I know what faith is," she muttered to herself as she tugged clothes out of her closet and organized them into piles. "I do!"

"Who are you talking to?" Gloria asked from the doorway, wiping down the woodwork as she spoke.

"God, I guess," Maggie answered and then corrected herself. "Actually, I think I reminded myself of something." She glanced at Gloria and then smiled. "'Faith is the substance of things hoped for, the evidence of things not seen.' I think I'd forgotten how to believe. Thanks, friend."

Gloria grinned and waved her cloth. "You're welcome, friend. Now, you want to tell me about that tall, handsome guy in the cowboy boots?"

Chapter Six

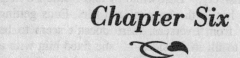

"**M**om? How many kids can we have to the party?" Katy peered up at her mother with a pleading expression she reserved for very special occasions. "It is our tenth birthday, you know, so how about ten each?"

"Twenty girls! Are you kidding? I'm not crazy yet!" Maggie poured herself and Grady another cup of coffee and stared at her daughters. "Although, if I fell for that line, I might just require the white-coated men." She noticed the glimmer of amusement in Grady's glowing eyes, and her guard immediately went up.

"Some people might even say this latest idea of yours qualifies you," he said meaningfully. "Taking on a whole pile of kids for two hours every evening? Nuts!"

"I happen to like kids," she told him sanctimoniously. "And they need to go to vacation Bible school. It's a rite of summer."

"Oh, I'm not debating that! But couldn't you have chosen a class to teach?" he asked with a twinkle in his eye. "Or taught a craft? Did you have to take on the directing of it?"

Maggie felt herself bristling and tried to control her temper. Over the past few weeks Grady had perfected the knack of getting her dander up, and lately he'd been doing it just for sport. Conscious of the girls, peering from one to the other, Maggie sipped her coffee slowly and counted to ten.

"I wasn't planning on directing the whole thing," she told him defensively. "Last winter, I told Nettie I'd help out. But with her in the hospital and Mrs. Enns getting that company from overseas, there doesn't seem to be anybody else to fill in. Besides—" she fixed him with a cooly sarcastic glance "—you should know how persuasive Minnie can be. She got you to take her to the Sunday school barbecue, didn't she?"

"Yeah, and she spilled ketchup all over his shirt!" Katy burst into a fit of the giggles as she remembered Grady's stunned face and pristine white shirt splattered with bloodred splotches. "It was so funny when she smacked that bottle and ketchup flew all over the place."

"Miss Hugenot did try to clean it up," Keeley reminded them, the beginnings of a grin tugging at her outer lips as she petted the kitten in her arms.

"Yes, I remember." Maggie blinked innocently up at Grady who had straightened from his lounging position at the far end of the table. "She almost had it off him and he was still wiping his face. That's when she knocked the bottle down and it dripped on his pants."

Katy and Keeley burst into peals of laughter at the look of disgust contorting Grady's handsome features.

"We were discussing vacation Bible school," he reminded them dourly. "And the fact that your mother doesn't have time to be running it. She's worn to a frazzle as it is."

"Well, thank you very much, Grady O'Toole!" Maggie stomped to the counter with her cup and plopped it into the dishwater, sending suds everywhere. "It's nice to know that I haven't lost that certain something every woman wants a man to notice—frazzle!" She stifled the ridiculous tears that begged release and scrubbed furiously at the cup.

Behind her there was the whisper of conspiratorial voices, but she resolutely ignored them, piling the lunch dishes in the sink with blatant disregard for their rims and edges.

"I'm sorry, Maggie," he murmured softly, his voice near the region of her left ear. "I didn't mean to upset you. Besides, you already know how lovely you are."

"I don't know anything of the kind," she replied, intent on keeping her face averted from him. "And I wasn't fishing for compliments. Weeding in the garden all morning is hardly the way to look alluring." She heard his quick indrawn breath and waited, but Grady merely picked up a tea towel and started drying.

"You don't need to try," he muttered after a few minutes. "You always look beautiful."

She twisted to stare at him and found his warm brown eyes fixed on her. There was a look on his face that told Maggie he wasn't lying and she held her breath as one tanned, work-roughened hand reached out to touch her cheek.

"You always look beautiful," he repeated softly. "It doesn't matter what you're doing. It's a beauty that shines through the field dust and the garden soil and the paint speckles."

He touched the tip of her nose where Maggie knew she had some remnants of the light blue wash she'd given her bedroom walls. And leaning down, he brushed his lips across hers.

Maggie was stunned at the reaction she felt from her toes upward. Her knees went weak and her hands moved of their own volition to tangle in the soft, worn denim of his shirt.

Grady pulled back a fraction to stare at her and then wrapped her in his big strong arms, his lips firmly on hers as he kissed her properly, his mouth warm and demanding.

Maggie kissed him back. There was something, some part of her that demanded she experience his kiss. It wasn't as though she hadn't wondered about him for weeks now, she told herself, as his arms pulled her even closer, his hands caressing her back in a soothing touch.

She had wondered exactly how it would feel to kiss him. And now she knew. It felt…wonderful!

"Mom, Mrs. Stone is here…" Katy's voice drained away as she took in the spectacle of her mother being kissed by Grady. "Uh, never mind. I'll keep her busy." Katy backed out the door and closed it carefully behind her.

"Well, that was embarrassing." Maggie laughed nervously as she pulled away from Grady and looked anywhere but at his eyes.

"I'm not sorry," he said gruffly. One finger tipped her chin up so his brown eyes looked directly into hers. "Although I probably should have waited until a more appropriate time. But Maggie, can't you see that you *are* a beautiful woman who deserves better than Brian Dalgleish?"

Maggie stared at the disgust on his face and in his tone, but not a word would come out of her mouth.

"You're not in love with him," Grady gritted through clenched teeth, swishing the towel over the rest of the dishes before he tossed it onto the counter and turned to face her. "I think you're blinded by the life you think he can give you."

"It's not such a bad life, Grady," she murmured, hanging the towel up and putting the dishes into their appropriate places. "It would mean opportunities for the girls."

"And you?"

"Of course me. I'd be able to work regular hours and be there when they needed me. We'd have a steady income, but most of all, Katy and Keeley would have some constancy in their lives." There was nothing more to do and she had to face him, but instead of finding his glance cool and condemning, his brown eyes were warm like liquid chocolate.

"Don't you have constancy here?" he asked quietly, his eyes penetrating the shell she tried to draw around herself.

"No! I have debts here. I have a lot of work. Sure, sometimes I even have some fun." She felt dread crawling up her spine again and finally, in a rush to have it out between them, spoke the word that haunted her. "But I have far too much fear to keep on living here."

"Fear?" His voice was shocked. "What in the world are you afraid of?"

"Margaret McCarthy, what is this strange child trying to do to me?" Emerald Stone burst through the door with Katy hanging on her arm and Keeley following behind. "I've been sitting on the veranda for almost ten minutes and the child just keeps babbling about you being busy. Now, are those dishes done, or not?"

Maggie nodded, knowing very well that it would do no good to argue with Mrs. Stone. Once she'd made up her mind, the matter was settled.

"Good. He," she nodded her head toward Grady, "has work to do, does he not?" Emerald stared at him balefully as if to say she knew very well that men had no place in the kitchen. "Then off you go! And take those two with you. Maggie and I have business to discuss and we don't need anyone around to bother us."

In five seconds flat, Emerald had shooed everyone but Maggie out of the house. She swiped her hands together in a dusting motion and breathed a hearty sigh before turning back toward Maggie.

"Now, Margaret, I would like to have a new outfit for my niece's wedding two weeks from next Saturday." And thus decreeing, Emerald pulled out ten meters of the boldest, ugliest fabric Maggie had ever seen. "If you could spare me a moment, I'd like to discuss cut and style with you."

"Of course, Emerald. It just so happens that I've got a few free minutes this week. I'd be happy to sew that up for you." Maggie tried to stifle the annoyance she desperately wanted to express. "Let's have a look, shall we?"

"She's a pain," Katy announced in a grim voice as the kitchen door closed behind them. "I tried to keep her away while you were kissing Mom, Grady, but she kept insisting. Keeley couldn't even hold her back."

"Nobody," Keeley said seriously, her face looking very adult, "and I mean *nobody,* can hold back Mrs. Stone when she wants something." Her big blue eyes were curious as they studied Grady. "Did you ever want something really badly, Grady? Something that you didn't get, even though you prayed and prayed for it?"

Grady thought of the tiny baby that had never had the chance to live. He thought of the years of dreaming of a family of his own. Dreams that had died in a miscarriage.

"Yes," he murmured, folding her seeking hand in his own. "I have."

"You have? What did you wish for?" That was curious Katy, peering up at him in interest.

Grady couldn't help himself. He reached out and patted the little girl's bright curls, his work-roughened fingers catching on the delicate strands.

"A little girl," he whispered, his voice breaking despite his attempts otherwise. "A little girl just like you and your sister."

"Are you going to marry our mother?" Keeley stared at the two of them, her frown marring the pretty oval of her face. "She doesn't want to stay on the farm, you know. She wants to get away."

Grady saw her cast a look of longing around the familiar landscape and wondered, for the first time, how Keeley would fare in the city. He searched for the right words.

"I think your mother has worked for a very long time to keep everything going," Grady said quietly. He sank down onto the lush green grass and waited for the girls to join him. "She's been trying to do everything."

"A farm does have a lot of work," Keeley told him seriously. "It's sort of like school. You can't always take a day or week off just because you want to."

"I know, sweetie." He smiled at her grown-up look. "And I suspect your mom hasn't had a day off in a very long time. She's always got another quilt to make, or books to work on." He cocked his head toward the house. "Or another dress to sew."

"She used to laugh a lot," Katy whispered, staring at her hands. "I can remember it. We'd make cookies at Christmas and Easter and stuff. I liked to put the decorations on." She scuffed her toe on the grass. "We never make cookies anymore."

"Katy McCarthy, that's a lie! Granny let us help her make cookies last week." Keeley's face was flushed and she glared at her sister. "That was the day Mrs. Bloomquist got the colors mixed up and Granny came out of the hairdresser's with pink hair."

Grady swallowed the laughter that rose in his throat. *So that's what had happened.* He smiled, remembering that brilliant fuchsia hair that had covered Kayleen Davis's head for five days. It had been the talk of the town.

"It's not the same as having Mom though, Keeley. Mom never just cut the shapes out. She adds things and fixes them up so they're different than all the other kids' cookies. I took some to play school once."

"Things are different now, Katy. Dad's not here anymore and Mom has to run things by herself." Keeley's eyes narrowed, surveying the thick green crop across the road. "She's having enough trouble keeping things going. And if we could just get a really good harvest, maybe Mom wouldn't feel so bad all the time."

"She feels bad because she wants to give us things," Katy muttered astutely, glancing at them both as she snapped her gum once more. "But I don't care about fancy clothes and stuff. I wouldn't mind a four-wheeler, though."

Grady grinned at the obvious hint about an upcoming birthday. Katy took every possible opportunity to impress on him the importance of a girl's tenth birthday. Her veiled hints about appropriate presents had included an aquarium, an ant farm, new uniforms for the Little League team she belonged to and roller blades. A four-wheeler was her most ambitious hint yet.

"I don't think your mom would appreciate that, Katy."

He mussed her curls with a grin. "Come on, girls. I need a little help with a project I'm working on. Only, you can't say a word to your mother. If she knew, I'd never live it down."

They danced around him like mosquitoes, trying to find out what he meant. But Grady just smiled and led them to a corner of the barn where he'd carefully hidden his latest labor.

"Uh...what is it?" Keeley peered at the plywood backdrop with its hinged sides. She struck her hands through the smoothly sanded holes and stared up at him, frowning. "You *deliberately* cut holes in this wood?" she asked in disbelief.

"Of course I did." He was strangely affronted that she didn't understand.

Katy glanced sideways at Keeley, who simply shrugged her shoulders and shook her head. Then they both sat down on a nearby bale of hay and waited for his explanation. Grady couldn't help feeling like a misunderstood schoolboy forced to stay late to explain his deeds.

"It's for vacation Bible school," he said at last, slightly exasperated.

"Oh, yes." Katy's big blue eyes were stretched wide open. "For Bible school," she said softly to Keeley, jabbing her sister in the side with an elbow.

"Uh-huh." They both stared at him in sympathy.

"Don't you get it? It's a backdrop for a puppet show!"

"Uh, Grady, our church hasn't got any puppets." Katy said the words slowly and carefully, her hand gentle on his arm. There was a soft sympathy shimmering in her gaze. "But it was very nice of you to think of it. Thank you."

"They'll have them by tomorrow," he told her smugly. "I ordered them from a place in Calgary."

"Wow!" Keeley, at least, appreciated his intentions. "So you can stand behind here and poke the puppets through and nobody will even know who's doing what." She beamed up at him. "It's great! What are you going to paint on here?"

"Well…" Grady scuffed his foot against the wooden floor in an imitation of Katy and drew in a deep breath of the fragrant hay smell. "That's a bit of a problem, you see. I can't draw a straight line."

"*Anybody* can draw a straight line," Keeley protested.

"Not me." Grady stared at his hands. "It's something to do with my eyes, they say. Even my glasses don't fix it completely. And I *was* hoping to have it ready as a surprise for your mom on Friday."

"What kind of puppets are they, Grady?" Keeley wanted to know, studying the smoothly sanded wood. "Animals or people or what?"

"The lady at the shop told me they're for a story about a missionary family living in the jungle of South America. There's a mother, a father, a boy and a girl and a dog named Luther." He watched her serious little face study the blank board before her.

"Luther's not a dog's name," Katy said disgustedly. "Where'd they get a dumb name like that?"

"It's not dumb," Grady murmured, hoping he wouldn't embarrass her. "Luther was the name of another sort of missionary a long, long time ago. Maybe that's why they called him that." He saw Keeley squinting at the board. "What do you think, sweetie?"

"I think we could do some trees and vines and stuff on here," she murmured. "But first it needs a white coat of paint to even things out. Can you do that?" She waited for him to nod and then continued. "I could draw some stuff on in pencil and then fill it in with paint later. Do you have paints?''

"No." He grimaced, stuffing his hands in his pockets. "I wasn't too sure what to get. Maybe we'd better take a trip into town to check things out. I'll just make sure that it's okay with your mom. You guys go and get into the truck.''

"Can we stop for ice cream after?" Katy asked around the wad of gum that pouched out her cheek like a squirrel.

"Only if you get rid of that gum," Grady retorted, grinning. "I thought your mother asked you not to chew it anymore?''

"She says it's the kind that 'won't stick to braces,'" Keeley stated dourly. "It sure sticks to the desks at school.''

"Katy!" Grady swung round to hide the grin that itched at his mouth when she hastily got rid of the ugly green glob. "You'd better not have any more when I get back," he ordered, striding off to the house before they saw him laughing.

Kids! Maggie sure had her hands full with this pair. And yet, she was so lucky.

Maggie snatched the sand pail full of water out of Greta Wilkinson's hand just before it was emptied on Grady's unsuspecting form and wondered why she'd ever consented to a beach party for the girls. This was more like a riot!

"Okay," Grady was saying. "Here's the raft." The words had barely left his lips when the raft lifted off the sandy beach and flopped down into the water. "Uh, you're welcome." He grinned, dusting his hands against his shorts. His brown eyes sparkled up at Maggie. "Just a little hyper, aren't they?''

"That's like being a little dead," Maggie informed him, sinking back down onto her beach chair. "Either you are or you aren't. There aren't any half measures. And I am," she added, closing her eyes and letting a sigh of tiredness escape. "Dead, I mean," she murmured, opening one bright eye to peer at him.

"Not quite yet." He laughed, catching the beach ball and tossing it back to the giggling girls in the water. "But relax for a while if you want. I'll watch them."

"All of them?" Maggie studied his face and privately wondered why Grady had hung around for so long. Sometimes, when his eyes got a misty, faraway kind of look, she was sure he wanted to be somewhere else.

"Okay, maybe not all of them. That Melinda kid asks too many questions. She's got more than Katy's even thought of."

Maggie groaned. "What did she ask now?"

"What does God do when he's on vacation?" Grady chuckled. "She didn't like my answer much."

"What did you tell her?" Maggie wondered out loud.

"That God doesn't take vacations. Even when we think He's busy somewhere else, God still hears His children and cares for them."

"Sure of that, are you?" she asked grouchily, thinking of the loan payment that would be due in September. It was a whopper.

"Absolutely positive," Grady said matter-of-factly. "But Melinda insisted that three weeks of vacation was the law and that God wouldn't be allowed to work it unless He got paid overtime." He shook his head at Maggie's wide-eyed look. "Then she wanted to know who paid God. Thankfully I didn't have to answer that."

"Why not?" She was almost afraid to hear this.

"Katy told her God got paid every Sunday when they

took the offering!'' He laughed heartily, his voice ringing out above the children's shrieks of joy, and Maggie caught her breath at the pure pleasure on his face. ''Those kids are really something, Maggie.''

''Yes,'' she murmured. ''They are. It was really kind of you to give the girls those bikes. That's an expensive gift for one child, but two? You shouldn't have done it.''

''Of course I should. How could I give one a bicycle and not the other? Honestly, for a mother, you're not well versed in fairness.'' He grinned knowingly when she sputtered angrily at the slur. ''Anyway, it was either a bike or a four-wheeler, and I'm well aware of your feelings on that subject, Maggie McCarthy!''

''You wouldn't have! Would you?'' Less certain now than she had been, Maggie frowned as she studied his face for an answer.

''I *was* considering it, but then I figured maybe you were right. They ought to be a little older before they go tearing around on one of those things. Next year, maybe.''

Maggie couldn't contain her thrill of excitement at the thought that Grady would still be around next year. She and the girls had really come to rely on his presence.

''By the way,'' she murmured a few minutes later, ''it's Friday today. How come you're not going in to Calgary for your weekly visit?''

He studied her for a few minutes as if he could see into her mind. Finally he spoke, but his words came out coolly, as if he didn't welcome her question. ''Everything is at a standstill right now. There's no need. Besides I saw somebody locally.''

She got lost in her thoughts of Grady and all the things they didn't know about him. Was he in love with someone in Calgary? Was that who he was making calls to? Or maybe he was really sick and had to go for treatment.

Maggie hated asking, but for the girls' sake she had to know. "Grady are you in some kind of trouble?"

"What?" He stared at her for one amazed moment and then burst out laughing. "You mean, am I visiting my parole officer every week?" He grinned. "Sorry to disappoint you, Maggie, but I haven't anything so exciting in my past." He took a deep breath and then lifted his head, his lustrous brown eyes meeting hers head-on.

"I had an investment company. Someone initiated a hostile takeover by spreading rumors that we were doing business illegally. I'm hoping to save what I can out of the whole mess. But I can't do that till my doctor gives me the all clear."

No wonder he had to work for someone else, Maggie thought to herself. *He must have lost everything but the truck and the camper.*

"I'm sorry," she apologized, her hand touching his gently. To her surprise he gathered it up and held it between his larger, work-roughened hands. "I had no right to pry. It's just that Emerald told me about Doctor Lee and I wondered if you were all right. Maybe you shouldn't be doing all that heavy work?"

"Good ol' Emerald." He didn't sound angry, and Maggie relaxed just a bit. "I suppose it's natural for people to speculate in a small community like this. That's something I'd forgotten about." He seemed lost in thought, unaware of her presence as he stared out at the glistening water rippling gently from a light westerly breeze.

"It's all right," she murmured finally. "You're entitled to your privacy as much as anyone else."

"You're a nice woman, Margaret Mary McCarthy. And trust me, in this day and age, that's a compliment!" He winked at her and let her hand go with a squeeze. "The truth is, I had a heart attack a while back. Stress induced, so they tell me. My doctor ordered me to rest and recuperate away from the city and my problems."

"A heart attack? So you decided to work on a farm?" Maggie shook her head. "That's really relaxing!"

"Actually it is," he muttered, staring at the calluses that covered his fingers and thumbs. "I do an honest job in the fresh air and the sun. A certain beautiful lady feeds me home-cooked meals and two little girls keep life from getting boring. I've never felt better. There's certainly no stress."

Maggie studied his tanned face, noting the healthy flush of color. "Grady, I don't think you should be—"

He cut her off. "I'm fine Maggie. Don't start fussing. And Doctor Lee checks on me. He says there's nothing on the farm that I shouldn't be doing. It's been really good for me." He lay back on the shore, his head cupped between his hands and stared at the sky. "What do you think that cloud looks like? I say it's a sailboat. One of the old-fashioned kind."

After a glance at the girls currently engaged in a sand-building contest, Maggie lay back on her towel and stared upward.

"No way," she disagreed after a moment. "See there." She pointed. "That's a puff of smoke from the dragon. There, underneath that ribbon. I can't believe you can't see it!"

"It's fairly obvious you don't know any science," Grady countered, shaking his head. "That's not a dragon. It's a dinosaur. Triceratops, I believe."

Maggie turned on her side to laugh down at him. "Triceratops, my foot! And I suppose you think the one beside it is a hippopotamus?"

He grinned, his breath near her ear. "Hey, maybe you're finally catching on."

She swatted his shoulder and found her fingers trapped in his. "I'll have you know I invented this game." Her voice died away at the look in his warm brown eyes, and she couldn't help leaning nearer when his mouth brushed across hers. It barely qualified as a kiss and yet Maggie hadn't felt this rush of stars to her head, or this giddy rush of feelings in a very long time. His mouth pulled away from hers but she couldn't break the intensity of his gaze.

"Are you married, Grady?" The soft words slipped out before she could stop them, and once said, Maggie sincerely hoped he'd answer her. The silence, however, was deafening.

"I was. Once." His voice was low and Maggie could hear the coolness. He was pulling away. Withdrawing. "We're divorced."

"I'm sorry. That must have been very painful." She wasn't sure just how to ask, but somehow she knew that it was important to know. "Do you have any children?"

His answer, when it came, shocked her to the depths of her being, and she felt as if the sun fell from the sky.

"Once I had everything. But now it's gone. Everything's gone." He got up then and strode down the beach, a lonely solitary figure, lost in the mists of pain she had glimpsed in his brown eyes.

"Oh, Lord," Maggie whispered fearfully. "Please be with him. Help him. I didn't mean to tear him up like that. I just didn't know."

Suddenly the pastor's words from last Sunday rolled through her brain. *I am, God said. I am in control. I am there when you think I'm not. I see. I hear. I know.*

It was a promise every bit as much as the rainbow that had covered the western sky had been a promise after the rain last evening. She just had to trust. Why was that so hard?

"Mom, we're starved. Can we have the wiener roast pretty soon?" Keeley stood staring down at her mother, her eyes swerving to where Grady walked far down the white sand. "Isn't Grady going to help?"

"Grady will come when he's ready, honey. But I think right now we should finish up here on the beach. You guys go gather some driftwood for the fire. Go down there." She pointed in the direction opposite of where Grady had walked. "I think there's a huge pile just over that rock. Okay?"

"Sure, Mom. Is everything all right?" Keeley's expression was worried and Maggie couldn't help the surge of love that she felt at the little girl's concern.

"Everything will be wonderful, sweetie. After all, God's looking out for us, isn't he?" She tried to sound sure of herself, but deep inside, everything was still a knot of questions.

"Yep! God, Granny and Gramps." Keeley grinned, pointing. "Here they come, Mom, and they've got presents." She swept up the beach and toward her grandparents with a whoop and a holler.

Maggie watched Katy follow and smiled at the looks on their faces as their grandparents wished them a happy birthday. But she couldn't help it when her eyes kept returning to the tall, lean, forlorn figure sitting hunkered down on a log, staring out over the water.

Chapter Seven

"**W**hy? Just tell me why the woman ever volunteered for this," Grady demanded of no one in particular as he hauled in the tons of stuff Maggie had tossed into his truck bed that morning. "And how did she sweet-talk me into helping?"

"Grumbling and complaining are a sin." Pastor Jim grinned as he grabbed one of the largest boxes and lugged it inside. "But since you provided us with the puppets and backdrop, I expect the Lord will forgive you." He sidestepped Tommy Williams and set his box down in the foyer. "The kids are a little excited about vacation Bible school," he explained.

"A little?" Grady winced as a shrill voice bellowed out in the vicinity of his left eardrum. "What do you call 'a lot'?"

"Just wait until Maggie gets them involved in one of those stories of hers. They'll be as still as statues."

"This I've got to see," Grady muttered, carrying in another armload.

"You're not going to be able to see anything, Grady.

You're going to be behind the backdrop. We're short a puppeteer," Maggie said as she walked over to the two men. Her bright eyes were studying him with a gleam that made his knees shake.

"Maggie, you promised!" he began. "You said that I wouldn't be needed in the school. You *said* that I could get started on that haying today for sure."

"But Grady," Maggie pleaded, her eyes imploring him with that wide-open appeal that Grady defied any man to resist. "You know I can't tell the story *and* manage a puppet. I'll help you with the haying this afternoon, I promise."

"You're not haying," Grady told her firmly. "It's far too hot, and besides, you've got that special quilt order to fill. I'll manage it myself. *If,*" he hinted broadly, "I ever get out of here."

He tried to sidestep her but to no avail. Her fingers wrapped themselves around his arm and she hung on.

"Grady, I *need* you. Please?"

He tried his best to get out of it. "What about Emerald Stone? I thought she was going to help you?"

"Emerald fell and hurt her leg. Has to stay off it. Besides, she doesn't like kids. Please?"

Who, Grady asked himself as he let her lead him behind the curtains of the stage, *could resist the woman?* Not him, that was for sure.

He sat behind the curtain, waiting as he listened to Maggie try to bring order out of chaos. At last the group were singing merrily along to the chorus. Then Maggie began her segue into the puppet show. He'd heard her practicing it at home.

"Did you ever wonder about God?" There was a murmur of excitement throughout the room. "What kind of things do you wonder? Janice?"

"Is God really invisible, or is that just a trick?"

Maggie, no doubt through long years of practice with Katy, fielded that one easily. "Anyone else?"

"Instead of letting people die and making new ones, why doesn't God just keep the ones He has now?"

Since Grady had wondered that himself, he listened and nodded at the pastor's answer. It *was* comforting to think that God had his child in heaven, watching over him.

"Okay guys, one more question. Tara?"

"I was just wondering how God could love everybody in the whole world. I only gots four people in my family and I have a hard time loving them all, 'specially at the same time."

"No, you can't." Maggie smiled. Grady could hear the mirth in her voice. "I have a hard time with that one myself, Tara. But that's because we aren't God. We're just humans. And today we're going to talk about God's love for a little boy who lives very far away in the jungle. His name is Tawi."

That was the signal for the puppets and Grady scrambled to get Tawi into place. Maggie—beautiful, *organized* Maggie—had taped the script into place above each hole and all he had to do was read his part at the appropriate place.

Ten minutes later he was drenched in sweat and profoundly glad he was finished.

"Now, that wasn't so bad, was it?" Maggie was smiling at him, and he couldn't help the charge of electricity he felt as he basked in that lovely smile.

"It was awful." He sighed, wiping his forehead. "I'll build the sets, I'll lug them here, I'll do all the grunt work. I'll weed the garden. I'll even paint something if I have to. But please, Maggie, please don't make me do that again." He folded his damp handkerchief carefully, stuffed it into his pants pocket and sank back on his heels, not caring a whit that he sounded like a whining six-year-old kid. If he remained standing, it would be a miracle.

"You did very well, Grady. Thank you for filling in." She wrapped her arms around his waist and hugged him. Grady, not caring who saw, hugged her back.

"You're welcome," he murmured when she finally pulled away. "I guess." The lemon scent of her hair clung to the air surrounding them. "Maybe it wasn't so bad. You need anything else?" *Like maybe another hug?*

"No, but thanks for asking. You go ahead and get started on the haying. "I'll see you at lunchtime."

Grady watched her walk away, his left hand slipping up to touch the spot on his cheek that she'd brushed with her fingertips.

"She's one rock-solid lady," Pastor Jim murmured, his eyes glinting as Grady's hand suddenly fell away. "Be an awful shame if she ever leaves."

"She wants to, though," Grady muttered, walking down the aisle with the minister. "She thinks she wants to live in the city and have a regular nine-to-five job."

"And I guess if things get much worse for her, she'll have to." Jim's voice was low and concerned. "I'd hate to see her leave the farm. She's carried a heavy load for so long, it'd be nice if she could get that crop of hers off and into the bin."

"It looks pretty good," Grady told him seriously. "Wheat's starting to form into good-size heads. Should be worth top dollar if we can get it off. I intend to ask some of the neighbors to help when the time comes." He glanced up at the blue sky. "I'd feel better if we could get that hay off, though. I don't think this weather is going to last."

"And Maggie's already obligated to vacation Bible

school." Pastor Jim nodded. "Yes, I see your problem.
But I might just have a solution." He studied Grady carefully for a long time and then nodded as if he was satisfied
with what he saw. "You ever worked with kids who've
been in trouble?"

"Yes. A little." Grady decided he'd have to give a bit
of information. "My company used to take on some of
the boys from the delinquent facility outside of Calgary.
You've heard of it?" When Pastor Jim nodded, Grady
relaxed a little and told him how many boys he'd trained
and in what capacity. "Are these young offenders?"

"Well—" Jim scratched his head doubtfully
"—they're young and they're certainly offenders. They
spread graffiti all over the high-level bridge a few weeks
ago, and even though they've cleaned it off, there's still
the matter of stealing that car and spilling manure all over
Highway 4."

"In other words, they've just started down the road to
ruin," Grady muttered, thinking. "What have you got in
mind?"

"Haying," said Pastor Jim triumphantly.

They spent the next few minutes deciding just how
they'd handle the boys, and it wasn't long before Grady
found himself agreeing to take on two extra boys. By one
o'clock they were heading out to start the largest field.
Maggie had frowned a little when the boys had shown up
after lunch. But Grady had shaken his head and she
seemed disposed to let it go. For now. He suspected the
dearth of garden produce waiting on the vines behind the
house had prompted her quick acquiescence.

"I want to go for as long as I can," he told her quietly.
"If you could manage a meal in the field, we'd appreciate
it. But if that's too much work, we'll catch something
later."

She'd favored him with a dour look. "Six sharp," she told him firmly. "I'll bring it out. You'd better be hungry."

He'd saluted smartly and turned and marched across the yard to the twins' fit of giggles. Kent and Randy, the two troubled youths, followed quickly, their sour looks erased for now.

Maggie watched the three of them drive off, a light feeling in her heart. She hated haying with a passion. It was hot, dirty, dusty work. "Which, come to think of it, is what most of farming is about," she muttered to herself derisively.

Katy and Keeley stood staring at her curiously. "Are you okay, Mom?" Keeley asked at last.

"I'm wonderful! And so are you." She pressed a kiss against their soft cheeks and replaced the hair clip hanging down Katy's back. "Now, here's the deal. If we can get those cucumbers and beans picked and put away this afternoon, we'll leave the peas till tomorrow."

"Gee, big deal," Katy muttered grumpily. "I thought maybe you had a surprise or something."

"Well, as it happens..." Maggie let the words hang, knowing her daughters wouldn't be able to resist her offer. "I thought maybe we could have a wiener roast by the creek tonight. You guys could toast marshmallows."

"Is Grady coming?" Keeley asked quietly amid her sister's loud jubilation. Maggie saw her tuck a piece of paper into her pocket.

"Maybe later. He wants to get the hay finished before it rains again. Why, honey? Don't you like it when it's just the three of us?"

"Yeah, I guess." Keeley's blue eyes were shaded by the sun hat she wore, and Maggie couldn't quite make out the strange look in them. "But it's more fun if he's there. Grady makes us feel like a family."

"And Mom's got somebody to talk to while we play," Katy reminded her. "The people said— Ow, Keeley, stop that!" She reached out and tugged her sister's neatly braided hair, sending Keeley off into a fit of anger.

"Girls!" Maggie raised her voice, her eyes open wide as she stared at them. "If this continues, we will not go to the creek or anywhere else. We'll finish hoeing the potatoes instead." Her daughters bent obediently and picked up their buckets, but not without angry glares tossed between them. Maggie walked behind them, her mind replaying their conversation.

"What did you mean, Katy? What people?" She saw Keeley's head give an almost imperceptible shake at Katy. "What did they say?" she asked more loudly.

"I can't tell you, Mom," Katy muttered, yanking the green beans off with a vicious twist that amazingly did little damage to the plant. "It's a secret. You know how you say we can have secrets if they're good. Well, this is a good one."

"Keeley?" Maggie fixed her daughter with a stern look but Keeley was busy hunting among the prickly vines for the pickling cucumbers she knew were used for dills.

"You said, Mom," was all Keeley would say.

Maggie sighed. Motherhood! It wasn't nearly as easy as it should be. But it was definitely worth it. "All right girls. But it had better be good." She watched them exchange a look that immediately set her motherly instincts on "red alert."

"Oh, it's good," they said. "Really good," Keeley added softly. "Some day you'll thank us."

"Oh, Lord," Maggie breathed silently as she picked

heads of dill and shook off the insects that always hid among the seeds. "Please let it be a good surprise."

The creek had dwindled down from its raging waters of spring's runoff but there was still enough to let the girls paddle around and cool off from the hot afternoon. As they giggled and laughed and chased the dog through the shallows, Maggie wondered if moving them would be the right thing. They'd had such happy times here.

"Well, isn't this a pretty sight." Grady's voice was low and intimate as he folded himself down beside her in the gloom of the evening. "It's nice when summer evenings are so long that it's still daylight at ten, isn't it?" he murmured, dropping another log on the flickering bed of coals.

"The girls love it. I usually let them stay up fairly late. After all, they can sleep in." She studied his damp brown hair as it curled onto his forehead. "How did it go?"

"Actually pretty well. I was glad I took the time to sharpen those knives on that relic, though. They wouldn't have cut butter." He took the stick with the hot dog on it and began slowly turning it over and over, browning it evenly. "I don't really need this," he muttered, sinking his even white teeth into the bun he'd wrapped around it. "That supper was enough to feed an army. Those ribs were something else."

"I'm glad you liked them. It's the lemon that brings out the flavor. Were the boys a help or a hindrance?" Maggie glanced at the girls downstream where they'd built a dam. She knew the moment they spotted Grady they'd come racing back, chatting and teasing with him. It made these few times together oddly special.

"They're smart kids," he said, biting into his hot dog. "They just got onto the wrong track. We talked about that after supper. They're coming back again to help with the baling later this week. I said I'd help them with a computer project in the fall in return for their help during harvest. They figured it was a pretty good deal.''

There it was again—that reference to a future here on the farm. Maggie hugged the knowledge to her and allowed herself to daydream as she stared into the flickering coals. It would be nice to have an evening now and then spent sharing the events of the day. Though the girls were still dependent on her, they were also more involved in their own lives. Particularly Keeley, who seemed to have developed more than her usual affinity with the computer lately.

"Maggie?" She turned at the light pressure on her arm and found Grady's face mere inches from hers.

"Yes?" She liked the way his grin tipped up the corners of his mouth lopsidedly when he smiled at her.

"You didn't hear anything I said, did you?" His eyes twinkled in the dusk of the sun setting over the riverbank. "You were lost in dreamland somewhere. Don't deny it."

"I wasn't going to." Maggie decided to just tell the truth. "I was thinking how nice it was to talk to an adult again. Which reminds me... Where are the girls?" She turned to look around.

"Don't knock the solitude." Grady chuckled. "They're fine. They're catching worms. I told them I'd take them fishing tomorrow afternoon while I wait for the hay to dry out. With this heat it won't be long before we can start baling." His voice dropped to a whisper. "I like talking to you, too, Maggie. It's just one of the things I like about this place."

Maggie got lost staring into his deep brown eyes. There were secrets there, she knew. And hidden pain. But there was tenderness and joy, too. She could see it in the tiny crow's-feet at the corners of his eyes when they crinkled with pleasure. Suddenly his words sank in.

"Fishing?" she repeated dazedly. "You're going fishing and you didn't tell me?" A slow burn started deep inside her brain and spread to her heart. "You're leaving me out of it?" She tried to mask the hurt she felt.

"Of course not!" Grady stared at her. "I just didn't think... Do you want to come?" he asked curiously. "I've never met a woman who actually *liked* fishing. We're using live worms, you know," he told her seriously, his dark eyebrows raised in a question.

As if I was made of icing sugar, Maggie huffed mentally. The one pleasure she dearly loved and seldom afforded herself and he was going to leave her out?

"Is there any other way?" She shrugged away from the warm arm that had oh so carelessly draped itself around her shoulders sometime during the conversation and wiggled backward on the blanket. "I've been using live bait for years. My dad and I used to spend hours on the Little Bow when I was a kid. Those pickerel could hardly wait for us to toss in our lines."

"Pickerel?" Grady peered through the dusky gloom at her. "They're not usually found this far south, are they?"

Maggie tilted her chin in the air and tossed him a superior look. *A fat lot you know, Grady O'Toole,* she thought to herself. "Pickerel like cold, fresh water," she informed him. "And the Bow River is fed from mountain streams and glaciers. It's generally cold enough to support pickerel." She glanced up when he shifted on the blanket. "Of course, now I don't need live bait. I have a special lure that's never failed me yet."

"All right," he admitted with that warm laugh that skittered across her nerves and made her feel cared for. "I concede my ignorance. I'll even confess that I was crass and unfeeling not to invite you along. Am I forgiven?" He pulled her up, drawing her very close to his lean, muscular length. "Would you do us the honor of joining us for a fishing expedition on the Little Bow River tomorrow afternoon, Margaret Mary McCarthy?"

His voice swirled around her like a cool mist after a blistering hot day and Maggie felt her anger melt away as she stared into those warm eyes. He was so…what was the word? Comfortable? No, that made him sound like a pair of old shoes, and Grady O'Toole was not nearly so mundane!

"Yes, thank you," she murmured primly, to hide the thrill she felt when his hands squeezed hers like that. "I love fishing. It'll be nice to get my fishing rod in the water again." She watched as he kicked wet sand over the fire and made a trench so the few smoking coals couldn't spread. "I'd better get the girls home. Tomorrow's bound to bring a big crowd out for Bible school."

"Why?" Grady asked from his crouched position on the sand. "Wasn't most of the town already there?"

"Well, we had about three dozen kids today. By tomorrow, the word will have spread that we have puppets. Besides, I promised a treat for anyone who brings along a guest." She laughed out loud at his shaking head. "It usually works fairly well."

"I can imagine." He dusted off his hands and plunged them into his pockets, studying her with an indulgent look that Maggie didn't quite understand. One hand came out to brush the blond fall of hair off her forehead. "Lady, you are a glutton for punishment."

"Aw, come on Grady," she teased, calling the girls once more. "The crop's growing like crazy, the weather's been wonderful. You've even got the hay off. Almost," she added at his frowning look. "Life is great. What could go wrong?"

"Don't even think about it," he muttered, shaking out the blanket and picking up the picnic basket. "By the way," he asked as the girls raced away in front of them, whooping through the thickly forested bush, "do you know what Keeley's been up to lately?"

There was something in his tone that had Maggie searching his eyes. "Keeley? No. Why?" Her heart thudded in her chest as she searched his face for some clue. "What's she done now?"

"Nothing that I know of. It's just that she spends so much time on that computer of hers. And then, when the mail comes, she's always there, waiting to sort it before Elmer even gets it in the box. She usually tries to hide it, but most days there's some envelope or letter packet for her."

"What do you suppose she's up to?" Maggie asked and watched the two blond heads tilt together as Keeley said something to her sister. "Maybe Katy knows."

"If she does, she isn't talking." Grady's face turned a deep red at Maggie's curious look. "I tried to pry it out of her days ago. No luck."

"Well, whatever it is, they'll spill it before long," Maggie muttered, grunting with exertion as she climbed the last steep hill. Grady's hand on her arm propelled her over the top. "They never could keep a secret for long," she panted, grinning at him happily.

They walked back to the house without another word, listening to the girls' excited jabber about tomorrow. When the twins had hugged Grady good-night and kissed Maggie, they climbed upstairs gladly, tired from their active day.

Maggie joined her hired hand on the front porch shortly

after that and handed him a long, cool glass of ice tea. As she leaned back in the old willow chair, her eyes studied the star-studded beauty of the heavens.

"They're up to something," she confided, tilting her head toward the window that overlooked the front yard. "I can hear the whispers from here. I'll bet Katy lets the cat out of the bag tomorrow."

But Grady wasn't so certain. She could see it in the way he studied that window for a long time, sipping his tea absently. And he never even commented on the falling star Maggie pointed out to him just before the old mantel clock struck midnight.

But she knew exactly when his attention shifted from the room upstairs to her. She could feel the crackle of tension in the air as he watched her from under the brim of his cowboy hat. And when he stood up and slowly placed his glass on a nearby table, Maggie knew he was going to kiss her.

She stood and moved into his embrace easily, relaxing against him when his arms fitted themselves around her waist. She could smell the bracing scent of his cologne mingled with the blooming hollyhocks and taste the hint of lemon on his breath when his mouth closed over hers.

"You're a very beautiful woman, Maggie," he murmured as his fingers disentangled themselves from her hair a moment later. His smooth soft lips brushed her cheek in a gossamer caress that almost made her forget where she was.

Almost.

"You're lucky, too," he whispered, his arms looped gently around her. "You have what most people long for." The words were so quiet, she barely heard them. "Land, a family and a place to call home." For once she had no desire to contradict him.

They stood there, staring at the stars in each other's eyes for a long time before Grady set her away, his lips touching hers one final time.

"Good night, Margaret Mary."

As he walked across the yard to his camper and the lights went on inside, Maggie flopped back down in her chair. The old yearning for something more, something better, rose up inside, deeper and stronger than ever as she started out across the yard.

What she saw wasn't that great. A rickety old barn that had been patched and repatched. Rusty farm machinery that ran on a piece of gum and a prayer. A drafty old house that cost her a fortune to cool in the hot Canadian summer and even more to heat in the winter.

"It might be home for now, Grady," she murmured to herself as she slipped inside and tugged the warped door closed behind her. "But it's just a place to stay until I can find something better. Someplace where we can have everything the girls and I need. And I will find it," she added fiercely as she climbed the creaky staircase to her lonely room. "I will get a better life for my girls and myself. No matter what."

Chapter Eight

❧

"Ah! This is the life." Maggie leaned back in her seat and jiggled her fishing pole slightly, waiting for the slight tug that would give her the next catch of the afternoon.

"Quit bragging," Grady muttered, casting out again. A disgusted look tipped his eyebrows down. "Two hours and not even a bite. What am I doing wrong, oh great fisherwoman?"

Maggie turned her face away, pretending to study her daughters as they searched the shallows near shore for minnows. The girls had long since tired of fishing with a pole and had opted for a swim, their minnow nets and the freedom to run and yell along the beach.

"I'm waiting," Grady muttered grumpily. "And if you even think about saying 'I told you so,'" he growled, motioning at the water, "I'll dump you overboard and return this monstrosity to your generous neighbor." His look grew even fiercer at the burst of giggles she couldn't contain.

"I'm sorry," Maggie said, laughing and lowering back into the chilly water of the lake the stringer holding the six lovely pickerel. "I told you, this is my lucky lure. It never fails to bring 'em in." She snapped it across the water with an expert flick of her wrist and glanced at him from the corner of her eye. "Would you like to borrow it?"

"No I would not." His voice was curt. "I'm using exactly the same lure. How many worms did you put on?"

"Didn't use 'em," Maggie asserted, jerking sharply on the line and winding it slowly in. "Don't need to," she said triumphantly as she lifted out another prime catch. She could feel his eyes studying her as she whipped the hook out of the fish's mouth and expertly strung it alongside the last. "It's all in the wrist action."

"How come it can't all be in the wrist when you change oil in your car, then?" he demanded, a trifle sulkily Maggie decided. "I've never seen anyone make that big a mess of an oil change."

"Changing oil is not my forte," she told him airily. It was hard to miss his "That's for sure!" seconds later. "You have some areas in which you don't exactly excel, either, you know," she reminded him primly.

"Oh, yeah! Name one."

"Well, for one thing, your color coordination is the worst I've ever seen." She nodded meaningfully at his faded pink shirt and bright red shorts. "The two of those do *not* belong on one body at the same time." She giggled at his offended look. "And especially not when the wearer is sporting such a sunburned nose."

"I got it this morning, teaching your children to water-ski," he reminded her sourly. "No, actually it was *trying* to teach you that took so long. I never had so much trouble with anyone else."

Privately, Maggie wondered if he spent as much time

and attention on all his other students. Even now she remembered the touch of his hands on her waist as he'd carefully fastened the life jacket and lifted her onto the dock. She could feel the tingle of electricity between them and recalled the way he'd pushed her hair out of her eyes and hauled her aboard after she'd been swamped in the waves of another boat. She'd been freezing when she got out of the water. He'd rubbed the towel briskly over her back and shoulders, stopping only when his face had been inches from hers and the girls had started giggling.

"I knew you'd keep nattering about that," she complained now, flushing hotly at his raised eyebrow. "I don't think it's very polite."

"Neither is saying my clothes don't match," he retorted with a grin. "Especially when *you* spilled the bleach on my shirt!"

Maggie could feel the heat traveling up her neck to her cheeks. "You're the one who came rushing into the house and shoved a great huge slug under my nose. What did you think I'd do—eat it?" She eyed the chilly water of the lake for one mad minute, then tossed away the idea of splashing him. He'd only retaliate.

"How else was I going to get you to take them seriously? I told you weeks ago that they were into the tomatoes and the carrots. You just couldn't accept my superior knowledge."

"Superior knowledge!" Maggie could have laughed out loud. "What superior knowledge? You don't know any more about gardening than I do." With an agitated flick of her wrist, she jerked in the hook a little too firmly and then had the embarrassment of freeing it from her T-shirt.

"Actually, I do," he told her smugly. "My mother is

the world's best gardener and she has passed on all her information to me. More than I ever wanted to know.''

''Your mother gardens?'' Maggie stared. ''Why?'' She couldn't imagine the parent of this tall, meticulous businessman pottering about getting her fingernails dirty. Once more she realized that Grady O'Toole was far more than just a farmhand.

''She loves it.'' He wound in his line and glared at the empty hook. ''This is very, *very* frustrating,'' he grumbled.

''Here, use my rod and reel,'' she offered kindly, rising from her seat and moving to sit on the hull of the boat. ''I've caught my limit anyway. I'll even leave the lure on.'' She grinned just to show there were no hard feelings.

''There's nothing wrong with this rod and reel or this lure,'' he contended angrily. ''Your sister said they're almost new.'' He tossed it against the seat with frustration.

''Oh, well, you see, that's the problem. Fish know when you're a serious fisherman and when you're just playing at it.'' She grinned sweetly. ''Borrowing a fishing rod? Well, that's pretty much playing around. Here, try mine. Please?'' She watched as he cast the line one, twice, three times without a bite. Grady never said a word but she could feel the tension building at his lack of success.

''Well, there's one sure thing,'' Grady said, and Maggie turned to frown at him, sensing there was some important point he was trying to make. ''There won't be any fishing like this if you move to the city. And I'll bet Brian doesn't find much joy in it, either.''

It was like a challenge and Maggie flushed at the scorn in his voice. ''Brian is a very nice man. He's been extremely considerate of us. And the girls like him well enough.'' She straightened her shoulders but kept her face averted from those knowing eyes.

"Is that enough for marriage? A father for your daughters whom they like *'well enough'*?"

"That isn't what I meant," she defended hotly. "Why can't you understand that I don't want to live and die without ever having done anything but slave away on this farm? I'm twenty-nine and I feel like I'm forty-five. The world is full of things that I've never seen or done. I'm dying here!"

"You're hardly dying!"

"I am dying inside," she muttered. "Do you realize that I'm almost thirty years old and I've never flown on a plane?" Maggie refused to look at him. "I've never been outside my own country, never been to a really formal occasion, never even eaten prawns!" She knuckled her fingers tightly, opening her eyes wide so the tears wouldn't fall.

"But you can plant a field of wheat straighter than an arrow, help a horse give birth, get a tractor running and with just a few kind words, can comfort any child that comes to you," he murmured softly from across the boat. "Isn't that worth something?"

"Don't you get it? When I finally die, I want to be somebody other than good old Maggie McCarthy from the farm. I want some exciting memories to take with me into old age. I want to experience life!"

He stopped winding for a minute. "Maggie, I didn't mean…"

"Yes, you did," she asserted, fixing him with a chilly look. "You seem to think that it's your right to comment on my wonderfully rustic life, my lack of choices. You have no idea what I need or want in my life."

"I know you think you're all alone in this. I know you think God has somehow abandoned you and left you to duke it out for yourself, but that's not true." His voice

was solemn, softly chiding. "God never leaves us or for-
sakes us. He's always there. It's like that poem about the
man who saw his life flashed in scenes and noticed that
sometimes there was only one set of footprints in the sand
of life. He thought he'd been abandoned. Instead, God
had been carrying him through the rough parts." Grady
lay her rod down on the seat and reached over, clasping
her hands between his. "I'm here to help, Maggie. And
you have lots of friends in town who would love to lend
a hand. If you'd ask."

"I don't want to go begging my neighbors for help,"
she informed him angrily. "I want to be independent and
manage things competently on my own."

"Hmm." He frowned. "Nobody can do everything
themselves, Maggie. And I can hardly imagine that Mrs.
Potter thought of it as begging when she asked you to
baby-sit her kids for a while last week."

"That's different!"

"No, honey, it isn't." He smiled sadly. "Everybody
needs people in their lives. Otherwise they become self-
centered and embittered. There's only one God, Maggie.
The rest of us are mere humans. We need each other."
He brushed one hand over the fall of hair that she could
never keep clipped back and tipped her chin, meeting her
gaze steadily.

"Can't you trust in God's promises, Maggie? Just a
little longer?" he asked softly. His eyes were warm and
she could have drowned in the peace she glimpsed there.
"I care about you, Margaret Mary McCarthy. And the
girls. I would never do anything to hurt you. Don't you
know that?"

They were words that Maggie had longed to hear for
so long. And she badly wanted to believe them, to relax
into the kiss that teased her lips and made her crave more.

But years of misplaced hope in a future that never arrived held her back.

"And what happens when you leave and go back to Calgary?" she whispered, drawing away from his touch. "What do we do then?"

She stared at him, remembering all the times he'd eased her load over the past weeks. Without even knowing how, Maggie realized Grady had assumed the hog's share of responsibility when it came to running the farm. She'd enjoyed this summer more than any other in a long time because of this man. But when he left, when he moved back to his company and his corporate business world, how could she go back to doing it all alone?

"You just keep trusting God to get you through this day and then the next." He cupped her cheeks in his hands, his thumbs brushing over her sun-warmed skin. "But I've got to tell you, lady, I'm not going anywhere. I like being right where I am. As long as you want me around, I'll be here for you and the girls. You're going to have to tell me when to leave."

And then he leaned in and kissed her with a soft sweetness that brought tears to her eyes. She would have kissed him back, would have told him that she felt safe and comfortable with him. Except that there was a whirring sound behind him and Maggie knew only too well what that meant.

"A bite! You've got a bite! Grab the rod," she squealed in excitement as Grady turned around. "Quick! It's getting away!" She watched in dismay as he missed grabbing the pole and heard the scream of line spinning out over the water. "It's a big one," she half whispered. "Really big."

She made a lunge for the rod which was now wiggling across the seat. But her fingers missed it by inches as the nylon line suddenly jerked and the rod flipped over the side of the boat.

"My lucky lure." She groaned helplessly, watching it flash downward in the crystal-clear water as the partially hooked fish swept past the side of their boat in what she believed was gloating victory. "My rod and reel!"

There was a sudden splash, and out of the corner of her eye, Maggie caught sight of Grady, fully clothed, diving over the edge of the boat. She stared as he dove downward in the water, saw him grab at something and then surface, gasping for air.

"For goodness' sake, Grady, get out of the water! You'll freeze! It's gone," she hollered in helpless frustration, watching him glance down once more. "Forget it."

He muttered something and dove again, swimming so far below the surface, Maggie couldn't make out his figure in the water. She was almost ready to jump in after him when he came surging to the surface, gasping for air. She yanked and pulled, trying to help him into the ladderless boat.

"It's gone," he sputtered, blinking up at her sadly. "I searched as much as I could, but it's gone. I'm sorry, Maggie. I know it was special."

"Doesn't matter," she muttered, pulling up the anchor and starting the engine as he toweled off. "That's the way life is, right? Don't ever get too attached to something, because sure as guns, you'll lose it." She deliberately drowned his reply by revving the boat's engine and then headed straight for shore.

"I should have known better than to dream," she whispered to herself, pasting a smile on her lips as they neared shore and her twins who were waving madly. Somehow she couldn't bear to look at Grady's sad face.

* * *

Back in Calgary and for a few hours and Grady O'Toole was sick of its honking horns and rushing traffic. He was sick of meetings that never ended and this ridiculous mental boxing match that had been going on for two days now and showed no signs of a winner. If anyone could come out of this a winner!

"How much do you want, Fiona?" he demanded finally, cutting across her lawyer's oily tones. He met her green-brown gaze straight on and flinched at the avariciousness he saw there. "You've got your own money, you don't need mine. The company's folded. I'm being investigated for something you know never happened. My name and my reputation have been dragged through the mud."

A sudden picture of Maggie's clear blue eyes rolled through his brain and Grady straightened. It was almost harvest time, and even though he'd finished baling the hay, Maggie would need his help to get that bumper crop off and in the bins. It was time to buckle down to business.

"What is it that you want?"

"Grady, I warned you not to speak." Harvey's worried tones hissed in his ear, but Grady brushed him away, his eyes never leaving the beautiful red-headed woman across the room who was suddenly a stranger to him.

"You've taken everything that you could get away with," he said sadly. "What more do you want?"

Fiona made as if to speak, but her lawyer intervened and the woman whom he'd once thought he loved leaned back in her chair and smiled bitterly.

"Mrs. O'Toole has not come here to cause harm—" the lawyer began, but Grady cut him off.

"She's not Mrs. O'Toole," he said clearly. "She never was. Never wanted to be known by my name. Why start now? And quit making speeches. What do you want?" He silently prayed, adding to a long chain of prayers for wisdom and guidance, and then straightened his shoulders. "Let's get down to business, shall we?"

A tap on the solid oak door of Harvey's office stopped the other man in midsentence as his friend's secretary poked her head through the door. Harvey got up and left, returning moments later with his usual implacable smile. He sat down, tapped his file folder against the mahogany table and spoke.

"I'm afraid Mr. O'Toole is not prepared to offer your client anything further than the settlement previously agreed upon. We will be filing a petition in the morning to have him completely absolved of even that responsibility. We have nothing further to say on this matter now. Thank you for coming."

Grady stared at Harvey in amazement. He wanted this thing over and done with, regardless of what it cost. He wanted to be free of this place and its memories. He wanted, he realized in stunned surprise, to be back on the farm with Maggie and the girls and see the look in their eyes when they ate dinner together tonight.

He was in love with her.

The knowledge staggered him and he shook his head a bit to clear away the fog. He loved Maggie McCarthy. More than he'd ever dreamed. He wanted to be there for her, share the girls with her and make their own special memories on that farm.

"In that case, my client will be filing a new petition of suit in the morning against Mr. O'Toole and any assets he may have." Fiona's lawyer named an amount that staggered Grady and sent his gaze winging to Harvey. But that man was smiling slightly, his faded blue eyes glimmering with excitement.

"Will you now? I'm sorry, Mr. Faraday, but I think, under the circumstances, that it would be against your client's best interests to file anything at the moment. In fact, I have here a waiver against any such future spurious claims. If you'd care to sign."

"Don't be ridiculous! Of course she won't sign. What are you up to now?" Mr. Faraday's eyes shifted around the table. "What is going on here?"

"What has been going on is a little smear campaign by your client. I have just received word that Judge Ronaldson has dismissed all your actions against us and disallowed the restraints that were placed on Mr. O'Toole's company. Shaughnessy's is free to open up tomorrow morning and resume business as soon as possible. If you persist in further persecutions, we will be forced to take legal action against yourself and your client." Harvey twirled his pen pleasantly, but his eyes were cold and hard.

"This is preposterous! Why would the judge suddenly do this?" Faraday's face was a comic mask. "Are we now to add bribery to the list?"

Harvey's voice was very quiet but there was a shaft of steel through it. "Perhaps you might wish to ask your client that, Mr. Faraday. It seems a witness has come forward. This witness swore to the judge that your client paid him sixty thousand dollars to falsify documents and spread heresay and rumor."

Harvey stood to his feet, gathered his papers and hooked his fingers under Grady's arm. "We'll leave you alone to discuss the matter," he said kindly. "I'm sure you have some questions that need answering."

As he stood staring at a woman he'd mistakenly thought he loved, Grady felt only pity for the angry, bitter woman who glared back at him.

"Why should you have all that money, Grady? You don't use it, you don't get any benefit from it. You just lock it away and pretend that it means nothing." Her face had drained of all color now and she rose slowly to her feet. "I could have used that money and doubled, no, tripled it. I could have made you the richest man in North America if you'd only taken my advice."

"You gained that advice in underhanded ways by manipulating people, Fiona," he told her quietly. "The money never meant that much to me. It's a legacy from a friend who wanted me to use it on something special. Once you could have asked and I would have given it to you."

She stared at him, hate broiling in her eyes. "For a child, Grady? Would you have given me your money if your child had lived?"

Pain came in waves then, rolling over him, almost knocking him down as he thought of the one thing he could never buy. Slowly he walked to the door, grateful for Harvey's support under his arm. He stopped there, and turning, let her see the agony and tears rolling down his cheeks as he thought of the child he would never know.

"Money is all you ever cared about, isn't it?" he said. "Being pregnant didn't stop you. You deliberately ignored all medical advice for the sake of a few more dollars. And it cost us our child, Fiona.

"I wanted that child, Fiona, more than you imagined. I dreamed of playing ball with him, of teaching him to swim, of handing over the company someday." The sheer pain of it made him stop and take a breath. He looked at her.

"Why didn't you stay in bed when you were supposed to? How much would it have cost you to leave the high-powered business deals behind? Why couldn't you forget about money for a few short months? Why couldn't you put the baby first?''

She shrugged. ''I had a job to do.'' Her face held no remorse. ''I never really wanted children anyway.''

Grady winced. ''I know that now. Too bad you didn't mention it before we were married.''

''I didn't think it was important.''

That one sentence said it all. There wasn't any point in going over it all again. Not now. It was too late, for all of them. Grady turned and left them all behind: Fiona, her lawyer and Harvey. He walked out of the office and into the street. With a rush of footsteps he was across the intersection and up the wide steep stairs of an old stone church that stood empty of afternoon visitors.

For a long time he sat, staring at the altar and the paintings of Jesus as a child, a young man and an adult. He knew he was crying, felt the tears dropping off his chin. But he didn't care. All that mattered now was the little body he'd never hold, the little fingers that would never wrap around his. The little voice that would never say ''Daddy''.

''Why?'' he demanded at last, staring at the stained glass window so high in the ceiling. ''Why?'' The words echoed round and round the empty sanctuary until once more everything was silent.

Grady leaned back against the padded seat and breathed in and out slowly, focusing on drawing fresh air into his tight lungs. As he did, his eyes fell on a picture of Jesus standing on a mountain, with crowds around. Underneath, words were printed, in a stylized hand, that he couldn't read from this far away. Slowly, unsteadily, Grady got up and walked over to the painting. Blinking to clear his vision, he focused on the script and then read it out loud in wonder.

"Who has known the mind of God? Or who has become His counselor? Oh, the depths of the riches both of the wisdom and knowledge of God! How unsearchable are His judgments and His ways past finding out."

"'His ways past finding out,'" Grady repeated to himself, thinking of all the things that had gone wrong without seeming reason. "You mean that I'm to trust that whatever happens, You're in charge?" he asked softly, staring straight ahead.

An image rolled through his mind, that of Maggie sitting in the boat listening to the smug, self-righteous words he'd offered, telling her that God was there, directing everything.

"Oh, I see." He sighed. "Practice what I preach, in other words." He gathered up his thoughts and once more focused on the beautiful picture hanging nearby. "'The depths of the riches of His wisdom and knowledge,'" Grady repeated, grinning now in spite of himself.

"I guess that means I can safely leave things up to You, right? Okay, God." He sighed again. "I'll try to let it go and focus on the future. I don't know what the plan is, but I trust You to handle it."

Satisfied, he walked to the door and stood staring at the city he'd lived in for so long. Suddenly he turned, walked back down the aisle and bowed in front of the cross.

"If it fits Your plans at all," he murmured softly, "could You somehow work things out for Maggie? I love her, God. And if this feeling is from You, You'll have to work through the situation for both of us. I'll trust You to do that. Amen."

And with a distinctly lighter heart, Grady walked out into the late-summer heat to head back to the one place where he still felt comfortable and at home. Maggie's farm.

But first he had a stop to make at a jewelry store. A very important stop. One that he fully intended would affect his future. If God willed.

Chapter Nine

"Anyone here?"

Grady could hardly believe it. There was no one home. He'd driven straight back to the farm, skipping supper in his urgency to return, and there wasn't a single soul waiting for him. Ironic, really.

"Trust," he repeated to himself as he changed out of the restrictive blue suit to his comfortable jeans and cotton shirt. "You've got to trust that all things work together for good for those who love God."

He grabbed three cucumbers from Maggie's garden and made himself a sandwich to accompany them inside the trailer while stifling down the worry that tugged on his brain. Where was she? It was getting dark and there was no sign of Maggie or the girls. That relic she relied on for transportation could have stopped anywhere between here and Timbuktu for all he knew. He decided to give her mother a call.

"Hi, Mrs. Davis? It's Grady. Have you talked to Maggie today?"

"Hello, Grady!" Kayleen's warm voice carried clearly

across the line. "How are you, dear? It's lovely out to-night, isn't it? I was just telling Herman that it's the per-fect night for a campfire. Perhaps you and Maggie could bring the girls for an hour or so?"

Grady swallowed, forcing himself to speak calmly. He didn't want to frighten Maggie's parents. Especially since he had nothing concrete to tell them. It was more a feel-ing, a nagging uncertainty.

"She's not here, Mrs. Davis. I was wondering if you had any idea when she might be back?"

"Grady O'Toole, I've told you more times than I can count to call me by my Christian name!" There was a short silence. "Not there? But I thought you had planned—no, wait a moment." There was some discus-sion that he couldn't quite hear and then Kayleen came back on the line. "Herman says she and the twins went to Calgary. To see Brian apparently. They're staying over."

The words were like a dagger through his heart. Grady thanked the woman and hung up, his mind unable to ac-cept the reality of what this decision meant.

He had no future with Margaret McCarthy. She'd made her choice and it didn't include him. Well, then, he'd have to learn to accept that. But he couldn't help asking why. Why now, when he'd finally faced Fiona and all the pain of the past, and come out feeling almost whole?

He did the chores mechanically, barely noticing the soft nuzzles of the animals. All Grady could think about was the fact that Maggie was leaving the farm behind for the "good life" of the city. Keeley would get her piano and ballet lessons and Katy would rejoice in the variety of sports once she got over the initial shock.

And Maggie? Maggie would get a home with a man who could support her so that she wouldn't need to slave away thanklessly on this farm anymore. She would have the security she'd always craved.

"But she won't have love," he murmured, staring at the night sky in all its glory. But maybe he was wrong. Maybe she did love this Brian fellow and would be perfectly happy in her new life. Grady was surprised how much that thought hurt him.

When the chores were done, Grady finally sank into one of the big scooped-out patio chairs he'd purchased from a local welder. The wrought iron was hard and cold against his back but he welcomed that. There wasn't any point in fetching a cushion. No need to try and soften things. Reality was harsh and it was time he faced it.

"I'll buy the farm," he murmured to himself, staring round at the freshly painted house and neatly mowed lawn now visible in the yellowish glare of the yard light. "It's the perfect place to get back to what's really important in life."

There were two quarters of land adjoining Maggie's that Grady had noticed For Sale signs on last week. If he added those to what she already had, the property would be more viable as an independent operation. And they were already producing.

"Alfalfa would make a good cash crop," he considered, remembering the dehydration plant just a few miles away. The plans whirled through his mind with surprising rapidity, and he fell to daydreaming about this new turn in his life.

But the videotape of the future stopped cold when he remembered that Maggie wouldn't be there. No lilting laugh to welcome him back from the fields, no mocking grin when the twins covered him with straw, no flush of appreciation when he brought home a bouquet of wildflowers from the back forty.

"How can I do this, Lord?" he murmured as the air rustled through the trees. "How can I plan a future alone?"

Like a refreshing drink of water, the words memorized so long ago floated through his brain, full of calm and reassurance. "Trust in the Lord with all your heart. And lean not on your own understanding. In all your ways acknowledge Him and He shall direct your paths."

"It didn't take me long, did it?" he chastised himself. "This afternoon I was going to trust You and here I am tonight, doubting again." He got up and shuffled toward the camper door, knowing that Maggie wouldn't show up tonight.

"Well, then, Lord," he mumbled, getting ready for bed. "I'm leaving it in Your hands. You brought me here for a reason and I'm ready to be used however You desire." Grady shut off the lights and climbed into the small, hard bunk. He felt better after saying that, but sleep did not come easy.

Saturday turned out to be long and tiring. Slim Tattersall came out to help him work on the combine and Grady couldn't avoid the questions.

"Maggie away?" Slim's eyebrows curved upward comically. "S'pose she and them girls deserve a little holiday. They been stuck out here on their own for a long time. Do them good to get away."

"Yes," Grady agreed quietly. "It will. Do you think this thing is going to run without breaking down? I'd hate to be in the middle of swathing and have to stop because a belt breaks or something seizes up." The red herring seemed to work.

"Most everybody has a breakdown during harvest," Slim muttered, yanking on the tired old belt. "Best thing would be to replace what you can and have extra belts on hand. Be Prepared—that's my motto." He spared a glance for the farmyard. "Cleaned things up a fair bit around here, haven't you? Makes a change. Herman used to keep a nice yard when he was here, but when the younguns took over, things got pretty run-down." He fingered the rusty metal hood of the tractor and frowned.

"Don't know how Maggie kept it going. Roger was a nice enough fellow but pigheaded as the day is long. Wouldn't take my advice about buying that last quarter along the river. Said he had to expand. Then up and dying like that! Sure left his wife in a fix." He shook his head sadly.

Grady vaguely remembered Kayleen talking about how Maggie's husband had spent his insurance money on something nonreturnable. Was this what she'd meant?

"Surely she had some savings?" Grady suggested, slipping the oil cover back into place. "Everybody puts a little bit by, don't they?"

"I reckon so, if they can spare it." Slim scratched his almost bald head and then slapped his cap back on. "But those two took out a loan to buy out Kayleen and Herman. Said they wouldn't be beholden to them. Bank payments come due a lot sooner than you think." Slim's eyes were astutely studying the old farmhouse. "Then when you gotta pay a hired hand." He shrugged. "Maggie worked in town at the supermarket for a while but her help out here kept quittin'. Not much of a loss. Most of 'em weren't worth a plugged nickel, anyway."

"There now. I think that should do it. Want to try?" Grady slammed the cover down and watched his neighbor swing up into the old worn seat with an ease that amazed him. "Give it a bit of gas," he offered helpfully.

Slim fiddled with the choke and then pressed the starter

but nothing happened. He clenched his jaw and tried again, finally eliciting a spark of interest on the fifth attempt. The motor spluttered indignantly for a few minutes, spewing out blue smoke in a huge cloud and then died.

"Thing's a pile of junk," Slim informed him curtly, climbing down. "Should have been retired ten years ago." He kicked one tire viciously. "Gonna take a pile of work to revive that hunk of scrap."

"I planned on that," Grady told him, grinning. "Want to help me out?" He waited for the older man's decision, ignoring the look of surprise.

"Didn't figure you'd be interested," Slim drawled, his eyes narrowed. "Big-city guys like you usually just buy what they need."

Grady stared. How did he know? "I, uh, that is, I'm not what you think."

"Sure y'are! I had some dealings with your company before it got shut down. Followed things real close." Slim chewed on the stem of wheat methodically before tipping his head back to grin at Grady. "Heard it's gonna be reinstated on Monday." When Grady didn't say anything, he continued. "S'pect you'll be moving on then." It wasn't a question but Grady answered anyway.

"No, I don't intend to go anywhere as long as Mag— Mrs. McCarthy needs help. I was raised on a farm and I've missed it." He opened the hood again and peered in at the rusted old motor. "I guess I'll have to lift this thing out, won't I?"

Slim shrugged. "Yep." His tone was quiet. "How come you don't just buy a new one? Seems to me you could afford it."

Grady stopped hooking the chain on the bumper, turned and met the older man's clear-eyed stare. Slim was concerned about Maggie, he could see that. And appreciate it.

"It's Mrs. McCarthy's farm, Slim. And she'd be offended if I bought something she couldn't afford. So I'm going to fix this machine if it kills me." He turned back to his work, hoping the man wouldn't threaten to expose him. He wanted to tell Maggie the truth himself. Sometime.

"Stubborn old thing probably will. Kill you I mean." Slim grinned from ear to ear, displaying a set of white, perfectly even teeth. Obviously there was more to the man than Grady had imagined. Slim's hand came out in a gesture of friendship.

"If we're gonna tackle this brute, I'd better call Buster McLean. He's the only one around here who's still got parts for these old clunkers." His hand was firm and reassuring as it gripped Grady's. "I don't aim to be telling anybody else's secrets," he added quietly. "I reckon you'll do the best you can for Mrs. McCarthy. Like you did with the spraying."

"Yes, I will." Grady met the older man's searching glance head-on. "The very best." After a long moment, Slim nodded. Then he was on the radio to his old chum, ordering him out to the farm.

"Now, Buster," Slim murmured half an hour later. "I don't want you taking any shortcuts. Me and Grady aim to fix this thing proper. And in time for harvest."

"By the look of that barley, that's gonna be pretty soon," Buster muttered, pulling on the chain that lifted the engine out of the combine. "Either pull or get out of the way, Slim. I got things to do."

"Like what?" Slim's disparaging look slid over the filthy overalls. "Change clothes, maybe?"

"Yeah! Give me that wrench, Slim." He smacked the

tool against the metal several times, and when nothing happened, laid a solid blow against it. Something shattered and lay in rusty disarray at their feet.

"You broke it! We don't need a wrecking crew here, knothead!" Slim picked up the pieces and handed them to Grady. "Maybe you didn't get it. We're aiming to fix the thing, not bust it up."

"Sometimes you gotta break eggs to make an omelet," Buster announced, twisting his head this way and that. "Now this here's your problem. I might have one of these at the shop but I can't get it right now." He dusted his hands on his overalls and picked up his tool kit.

"Why not? You got a hot date or sumthin'?" Slim snickered. Grady saw the other man's barrel chest puff out and contented himself with watching this confrontation.

"You really are a silly old fool," Buster said, affectionately slapping Slim's thin shoulder. "The social's on tonight. Right after the chuck wagon races. I ain't aiming to miss that." He stomped out the door and lunged into his truck. "That guy with the real loud voice is singin' at the bandstand later, too. My wife's determined I gotta hear that." He shook his head mournfully. "I can't abide loud music."

Grady watched Slim's head snap back. The other man's face tightened, eyes wide as if lightning had struck. "Almost forgot." Slim handed Grady his wrench and stalked across the yard. "I'll have to do this later, son. I've never missed a chuck wagon race yet, and I ain't starting now."

They were both in their trucks, motors running, before Grady woke up. "Wait a minute," he called. "What races? Where?" He saw the pitiful looks they cast his way before Slim glanced across at Buster and shrugged.

"You better tell him, Buster. No sense in him missing

all the fun.'' With a chuckle, Slim drove off down the driveway.

"It's the local fair," Buster said, wedging himself in behind the wheel of his truck. "Not the Calgary Stampede by any means, but our own little production. Since it's near the end of the season, we get a lot of the fellows from the chuck wagon and chariot circuits stopping off. Makes for some interesting races.''

Grady was well acquainted with Calgary's annual event. Visitors from around the world had been coming for years to see professional riders rope calves and ride broncos. The prizes for most Stampede events were worth a lot. But he was interested in watching the way a small town like Willow Bunch handled such an event. Besides, it would get him away from the farm and his own morose thoughts.

"Where is it held?" He scribbled down Buster's directions and waved the big man down the driveway, wincing as Buster's souped-up engine roared away.

The fairgrounds were smack-dab in the middle of town, surrounded by tall, wavering spruce trees that were supposed to protect the residents from the noise of horns blowing and hooves digging into the watered-down dirt. If there were any residents at home, that was.

Grady could hardly imagine that any one of the five thousand residents of Willow Bunch had stayed away. They were jam-packed on the stands around him, avidly watching a tractor pull a huge load of cattle feed across a chalk line. The winner got to keep the feed.

"Come on, Travis! Put your foot down!" The tiny blonde behind him had a voice suitable for one of Maggie's opera singers, Grady decided, and then wished he hadn't thought of Maggie again.

"May I sit beside you, Mr. O'Toole?" Minnie Hugenot plopped down on the bench and offered him a French fry. "It's pretty warm, isn't it?" She glanced around him curiously. "Where's Maggie?"

It was the fifth time someone had asked him that in the last ten minutes, and Grady forcibly restrained himself from the curt reply that itched inside his brain.

"Uh, she's away, Miss Hugenot. I'm not sure when she'll be back." He tried to concentrate on the two massive tractors entering the track. "Sure good weather for a fair," he murmured, but Minnie ignored that.

"Don't you worry, honey," she consoled him, patting his arm. "Maggie will be here. She never misses the chuck wagons. Maggie and those girls of hers could out-yell most of the folks here." As the woman behind him bellowed more orders to Travis, Grady rolled his eyes. "Yes, even louder than that." Minnie giggled.

"Hey, Grady! We're going to look at those newfangled foreign rigs Bob Reynolds just got in. Wanna come?" Slim stood at the bottom of the bleachers, clearly unembarrassed by the attention he was drawing.

But Grady barely noticed. His attention was centered on the slim, blond-haired woman carrying three cups. Two little blond heads followed closely behind.

"There she is now." Minnie beamed. "Maggie! Maggie McCarthy, you get up here and talk to this lonely man right now!"

And Grady was so glad to see her, he didn't care that half the heads in the crowd turned to stare at them. He tried to control the joy that sprung up inside by reminding himself that Maggie might well be tied to another man by now, but when his eyes caught a glimpse of her empty ring finger, he couldn't help the grin that spread across his face.

"Hi." Maggie leaned in front of Minnie to smile at him and Grady strove to remain calm.

"Hi, Grady," the girls chorused. Their faces were wreathed in smiles and Grady couldn't help wondering why they looked so happy.

"Hi, yourselves." He grinned back. And then stared at his hands, trying desperately to think of something to say other than, "Where have you been?"

"Hello, Miss Hugenot," Keeley murmured dutifully. She shuffled her feet for a moment and then grinned at Katy. "I think Mrs. Copperfield is looking for you to help her in the booth. They had a whole bunch of people lined up when we came past."

"Good gravy!" Minnie said explosively, hustling to her feet. "I just finished a shift! Folks seem to be mighty hungry today." She gathered up her huge handbag. "Still, it's for a good cause. Slide over here now, Maggie. That's right. Leave some room at the end so folks don't have to clamber over everyone. See you later."

As they wished Minnie goodbye, Grady couldn't help but notice Katy's smug nod at Keeley. But there was no point in asking them what it was all about. He was pretty sure they wouldn't tell him anyway. He turned his attention where he'd wanted it in the first place. Back on Maggie.

"Did you have a good trip?" he asked softly. "Your mother told me you went to Calgary. Everything okay?"

Maggie's big blue eyes met his straight on as she nodded her head. "I think so," she murmured. Her voice dropped to a whisper. "I went to see Brian."

Grady forced his face to remain impassive and kept his rump planted right where it was even though he wanted to run howling into the hills. "Oh."

"I wanted to tell him that I couldn't marry him after

all.'' She flushed under his intense scrutiny, but to Grady she was just more beautiful. ''Then the girls and I had a little holiday at Calaway Park.''

Grady listened as the twins burst into excited speech about their day at the amusement center. But while they talked about the rides they'd enjoyed, he concentrated on Maggie. And praised God that she hadn't been drawn in by the allure of Brian and all that he could offer her. Now, if he could just get a few minutes alone with her, maybe he could make her understand how much he'd missed her.

''Thanks for minding the farm for us,'' she whispered as the last tractor left the track. ''I really needed a break and so did the girls. They haven't had a holiday in a long time.'' Her fingers squeezed his and Grady squeezed them back.

''You're welcome,'' he said softly. ''You're very welcome.'' And when she would have pulled away, Grady hung on, enveloping her slender fingers in both his hands.

The chariot races took over then and Grady watched amused as Katy and Keeley alternately cheered and jeered the teams they picked to win.

''They have a small wager going,'' Maggie explained as he watched Katy hand Keeley a pack of gun. ''But they pretend they don't because they know I have a strict rule about gambling.'' She raised her voice on the last few words and was rewarded with two cheeky grins.

''Oh, Mom!'' Katy rolled her eyes heavenward and snapped her gum at the same time. ''It's just a game!''

But it was a good game, Grady agreed. ''I'll take the red-and-white striped chariot, girls. I think those ponies are going to clean house.''

The three females surrounding him looked at each other and burst out laughing.

''Oh, Grady,' Maggie said, wiping the tears of laughter

from her eyes. "Thank goodness your expertise is farming and not horse racing." When she wouldn't explain further, Grady contented himself with watching the teams set up, mentally chiding the gorgeous brown geldings to prove her wrong.

"Can't beat that for a start," he informed them as the colorful rig rushed to the front. "Look how they're pulling away from the pack. I knew those horses could go."

And go they did. Across the infield, off the track, dodging chuck wagons that were just entering the ring. The driver seemed to be fighting with the horses as they pranced merrily past the stands. He finally lost his hold on the reins and fell out the back, losing his shoes and his baggy pants in the process. Underneath, he sported bright red boxers with a huge heart on the rear.

"He's a clown," Grady told them disgustedly. "A team like that and he's a clown!"

"A very good clown," Maggie corrected him. She was laughing openly at him now, her lips spread wide as her eyes glistened in the bright sunshine. Automatically Grady leaned forward and pressed his lips to hers, uncaring of the interested spectators surrounding them. The kiss lasted for only a second or two before Maggie pulled back, flushed with embarrassment. But for Grady, it was enough to start with.

"*Now* we're square," he murmured, for her ears only.

Maggie couldn't believe Grady O'Toole had kissed her in front of God and the entire population of Willow Bunch. Now everyone would be talking about them! Still, she couldn't help the hand that slipped up to touch her lips where his had rested.

"I, uh, I don't think this is a very good idea just now," she murmured, trying to control the heat in her face. "Everyone's watching."

Grady studied her serious face before turning back to the track. "Okay," he agreed softly. "But we need to talk. At least, I need to talk to you." She saw the uncertainty touch his face. "If you want to, I mean."

"Oh, yes, I want to," she agreed quietly, heart pounding as she considered all the things she wanted to tell him. "Later."

The chuck wagons ran faster that night than in previous years. Or it seemed that way to Maggie. And as she watched Katy's and Keeley's bright heads bent over in conversation with Grady, she whispered a prayer of thankfulness toward heaven.

This seems right, she thought, happily content to let the girls occupy his time. *He's kind and considerate. He knows by now that I haven't got a dime and yet he stays on. The girls like him.*

Those thoughts occupied her mind until it was time to leave the grandstand and move into the teeming crowd of people. At last they were on their way home with Grady's truck following close behind.

"Mom?" Keeley's voice was soft in the darkness. "Do you like Grady?"

"Of course I like him, sweetheart! He's been very good to us." Some motherly sense told Maggie what was coming.

"No, Mom! I mean do you like, love him? Like in the movies?" Keeley's serious face tilted upward, waiting. "'Cause if you do, well, Katy and I like him, too. We think he's great."

"I know you do, honey. And Grady is a really nice man. But I think it's too soon to be talking about love. We hardly know him."

"I know him really good," Katy piped up from the

back seat. "He doesn't care if I ask questions all the time. Not like Brian."

Maggie frowned. "What questions did you ask Brian, Katy?"

"I asked him if he figured God meant for giraffes to look like that." Maggie could hear the snap of gum but ignored it. "Just seems kind of odd that He'd do it that way. You know?"

"What did Brian say?" Maggie could imagine that Brian had not understood the little girl's enquiring mind. It was one of Brian's shortcomings that she hadn't wanted to admit to herself.

"He said I was being sac...sac...something." She snapped her gum again. "But I wasn't, Mom. Honest. I wonder why, if God can create such a great invention as the photocopier, He would make giraffes look like they do?"

Maggie stifled her laughter and turned the car into her driveway. "Anything else?" she asked, tongue in cheek.

"Well, I said that if we came to live with him, Keeley and me would like our own bedrooms. I mean, you wouldn't want us to end up like Cain and Abel, would you? I bet if their mom had given them separate rooms, they wouldn't have killed each other." Katy stopped and Maggie could see her, in the rearview mirror, twisting her pigtail as she remembered that conversation. "He got kind of red-faced and told me not to be sac...that word."

"We're not going to live with Brian, Katy. I'm not going to marry him, remember? So I don't think you have to worry about it anymore. You'll still have your own rooms here in our house."

"Yes!" Katy high-fived her sister in a jubilant cry of satisfaction, before yanking open the car door and racing over to Grady's truck. "We're not moving," she announced, hugging him tightly.

Grady's warm brown eyes met Maggie's, sending his own message, and she felt warmed by his gaze. "Yes, I know," he murmured, hugging Katy back. "And I'm glad. Very glad," he repeated as Katy raced around the yard, yelling at the top of her lungs.

The girls were overexcited, and it took an hour before they were finally settled in their beds. They insisted on Grady coming in to kiss them good-night, and Maggie noticed that he seemed thrilled with the idea. She stood outside Keeley's door, listening to their conversation.

"Are you going away, Grady? Or are you going to stay and help my mother with the harvest?" She sounded fearful, and Maggie wished she hadn't let the girls see how much the farm had taken out of her this year. At ten years of age, they shouldn't have to worry about her.

"I'm staying right here, Keeley. For as long as your mother needs me. You can count on that. And if you and Katy ever want my help, or just want to talk, I'll be here for you, too. No matter what happens. Okay?"

Maggie heard the heartfelt sigh clearly. "Thanks, Grady. It's just that I can't help wondering about things. You know?"

"I know exactly what you mean. And if there's anything else bothering you, you just ask me." There was a minute of silence and then Grady spoke again. "Keeley? Was there something else?"

"Well, I was just wondering." The little girl's voice dropped to a whisper and Maggie had to lean in to hear. "My dad died a while ago. And my mom's been alone ever since. She never complains or anything," Keeley rushed to explain. "But sometimes it would be nice if she had an adult to talk to, don't you think? Somebody who tells her she's beautiful and makes her laugh.''

Maggie blushed. It was humiliating to have your daughter trying to match you up, and she was ready to go charging into the room when Grady spoke.

''I like your mom, Keeley. I like her very much. And you're right—she is very beautiful. But I think it would be best if I told her that myself, in my own way.'' Maggie heard the tender note in his voice. ''Without the help of two little girls who are very tired and really need their sleep. Get my meaning?''

''Good night, Grady.'' Keeley giggled.

Maggie went downstairs to make tea, smiling as she filled the kettle. Her daughters might be meddling, but they weren't stupid. They knew when to back off.

''They're in bed and the lights are off,'' Grady said, walking into the kitchen. ''But that's all I can guarantee.''

''That's good enough for me.'' Maggie laughed. ''Thanks. If you'll take the cups, I'll bring the teapot out in a minute.'' She deliberately kept her eyes focused on the counter in front of her, waiting as Grady stood watching her. Finally she heard him walk through the door and breathed a sigh of relief.

You can get through this, she told herself sternly. *Just pretend that you didn't hear a word.* But no matter how much she pretended, Maggie couldn't help remembering the look in his eyes earlier this evening when he'd kissed her.

''Oh, get on with it, woman,'' she muttered, grabbing the teapot and opening the door. ''You're no schoolgirl!'' She shivered as the warmth of the evening and the intimacy of being alone with him suddenly hit her.

''Whatever happens, Lord,'' she pleaded, ''please help me say the right thing. Don't let me hurt him.''

Chapter Ten

Grady wasn't on the screen porch. Instead he sat stretched out on a redwood lounger on the grass in front of the house. He'd pulled up a table and a chair for her, as well.

"It's hard to believe God made it all in six days, isn't it?" he murmured, staring at the star-studded, black velvet sky. "Perfection." He grinned at her, his teeth flashing. "And you look lovely, too."

"I always did think plain old denim and ordinary white cotton was my forte," Maggie scoffed, sipping her tea.

"It wasn't so much the color of the fabric I was referring to," Grady murmured, his eyes warm as they moved over her worn jeans and white cotton shirt. "You always look lovely. It's something that comes from inside, not from what you wear. You wouldn't be any more lovely if you were dressed in silk."

"Still," Maggie said with a laugh, "I wouldn't mind trying it out once." She stopped at the look on his face. "I'm sorry. That was rude." She inclined her head. "Thank you for the compliment."

"It wasn't really a compliment, Maggie. It was the truth. I've seen your real inner beauty every day that I've been here. When you're talking with the girls, or leading Bible school or losing your fishing pole to a klutz. I think you're pretty special, Margaret Mary McCarthy."

"Oh. Well, thank you." Maggie placed her cup on the table and stood, trying to look nonchalant as she searched for another subject. Why was she so nervous?

"Maggie?" He was behind her, his hand on her arm. "I wanted to tell you something." She nodded her head and he continued. "I was in Calgary yesterday. The business with my company is all settled. Finally."

"So you can go back now?" It was hard, so hard to say those words. "Well, I wish you all the best, Grady. And I want to thank you for helping us out." She would have said more but for the lump in her throat. The silence yawned between them until she finally glanced up, surprised when his hands moved to her shoulders.

"I'm not leaving, Maggie. Not unless you want me to. I don't know what will happen about the company. I don't think I want to do that anymore."

"What *do* you want to do?" Maggie didn't know where the courage to say those words had come from, but she waited anxiously for his reply.

"I want to stay here, on the farm. I want to help you harvest this crop and watch the snow fly while we plan next year's. I want to watch the girls go off to school and be here when they get off the bus at night."

"Oh." She didn't know what to say to that.

"I love you, Maggie. I believe God sent me here, to meet you and the girls. I think He wants us to be a family and serve Him together. I think Katy has the right idea with her verse." His arms were completely around her now, holding her tenderly, his head just inches away from hers.

"Katy? What verse?" His eyes held hers, intent in their scrutiny. Maggie couldn't look away, even if she'd wanted to.

"'Two are better than one because they have a good return for their work. If one falls down, his friend can help him up. But pity the man who has no one to help him up...and how can one keep warm alone. Though one may be overpowered, two can defend themselves.'" He recited the words softly.

Maggie frowned slightly, trying to recall just where she'd last heard that.

"It's from Ecclesiastes," Grady murmured. "She painted it on a plaque at Bible school. I think we'd make a great team, Maggie." He kissed her tenderly, his lips asking a question Maggie knew she'd have to answer. "Maggie?"

Help me, she prayed fervently. *I can't make a mistake here.*

"I think I do love you, Grady," she murmured at last, watching the glow in his eyes dim just a little. "I like you very much. You're warm and kind and gentle and you've been here for me so many times." She eased away from him and took one step backward. "I think being married to you would be the most wonderful thing any woman could wish for, and I know I'd be happier than I've ever been."

"But?" He smiled at her grimly. "There is a but, isn't there?"

"But I don't want to stay on the farm, Grady. I want to be free of the never-ending debts and drudgery. I want to feel young and carefree, to go to a concert in the park, watch the girls enjoy life that isn't confined to good old

Willow Bunch." She glanced up at him despairingly. "I've told you all this before."

"But we can do that, Maggie! We'll go for holidays and take the girls on weekend excursions. We can even go to Disneyland after Christmas, if you want."

"But I'll still be stuck on the farm." She felt terrible saying it, but she'd spent too many years denying reality. Now was not the time to start pretending life would be grand just because she married Grady.

Maggie watched the pain flood his eyes and knew she'd hurt him. "It's not you," she cried. "It's this place. I've slaved away here for years, trying to make a go of it, and it just isn't working."

"Maggie, the crops are going to be bumper this year! You'll be well on the way. And of course I expect to put some money into the farm, to share the load with you. We can have a wonderful life here, if you'll just give us a chance."

"You're not pouring more money into this place," Maggie informed him sternly. "Don't you see? That's been the problem all along." She shook her head firmly. "No, somehow we've got to become self-sufficient, and until I can contribute my share, I don't want to be dependent on anyone. It wouldn't be fair to dump all my debts on you."

"Maggie, I'm not trying to buy you!" His words were harsh. "I want to share the farm with you. I've got money, I can afford it. And we can make it into something to be proud of *together*. Don't you see?"

"No," she persisted stubbornly. "I don't. All I see is this huge millstone that will drag us both down, regardless of how wonderful things look now." Maggie felt her heart sink to her shoes as she said the words, but she refused to let that sway her. This wasn't God's will for her; it couldn't be. Not when everything that was in her cried out to get away from this place.

But what about Grady? a small inner voice chided. *Are you prepared to go through life without him?* A resounding no rose up in her throat and she struggled to understand the confusion in her mind.

"Please understand," she murmured finally, lifting her head to see the pain on his face. "I've worked so long to be independent. I need to know that I can take care of myself and my children no matter what happens." There was no point in prevaricating, she decided. He might as well know it all.

"I was devastated when Roger died. But it was worse when I found out how strapped we were financially. I felt abandoned and not very capable of standing on my own two feet." She sighed. "I know everyone means well. My friends have stuck by me when no one else believed I could put food on the table, and sometimes they've even put it there for me. But I'm tired of being the local charity case. I want to be able to hold my head up, knowing that my girls aren't being denied their chance."

She searched his face for some sign that he comprehended her feeling of failure. "Can you understand what I'm saying, Grady?"

"All I really want to know is whether or not you love me?" he reiterated firmly. "Everything beyond that we can work out."

"All right! Yes, I love you!" She glared at him in frustration. "But that's not the point."

"Yes, my darling Margaret Mary, that is exactly the point." She heard the relief in his voice and moved willingly into his arms as he tugged her close. His kiss was exultant. "If we start from the right place, God will lead us to the next step. You're not alone anymore, sweetheart. We're in this together.''

As she returned his hug, Maggie considered his words. Maybe it was possible. Maybe love really could conquer all. Maybe this time, she didn't need to be afraid.

"Are you with me, Maggie, my love?'' His voice was soft and cajoling and she couldn't deny him.

"Yes,'' she whispered at last. "I'm with you. But let's go slowly and figure out each step as we go along.''

"All right!'' He grinned at her, his eyes blazing with new light. "How about this?'' Grady's hands enclosed hers, holding them tightly. "We'll be engaged. For as long as it takes you to see that this farm can be a wonderful home for us. Together we'll take that crop off, sell it, pay down your loans and then you're going to marry me. Deal?''

It sounded too good to be true. Grady, strong, reliable Grady would stay by her side. They would support each other. And, please God, if they got this crop off, they could start planning a future together.

"Deal,'' she murmured.

"See, I told you,'' Keeley whispered, poking her sister in the side. "The lady said *'get 'em together and keep 'em together'* when she sent that last E-mail. So far it looks pretty good.''

Katy turned her eyes away from the window as her mother kissed Grady. "Yuck! I can't stand all that mushy stuff!''

"You don't have to,'' Keeley said reasonably. "They do.'' She leaned a little farther out the open window and smiled. She pulled her head back in at Katy's insistent tug. "What?''

"How do you suppose that woman knows all this stuff about making people fall in love?"

"She's a writer, isn't she?" Keeley reminded her sister. She pulled the curtain back into place and flopped onto her bed. "She writes about this stuff all the time."

"All the time?" Katy could hardly believe it. "Gee! How can she stand it?"

"Lots of people buy her books, dummy. She must know what she's talking about. I'm gonna ask her the next step." Keeley skipped over to her computer and flicked it on, waited a moment for it to boot up and then clicked on the E-mail icon. "It's a good thing I read that book she sent me. It had a lot of helpful hints in it."

"Yeah, but that was for *writing*," Katy reminded her. "This is real life. *And* it's our mother!"

"Still, everybody likes a happy ending," her sister muttered, typing out a few short sentences. "There, now she'll see where we are. I think we're past stage four, don't you?"

"Why don't you go in a chat room with her?" Katy demanded, popping another bubble. "Then you could ask all the questions you want."

"Because I don't want to! This is better." She frowned at the keyboard, erased a few lines and then continued tapping. "Anyway, I don't know how."

"Well, I wish you'd get it over with, that's all," Katy grumbled, tossing her ball in the air and catching it. "I wouldn't mind playing my computer games once in a while, you know. That *is* why I got them."

"This is more important," Keeley muttered. "Mom needs us now and we can't just desert her. Besides, *you're the one* who doesn't want to leave the farm. If Mom and Grady get married, we'll be able to stay here."

"Like you want to!" Katy sneered. "You know very

well you've been begging for a new piano teacher for months. And there's no drawing teacher in Willow Bunch.''

"No." Keeley flicked the computer off and swiveled around on her chair. "But I could go to the city once a week to take art lessons. Or piano. We wouldn't have to live there." She climbed into bed and made room for her sister to sit on the end. "The truth is, I don't really mind where we live. But I do want Mom to be happy and I think she would be with Grady."

"You like him a lot, don't you?"

"Don't you?" Keeley countered. "He's fun to be around, he knows about all sorts of things and he's not afraid to talk about God. I didn't like to ask Brian anything!" They looked at each other and grinned.

"At least he's out of the picture." Katy blew a huge bubble and let it snap all over her face. "That's what I think of Brian." She giggled, enjoying Keeley's look of disgust. "Why were you talking to Grady 'bout God?"

"Because I wanted to ask him something." She stopped abruptly but when Katy merely raised her eyebrows, Keeley continued softly, whispering so that they couldn't be heard. "You know how Mrs. Stone's been going over all those armies that God killed in the Old Testament?" Katy nodded. "That kinda bugged me. I mean, is that all God does—punish people? It goes on and on. 'He killed this bunch and smote that one.' It's scary!"

"Yeah, but they were fighting against God's people," Katy informed her. "God didn't like that. They deserved it."

"But that's just it. I do lots of bad things. I deserve to be punished, too." Keeley stared at her hands. "And I was scared."

"What did Grady say?" Katy was sitting up straight now, her gum forgotten as she studied her sister's face.

"He said that God is just like our father, only He's a heavenly father and that I should think of Him as my dad and not as a policeman."

"We don't have a dad." Katy's voice was flat.

"That's what I told him! So Grady explained some more." Keeley's forehead creased as she sought earnestly for the right words to tell her sister. "See, Katy, God doesn't like it when we do something wrong and He wants us to ask for forgiveness. But He doesn't hold it against us. He forgives us because He made us and loves us and knows that everybody makes mistakes. That's why He sent Jesus to die for us. Only you can't go making the same mistake over and over. You have to learn from it and not do it again."

Katy shuffled uncomfortably on the bed. "You mean like throwing spitballs in school?" she muttered at last.

"Yes, exactly like that." Keeley shook her head in disgust. "And come schooltime, you better not start doing that again," she reminded firmly. "You told the teacher you were sorry. If you were really sorry, you'd stop. You can't be sorry if you keep right on doing it!"

Katy nodded. "Yeah, I get it," she muttered. "But sometimes I do things wrong even when I know better. Does that mean God won't forgive me?"

Keeley shook her head firmly. "Grady said that if we confess that we did wrong, God will forgive us and wipe our mistakes as far away as the east is from the west."

"I don't get it," Katy announced, her forehead wrinkled in puzzlement. "That's infinity. East doesn't ever meet west."

"I know. Isn't it great?"

They grinned at each other in sudden understanding and

then guilt as they heard the front door open and shut. Katy wriggled off the bed and headed soundlessly for the door where she turned back to grin at her sister.

"I just hope Mom is as understanding when she finds out what we're up to," she whispered, grinning from ear to ear. "And if she's mad, I'm going to explain that it was all your idea." She scurried out the door and across the hall as the bottom step squeaked a warning.

"Mother! What's happened to your hair this time?" Maggie stared at the tiny woman coming through her kitchen door. "Ow!" She jerked her fingers back from the bubbling pot of raspberry jam and then resumed the steady stirring motion.

"Maggie, you've filled that kettle too full. I suppose you were trying to maximize the berries and minimize the sugar again?" Kayleen shook her head at the thick red mass and moved to pour boiling water over the jars in the sink. "I hope it gels," she muttered.

"If it doesn't, the girls can eat it on ice cream," Maggie told her, removing the pot from the element and then skimming the light pink foam off. "What happened?"

"Oh, I tried to get a perm. You know the Peters girl?" At Maggie's distracted nod she continued. "Well, she's trying out for her licence this month and she wanted to practice one last time. I let her."

"And in the process you lost four inches of hair?" Maggie took the measuring cup from Kayleen's hand with a muttered thanks and began scooping the thick syrupy jam into jars, snapping on the lids as she went. "What really happened, Mother?"

"I just told you." Kayleen poured herself a cup of coffee and sank into the nearest chair, patting her shorn head.

"She used too much solution and left it on too long. There wasn't any other option but to cut off the damaged parts."

Maggie poured the last of the jam into its container and slipped the lid on before inverting the jar on the counter and setting the Dutch oven in the sink. At last she turned and studied her mother thoroughly.

"I like it," she said finally. "It makes your eyes look huge." The soft feathery silver strands lay close against her mother's head, a curling tendril caressing her cheek here and there. "You look young and carefree."

"Your father will have a fit," Kayleen said calmly. "But he'll get over it. And he won't be able to gripe about how much time it takes me to get ready for church anymore." She smiled, patting the lavender sac at her feet. "He'll have even less to say when I show him my new nightie."

"Mother!" Maggie gasped, laughing appreciatively. "You are the most devious, conniving woman."

"It's not devious," Kayleen argued. "It's common sense. Herman likes me to look my best." She preened a bit. "And believe me, I do look good in that."

"Mother, have you lost weight?" Maggie studied the pronounced cheekbones and angular chin line. "Your face looks thinner."

"Why, thank you, dear!" Kayleen beamed. "I've lost twelve pounds now. And I don't feel nearly so dumpy. I think feeling good about yourself makes such a difference to a woman's looks." Her eyes slid over her daughter. "You look pretty good yourself. Anything you want to tell me about?"

"No. Nothing." Maggie turned away to pour herself a cup of coffee and then sank down into a chair, ignoring her mother's knowing look.

"Margaret Mary McCarthy! You tell me right this minute what's put that sparkle in your eyes!"

"Or what?" Maggie giggled. "You'll put me over your knee?" She laughed out loud at Kayleen's glowering face.

"And don't think I can't," the tiny powerhouse threatened. "Now tell all."

"Grady has asked me to marry him." Maggie could hardly believe it herself. Was it any wonder she whispered?

"Excellent!" Kayleen rubbed her hands together. "When's the wedding?"

"Mother! We haven't decided on a wedding. I'm still thinking about things." The old yearning rose in her but she stifled it down.

"What's to think about? That man out there—" Kayleen jerked her thumb toward the barn "—wants to marry you. Presumably he loves you?"

"He says he does."

"Then what's the problem? Is something wrong, dear? Don't you love him?"

"Of course I love him. That's not it." Maggie flopped back in her chair and stared at the dingy old ceiling. "I'm just not sure. We're so different."

"Different? How?" Kayleen sat silent, waiting, Maggie knew, for her to open up.

"Grady wants us to stay on the farm. He wants to build it up. He thinks this place is better than sliced bread!" She glanced around the tired old kitchen dismissively.

"There was a time," Kayleen said quietly, "when you thought that way, too."

"Well, I've smartened up since I was eighteen. I feel like the farm is dragging the very life out of me," Maggie burst out. She grimaced as the pipes began a high-pitched whine. "Every single thing in this place needs fixing!"

"There's nothing that a new coat of paint wouldn't fix," her mother stated calmly, glancing around.

"Mother, get real! This ceiling's about to fall down from being waterlogged. And why? Because the toilet upstairs keeps plugging. There are trees growing into the sewer lines or something, and it'll cost hundreds to fix. The washer conked out again last night. It needs a new motor." She got up and walked to the living room.

"Why is it so dark in here?" Kayleen peered through the gloomy room and found the light switch. She clicked it several times. "The power's off."

"On purpose. Last night I woke up to the sound of voices. I thought it was a burglar but it turns out it was just the TV going on and off. Grady says there's some kind of short in the line and he turned off the breaker. Not before it burnt out the inside of the VCR though." She yanked the back off the black box and showed her mother the mass of melted wire inside. "I can't afford to get another one."

"Thank the Lord that it didn't start a fire before Grady found it, Maggie!" Her mother breathed a prayer of relief and tripped on the edge of protruding carpet. There was a tearing sound as Kayleen sought for a hold on something that might stop her fall. "Darling, I'm sorry. I didn't mean to tear it up but my heel caught." She would have said more but Maggie held up her hand.

"Forget it, Mom. It was old when we were kids. It should have been replaced long ago. I'll get Grady to cut it off and tack it back down." Maggie walked slowly back into the kitchen and sank into her chair. "Do you see what I mean? And that's only in the house."

"Perhaps your father and I could get you a new carpet. Something not too expensive but sturdy."

"No. Mom, you and Dad cannot keep spending your savings to get me out of a hole I dug myself into."

"If you can get the crops sold, you should be better off."

"If. If it weren't for bad luck, I wouldn't have any luck at all," Maggie scoffed bitterly.

"Why, Margaret McCarthy! We do not rely on *luck* to get us through this life. We rely on our heavenly Father." She patted Maggie's hand kindly. "Are you doubting Him?"

"I'm doubting everything," Maggie confessed. "I feel as if I'm dying here, Mom. Dying slowly, but surely."

"We're all dying, dear. From the day we were born."

"But don't you see?" Maggie explained tearfully. "I feel like I've never really lived." She swiped her hand across her cheeks. "I know you and Dad tried to tell me to get an education before I married Roger. You thought I should see something of the world before I decided on the rest of my life. You were right, Mom. You were right!"

"No, honey," her mother answered thoughtfully. "I don't think I was."

Maggie stopped midsob and stared. "What?"

"God has a plan, Maggie. We can't know it or understand it, but it's still there. I believe He wanted you to marry Roger and have those two darling girls. And hard as it may seem, I believe Roger's dying was part of His plan also. Now Grady's here. Is that coincidence? I don't think so. It's just another piece of the puzzle that He's so wonderfully fitting together."

"And what about me? What about this need I have to be free and young before I get much older?" Maggie made no attempt to hide her anger. "I want a place where

I can be comfortable, not constantly looking ahead to the next chore.''

"Well, darling, pardon me for saying so, but I think you're fighting against the plan. It reminds me a bit of Job."

"Job? You mean I've got boils and pestilence to look forward to?" Maggie rolled her eyes.

"Maybe." Kayleen smiled at the disgusted look on her daughter's face.

"Gee, thanks so much, Mother. Boils, huh? I feel much better now."

Kayleen continued, unperturbed. "Job had everything and he lost it. All of it. It wasn't because he was sinful or even that he did something wrong. He knew that. What he didn't know was 'why'?"

"Exactly. Why?" Maggie glared at her mother balefully. "Why me? Why now? Why here? Why?"

"Maggie, you cannot know the mind of God. You simply cannot because you are not God. The majesty and sovereignty of God isn't understandable to the human mind."

"In other words, there is no answer." Maggie frowned, trying to wrap her mind around the words.

"Yes, darling. There *is* an answer. But you may never know what it is. Then again, you may, some day, understand. But that doesn't matter."

"Well, then, what does?" Maggie looked at her mother.

"Handling each day that God gives you the best way you can. Problems will always come up, Maggie. You take them one at a time, do what you can and plan for the future to the best of your ability. There's only one sure thing in this life." She smiled. "The promise that whatever happens, God is still there, waiting and watching, ready to help us take the next step. He promised.''

"You mean, why worry?" Maggie shrugged. "That's a pretty tall order."

"Yes, but you've got help." Kayleen thought for a moment. "Sweetie, if you spent your life worrying about Mount Vesuvius, would that stop it from blowing up when the time came? Of course not. Worrying is only beneficial if it helps you change something. If you're worried that the electricity might cause a fire in your living room and burn you and the children, then, yes, you do something about it. But to fret and stew about things that may or may not happen is pointless.''

Maggie felt her mother's hand on her head and leaned into that caress as if she were still a young girl, needing reassurance.

"Honey, God is all-powerful. Beside Him, we are nothing. But He promises that if we pray to Him, He will hear us. We can't even understand the miracles of nature and how He created them. But we do know that God is sovereign, in control and knows things we can only dream about. Our job is to follow where He leads us, one day at a time. Can you do that?"

"I'll try, Mom." She shuffled to her feet and moved toward the stack of pots in the sink. "I guess I've become a real whiner lately. It's a wonder anyone still speaks to me." She leaned backward into her mother's hug. "Thanks for reminding me."

"Don't give up, darling. 'Trust and see that the Lord is good.' I've proven it over and over in my own life." She picked up a tea towel and dried the pots one by one. "What's next on the agenda?"

"I've got to do something with that zucchini," Maggie muttered, staring out the window at the offending plants.

"I'll take some," Kayleen offered. "I thought it would be so wonderful to have only a flower garden after spending so many years planting that great huge plot out here. But you know, I really miss the first taste of those fresh vegetables. Next year I may plant some beets and potatoes in town. Just a few," she cautioned Maggie with a wink.

"Don't be silly! There's more than enough for you out here," Maggie chided. "Come on, let's go see what you'd like. We've been eating new potatoes for a while now."

"Your father loves those." Kayleen grinned as they walked along Maggie's garden. "I'll take a few. By the way, do you want to go blueberry picking tomorrow? I thought I'd get a few since Herman is champing at the bit to get out into the wilderness, as he calls it."

"Ha!" Maggie grinned, remembering this ploy from the past. "You just want someone to visit with while Dad disappears into the underbrush, searching for bigger and better berries." She watched her mother flush prettily.

"There are a lot of bears about, you know," Kayleen murmured. "It's dangerous to be alone in the woods."

"Oh, right!" Maggie giggled, digging another hill of potatoes. "If you take ten zucchini, I promise I'll come," she compromised and watched amazed as her mother picked out the largest specimens. "But not tomorrow. I promised I'd take the girls to get their school supplies. Can you believe school starts next week?"

"I can believe it," Kayleen said, nodding at the lush golden field across the road. "That wheat looks almost ready."

"It is. Grady says it could come off number one. Which would be wonderful since the price has jumped. Grady says it's gone up because a lot of people didn't plant wheat this year. I guess they remember last year's disaster."

"Does Grady know a lot about farming?" Kayleen studied her daughter curiously.

"Seems to. But he knows even more about the markets. He had a company in Calgary that did a lot of business in that area. He studies the papers for hours. He's even got next year's crops figured out."

"Had a company?" Kayleen repeated frowning. "What happened to it?"

"He sold it or something. It had to do with his ex-wife." Maggie set several beets into her pail and moved on to the carrots. "He hasn't said an awful lot about it."

"Does he have children from this marriage?" Kayleen's face was serious as she watched the object of their conversation emerge from the toolshed.

"No. I asked him that once and he got all cold and withdrawn as if he was hurting. I don't know what it's all about but I suppose he'll tell me when he's ready."

"Probably," Kayleen agreed. "The girls seem to adore him." They both watched as Grady hunched down to show Keeley something on her new bike. Katy moved to slide her arm around his shoulders and he drew her into his free arm.

"Yes, they do. And he really cares for them, Mom. I always wondered if Brian merely tolerated them for my sake."

"I never liked Brian," Kayleen said firmly. "He was too full of himself."

"Mother! You never said a word."

"Of course not." Kayleen carried her zucchini to the trunk of her car. "That was your decision, dear. I will always support you whatever you decide."

"Thanks, Mom. You've always been there for me." Maggie hugged the woman's narrow shoulders.

"That's what mothers do. You'll learn that sooner or

later. By the way—'' she helped Maggie store the other vegetables in a corner of the trunk ''—your sisters are coming down for the long weekend. Beth can only come for Saturday, she's on duty after that.''

''What about Cathryn and Dorothy?''

''The whole weekend. Kids and all.''

''Put away your good china, then,'' Maggie ordered, her voice droll. ''And make sure your insurance is up-to-date.''

''Maggie, that isn't nice,'' Kayleen reprimanded, frowning.

''Nice, no. Truthful, yes.'' Maggie slammed the car door shut and watched as her mother put the car into gear. ''Bye, Mom,'' she called. ''And thanks. For everything.''

''Patience,'' her mother reminded. ''And trust in the promises.''

''I'll try.'' She eyed the grain fields with a practiced look and reviewed this morning's grain quotes in her mind. ''Although it would sure help my faith if we could get sixty bushels to the acre and haul it to the elevator without any problems.''

Chapter Eleven

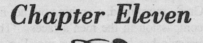

Grady winced at the noise emanating from the old farmhouse and grinned to himself. So this was what it was like to be part of a big family. The only child of only children, he'd never known the joy cousins found in each other's company.

"Bradley Richards, you are a bully! Leave that kitten alone." That was Katy, as vocal as ever when it came to her pets.

Here in the yard a group of children stood waiting their turn on the trampoline Maggie's sister had brought with her from Calgary.

"Until we get a fence up with strong sturdy locks, there's just no way I'm having that thing in my yard," she'd insisted. "The entire neighborhood comes over whenever they feel like it and we're liable if anyone gets hurt. Your girls might as well use it till then."

"If I had my way, I'd leave that thing here permanently," Dorothy's husband, Ron, muttered, grinning at Grady. "The thought of the lawsuits it could engender scares me to death."

"It's a crazy world when everybody starts suing every-one else," Matt agreed. He studied Grady. "Grady O'Toole. Aren't you the guy who owns Shaughnessy's?"

"I did," Grady told him. "Before it was closed down."

"We heard about that." Ron nodded. Both men were lawyers and Grady knew the news had probably spread through the legal community like wildfire. "Are you go-ing to start it up again?"

"No," Grady murmured, searching but not finding any-thing but compassion in the men's faces. "The pleasure in Shaughnessy's has been lost for me. I'm thinking of staying on here."

"As what? Hired help?" Matt scoffed. "You're not a farmer."

"I could be. But I was thinking more in terms as a member of the family. Maggie's family." Grady watched as surprise lifted the men's eyebrows. "I'd like to take this place on and make a go of it."

"You do have a reputation of revitalizing broken-down companies," Steven Richards mused, glancing around the yard. "But farms?"

"He's going to need every bit of that reputation to re-vitalize this place." Matt frowned. "I thought Cathryn said Maggie wanted to move."

"That was the whole point of Brian, wasn't it?" Ron glanced from one to the other. "Can't say I miss him much. Grady's a much better asset."

"That depends." Matt grinned, rubbing his hands to-gether. "Know any football?" he asked with a laugh.

"Used to play on the all-star team," Grady told him. "Why?"

"Because we haven't had a decent game of football in years, that's why," Ron said, tugging off his dress shirt so there was only a T-shirt covering his chest. "It's about

time we brought back that tradition.'' The others agreed
and within seconds they were searching for a ball.

He was in, Grady marveled. Just like that. No embarrassing questions. His connection with Maggie made him
part of the family. It was a situation he wasn't about to
question.

"You city guys think you can run in those fancy
pants," he called out, noticing that they all stood waiting
at the edge of the lawn. "Wanna borrow some jeans or
something?"

"City guys? Buddy, all three of us were born and raised
in the country. Cut our teeth on prime rib and T-bones.
You'd better watch it." Steven was a different man without his horn-rimmed glasses, and Grady had to marvel at
the speed with which he'd organized everyone into teams.

It was a hilarious afternoon. Grady caught as many
passes as the next guy, but he wasn't used to running in
his cowboy boots. After hitting the ground solidly for the
sixth time, he sank to the grass and pulled them off, leaving his feet bare in the thick springy grass. It was a strat-
egy that worked for he made two touchdowns in the next
five minutes.

"Aha! The man's been holding back," Matt called,
take a swig from his wife's full glass of lemonade.
"You'd better give me a kiss for energy, darlin', or I'm
liable to pass out here and now." Cathryn flushed a bit
self-consciously and tried to turn away but he kissed her
anyway, in full view of the crowd, and then went jogging
back into the fray.

"Dad," Maggie's nephew, Bradley called. "You'd better get some energy from Mom, too."

Steven obediently walked over to his wife and took her
in his arms, tipping her dramatically over one arm as he
kissed her.

"Ooh!" the children cried from the sidelines.

"Hey, my dad's gonna make the next one. Aren't you, Dad?"

"Not unless your mother can outdo her sisters." Ron smirked, standing in front of his wife. "What say, Doc?" Beth never said a word, but Grady figured the kiss she planted on him should turn him into a Hercules.

That left him and there was no way Grady was kissing Maggie in front of this rowdy crowd. Unfortunately, the twins had other ideas.

"Come on, Mom! You gotta kiss Grady so he'll win!" Katy was hopping up and down in her excitement. "Come on."

"No, Katy. It's all right. I can beat these guys with my feet tied up." He didn't even glance at Maggie, but suddenly she was standing there in front of him, head tipped to one side with her ponytail dancing in the wind.

"What's the matter, Grady?" she demanded, hands on her hips. "You never minded kissing me before."

Everyone was staring at him and Grady had never felt more embarrassed in his life.

Grady kissed her the way he'd wanted to all day. He kissed her so completely, that it was some time before he heard the voices.

"So what is this?" Bradley the referee demanded. "Halftime?"

"I dunno. Maybe their lips are stuck together." Katy stood staring at her mother in Grady's arms. But she didn't appear to be the least bit worried.

Grady moved back slightly and stared into Maggie's wide blue eyes. She seemed as bemused as he as she pressed one hand against her mouth. The other hand lay against his chest, right over his thudding heart.

"I love you, Maggie McCarthy. And I don't care who knows it." But he said the words for her ears alone and was gratified to see the tiny flicker of a grin at the corners of her mouth.

"Nobody ever said I was shy, either," she whispered, and stood on tiptoe to reach his mouth. "I love you, Grady."

"We've got a game going here, folks. If you want to keep that up, I suggest you move off the field." Matt's tone was smug. "Maybe you should set a date."

"I, uh, think we should continue this later, Grady," Maggie mumbled, pressing away from him a second time.

"Yeah," he agreed. He let her go, but his eyes followed her figure and long legs to the edge of the grass.

"You okay?" Steven asked, clapping him on one shoulder. "I can get Beth's smelling salts if you want."

"Nah, leave him alone," Ron chided. "Maybe this'll slow him down a little and give us an edge. Us old married guys need an advantage."

"You should have slowed down a little," Maggie muttered as she stood many hours later dabbing liniment on his chest, reminding him of his childishness. She clicked her tongue at the bruise that stretched over one shoulder and down his torso. "Matt plays racquetball every day, you know. He's tougher than nails. And Ron lifts weights like a pro." She sniffed as he winced. "It's a ridiculous game anyway."

"It's a wonderful game," Grady contradicted, tugging her close. "I had a wonderful time with your family. But some moments were more memorable than others." He pulled her head down and kissed her softly. "Thank you."

"For what?" She stared at him curiously.

"For helping me feel like one of the family. I like your sisters and their husbands, Margaret Mary." His arms rested around her waist. "They're real people."

"That was evident by the amount of food they consumed. That huge bowl of potato salad Mom brought is completely gone. Ditto Matt's steaks and Ron's burgers."

"Did Steve really make that dessert?" Grady watched her nod. "It's hard to believe a man with that many degrees can do all that stuff. There's obviously more to a radiologist than meets the eye."

Maggie frowned severely. "That joke is growing very old," she warned him. "Find something new."

"This is new." He tugged her a little closer. "I can't remember the last time I had the pleasure of kissing you in private." He did it again just to make sure he hadn't lost the knack.

"And I guess that's going to have to last you for a while," she whispered, pulling away. "Here come the troops again."

Grady tugged on his shirt just as the door flew open and Katy popped her bright head in. "Aren't you and Grady ever coming out, Mom? The fire's just going good." She spied the bag of marshmallows on the table and snatched them up before racing away. "Hurry!"

"Maggie?" Grady watched as the woman he loved rinsed her hands. He dried them carefully and then slipped the ring he'd found days ago onto her finger. "Please marry me? Soon?"

She stared at the wide gold band with its brilliantly glittering sapphire and the ring of diamonds that surrounded it. As he watched, tears formed at the corners of her eyes.

"Oh, Grady," she whispered, throwing her arms around his neck. "Why did you have to pick today?"

"Because it's been such a wonderful day." He smiled, wiping away her tears. "And because I couldn't carry that around in my shirt pocket any more. I love you, beautiful Maggie. I want to marry you. I bought the ring because it reminds me of your eyes." He had a sudden thought. "If you want something else, we can always exchange it." She started crying harder and sudden doubt assailed him. "Maggie?"

"I will marry you, Grady. Soon," she blubbered. He handed her a tissue and waited till she'd mopped up her face. "I love you, too. But just for tonight, could this be our secret? Just between you and me?"

It wasn't what he wanted to hear, Grady admitted. He wanted her to be as pleased as he was. To shout it so the whole world could hear. But she hadn't said no. Maggie McCarthy had said she wanted to marry him and that was what he wanted most of all, wasn't it?

"Sweetheart," he whispered, holding her tenderly. "We can do anything you want. I love you, and no matter what, I'll always be here. Count on that. Okay?" She nodded and he kissed her one last time before enfolding her left hand in his and walking back out to her family.

As they sat far into the night, singing old-fashioned songs around the campfire and toasting marshmallows golden brown, Grady held on to Maggie's hand and thought how lucky he was to be included in this big, boisterous family. The older kids tented in the front yard. The younger ones lay fast asleep in their parents' arms.

It was so exactly what he'd dreamed of for so long, he couldn't help but whisper a prayer of thanks. And when Matt led out in the doxology, Grady willingly sang along.

"God from whom all blessings flow," Herman repeated, snuggling up against his wife. "We have a caring God, don't we, my dear."

Kayleen pressed her head against her husband's shoulder and sighed. "Too big, too kind, too wonderful to understand," she agreed happily and then got to her feet as a baby cried out, shattering the solitude. "And I think it's time we went home." She pressed a kiss against Maggie's cheek and hugged Grady. "Thank you, my dears. We had a wonderful time."

Grady stood and watched everyone leave, holding Maggie protectively at his side. He waited while Katy and Keeley bid them good-night and went quietly up to bed. He even waited while Maggie fussed with the toys left lying around and dishes not yet put away. Grady stifled the small voice that asked why she hadn't told her parents or shown anyone the ring and concentrated on the here and now.

He waited as long as he could and then he grabbed her hand and pulled her back to the fire pit, sinking down onto the blanket that still lay there. He leaned back against the chair and pulled Maggie into the circle of his arms, sighing deeply when she settled against him.

"What was that for?"

"That was a sigh of pure contentment," he told her seriously. "And when things get rough and you get mad at me and the girls won't listen, I'm going to remember this perfect evening when you and I got officially engaged. I'm going to think about how we all sat around the fire together and sang songs and I'm going to remember the way you kissed me good-night."

"I didn't kiss you good-night," she replied, frowning, tilting her head to one side to stare at him.

"I know." He winked at her, watching the glint of awareness light her beautiful eyes from inside. "But I have very high hopes that you will soon. Please?"

He would never tire of that lilting laugh, Grady told himself as she turned and wrapped her arms around him. Not ever.

Chapter Twelve

❧

"Maggie, my love, that is the sweetest smell I've inhaled in years. Fresh apple pie!" Maggie watched as Grady closed his eyes and sniffed while curving one arm around her waist. "I can wait just long enough for you to kiss me."

Maggie complied and saw his eyes widen as he saw the ring he'd given her days ago, now strung on a chain around her neck. She tucked it back into the neckline of her blouse and flushed.

"I don't want to damage it by getting it full of flour and lard or ruin it when I do work outside," she told him, turning away to cut a piece of pie. When he didn't speak, she finally admitted the truth. "And I still don't want to tell anyone. Not yet."

"Waiting for a better offer?" he teased, but his laugh didn't ring quite true.

"No, that's not it," she told him seriously. She watched as he took the first bite and then poured two cups of coffee before sitting down in the chair across from him. She added two dollops of cream, which she knew he liked, and then pushed the mug across toward him. "I just want a little time to think everything through, Grady. Is that so wrong of me?"

"No, of course not," he mumbled. "It's good to be sure. I guess I just assumed that you *were* sure about us."

"I'm sure about loving you." She fiddled with her cup. "It's the rest of it that bothers me. I guess I just have to deal with this in my own way, Grady. Please don't be mad."

"I'm not mad." He grinned. "I'm the happiest man on this side of the planet. I've got what I always wanted."

"What's that?"

"Three gorgeous women. And a slice of the most delicious pie I've ever eaten. Life is good." He leaned back and patted his washboard-flat stomach.

"You're good for my ego." Maggie laughed. "But 'gorgeous'? I'm sure!" She touched the scarf that held her hair off her face and thrust out her stained fingers. "I've been fiddling with that auger all morning."

Grady winced and dropped his dark head into his hands in dismay. "Maggie, I asked you to please leave the machinery to me. I'll get to it."

"If we're going to start swathing this week, it needs to be done," she reminded him. "I want to at least start out with no breakdowns." He muttered something about her being the cause of the breakdowns, and Maggie glared at him. "I heard that."

"I'm sorry." Grady brushed a kiss across the top of her head in consolation as he took his dishes to the sink. "I'm going to do a round on that barley field now. I think it's about time."

"But what about the winter wheat in the south quarter? It should be ready, shouldn't it?"

"Not quite. Besides, I'd like to take it off straight if I

can. This crazy weather we've been having isn't reliable enough to leave anything in the swath for very long." He walked to the door and stopped to look at the pail of crab apples on the counter. "What are you doing with those?"

"Oh, jelly, I suppose, though I don't know why. We'll never eat all the stuff I've canned and frozen this year. Just look at this." Maggie opened the pantry doors for him to see row upon row of preserves, jams, jellies and pickles lining the shelves. "That's a twenty-six-cubic-foot freezer over there and it's stuffed, too."

"I happen to love crab apple jelly, just about as much as I love you. Besides, now you'll be able to celebrate Thanksgiving with a full heart." He grinned, tugging his gloves out of his pocket.

"But I haven't even started on the pumpkins yet! What am I going to do with it all?" Maggie closed the pantry doors automatically as she glanced out at the yellowish-turning-orange vegetables that dotted the garden. "I could make a fortune at the farmer's market selling only pumpkins!"

"I don't think so. Everyone around here seems to have lots. I guess you'll just have to make a whole bunch of pumpkin pies," he teased, rolling his eyes. "What a hardship! But I'll face it like a man."

"Oh, get out of here!" She tossed an oven mitt at him, unable to stop the burst of laughter at his offended look. He advanced menacingly toward her and Maggie retreated. "No, don't you dare!"

But it seemed Grady O'Toole did dare and within minutes had her doubled over in laughter as his fingers tickled her mercilessly.

"Truce. Truce!" Slipping beyond his reach, Maggie wiped the tears off her cheeks and frowned. "How did you know about that particular weakness of mine, pray tell?"

"I have my sources," he whispered, advancing close enough to brush his lips against her ear. "Two short but very reliable and informative sources. No, don't put that…abomination over this gorgeous hair again. It should be illegal to cover such beauty."

Pleased that he found her attractive, Maggie tucked the scarf into her pocket. "Well, I have to do something with it," she muttered, blushing. "It's getting so shaggy."

"I like your hair long," Grady murmured, running his fingers through it. "It's beautiful. And so are you." He kissed her then. "Enough of this mushy stuff!" His eyes glittered as he set her gently away from him. "I've got to get to work. Are you going to be around?"

"Yes, I'm going to start on a new project. Why?" She hated to pull her hands away from his shoulders. She wanted to be held, safe and secure in that gentle embrace, just a little bit longer. Just long enough to shut out the worries that plagued her late at night when she was all alone and couldn't rush off to another job.

"Because I might need you to bring the truck over. If that barley's ready, I'll keep going." He waited till she nodded, then stepped back and picked up the gloves he'd dropped at her feet. "I love you, Maggie." With a peck on her nose, he was gone.

"I love you, too," she murmured. But Grady had left and the words hung in the silence of the kitchen. "There's no point in fussing about things," she reminded herself sternly. "The Father knows what you need before you ask Him. Now relax and do your part."

Maggie carried her coffee into her workroom and set about piecing together her Thanksgiving quilt. She made one every year and then gave it to the church ladies for the silent auction they held to raise Christmas funds for missionaries.

A pumpkin motif seemed appropriate and Maggie set to work planning the pattern, unaware of time until the door slammed open and Katy's voice echoed through the house. "I'm home."

"I can see that. How was school?" They talked for several moments before Maggie realized that her older daughter had not come in. "Where's Keeley?"

"Um, well, you see, that is…" Katy stumbled over the words, her cheeks flushed, eyes downcast. "Keeley sort of had to stay after school."

"Keeley did?" Maggie stared. "Why?"

"I think she should tell you, Mom. I don't want to be a tattletale." Katy walked regally from the room, head held high.

"Since when?" Maggie called, but Katy ignored her, trudging up the stairs with solemn dignity. The telephone pealed out just then, preventing any further conversation.

"Mrs. McCarthy, this is Janice Fortescue. I thought I'd let you know that I'm keeping Keeley after school today." Maggie listened as the teacher spoke and felt the knot of tension in her shoulders wind ever tighter.

"No, Janice. That's perfectly fine. If you feel she deserves to then I support you wholeheartedly. I'll pick her up in half an hour? Thank you." Maggie hung up the phone automatically. "Katy McCarthy, you get down here right this minute!"

But Katy, it seemed, had snuck out the back door and was nowhere to be found. Maggie scrubbed her hands in the sink, soapy water flying everywhere as she mumbled dire predictions the entire time.

"Maggie?" The radio blared from the kitchen. "Are you there?"

"Yes, I'm here but not for long." Maggie forced herself to speak calmly and clearly. "I'm on my way into town to get Keeley. She had to stay after school."

"Keeley did? Why?" Grady's voice reflected her surprise.

"I don't know, Grady. But I intend to find out. By the way, if you see Katy around, grab her by the seat of her pants and hang on to her. I intend to have a heart-to-heart talk with both of them when I get back. Bye." She snapped the button down and then pressed it again, anxiety rising. "By the way, how is the barley?"

"Ready to go. That's why I was calling. But don't worry, Buster's here. I'll get him to drive over and bring the truck. I'm nearly full now. See you later."

"Yes, all right. I'll bring supper out at six. Bye."

"Maggie?"

"Yes?"

"I don't know how to say this other than to say, don't jump to conclusions, okay? Let her tell it in her own way."

"Grady, I'm the girls' mother! I've had ten years of practicing. I think I know how to deal with this." Upset that he would question her judgment put a harsh tone on her words.

"I know you can. Just calm down, okay? Nothing can be that terrible." When she didn't answer, he sighed heavily. "Bye, love."

"Goodbye." Maggie grabbed her purse and stormed out of the house. "As if I don't know how to handle my own children," she sputtered. "Who does he think he is?"

A tiny inner voice chided her for blaming Grady when all he was trying to do was help. He loved the girls and cared deeply for them. He loved her, too, the voice reminded Maggie.

Then he should trust me to do the right thing. The words rolled round and round inside her head, and suddenly Maggie realized that the same thing applied to her position with God. She was always telling Him what to do and how to do it, when she could and ought to be trusting Him to do the right thing.

"Sorry, Lord," she murmured, pulling into the school yard. "I've goofed again."

As she walked up the stairs and into the old, mustysmelling building, Maggie ordered herself to be calm and rational. The sight of her daughter, seated at the front of the room, head down as she read from a thick heavy book almost shook that determination, but Maggie held on. Barely.

"Miss Fortescue, Keeley." Maggie stood in the doorway. "What seems to be the problem?"

"I didn't mean to hurt her, Mom, really I didn't!" Keeley dashed into her mother's arms, sobbing as if her heart was broken.

"Hurt who? Keeley, what is the matter?" Maggie wrapped her arms around her daughter and held her tight, amazed to find the little body shaking.

"Keeley slapped Ginny Patterson. Ginny fell backward and hit her head on the cement curb surrounding the playground. I'm afraid she had to have some stitches."

"Keeley?" Maggie gaped at the daughter who had always been so quiet and restrained in her emotions. "Will you tell me what happened?"

"I—I s-s-slapped her." Keeley hiccuped and sniffled. "And I'm glad!"

"Maybe you are," Maggie muttered angrily. "But regardless of your feelings in the matter, we do not go

around slapping people. What happened?'' When Keeley
didn't speak, Maggie glanced at the teacher.

"I'm sorry," Janice said, shrugging her shoulders.
"You know as much as I do. Keeley won't say anymore."

"Yes, she will," Maggie muttered, pressing her daughter down in a nearby chair. "And right now, Keeley McCarthy. I want an answer."

"Ginny's mean and nasty," Keeley told them indignantly. "She steals and she lies!"

"That may well be," Maggie replied, and sat down.
"But we're not going to go around decking every person
we don't happen to personally like, are we?" She watched
for the negative shake of Keeley's blond head. "Now
what, exactly, did Ginny steal, and what lies did she tell?"

Maggie returned her daughter's stare with steely-eyed
determination, holding her features in her best mother-the-
discipliner look. "Well?"

"She said I was always gonna be an orphan, that nobody would ever want Katy and me for a part of their
family." Keeley sniffed mournfully.

"But you know that isn't true. You and Katy and I are
family. We have each other. You're not an orphan." Maggie watched the blond head bend. "What else?"

"Well..." Keeley stalled for time.

"Keeley, I was very busy when Miss Fortescue called.
But I took the time to come here because I'm concerned
with the way you've been acting. You know better than
that. Now, what else?"

"She said nobody would ever marry you and be our
dad 'cause they'd have to take on our ramshackle farm,
and everybody knows we don't even have enough money
to pay our bills, let alone buy anything new!" Keeley
glared at her mother belligerently.

"I always pay my bills," Maggie murmured, softly

enough that Keeley would hear, but fully aware of the teacher seated nearby, listening to this very personal discussion of her private affairs. She felt humiliated. "And nothing you've said so far explains why you slapped Ginny." Maggie thought over the conversation. "You said 'she steals.' What did she steal, honey?" Keeley muttered something that Maggie didn't catch. "Pardon?"

"My papers. She stole my papers!" Keeley burst out angrily.

"What papers?"

"These papers," Janice Fortescue murmured, holding out a sheaf of white computer printed sheets. "I picked them up off the ground."

There was a look of shared commiseration on her face that Maggie didn't understand. She accepted them and glanced down in perplexity. Her eyes popped open at the big bold title on the first page.

"How To Help Your Mother Snare That Man," she read out aloud. Her shocked eyes flew to Keeley's. "Where did this come from?" she demanded.

"I, um, that is, a lady I've been E-mailing sent it to me," Keeley mumbled, shame-faced. "She writes romances, Mom, and I figured she'd know a good way for you to meet someone. Then when Grady came along and you seemed to like him, I figured it would be nice to have him for our dad. You like him, Mom, I know you do." Keeley's belligerent voice was full of tears. "And Katy and I think he's the best almost-dad we've ever had. He really listens when we tell him stuff."

"But Keeley," Maggie gasped as she sorted through the documents that explained several ways couples could get to know each other better. "To talk to someone I don't even know, about my private affairs!" She stared at the pages with distaste. "I just can't believe you'd do this. Why, Keeley?"

"Because Katy and me want a dad, that's why. I'm tired of worrying about you and about what's going to happen when we leave here! I got sick of hearing you crying at night. You did, Mom," she accused when Maggie's head jerked upward. "Before Grady came, when you thought we were sleeping, you'd get up and go in the kitchen and make hot chocolate. I followed you once and you were crying." Keeley's eyes filled with fresh tears. "After Grady came, you weren't nearly as sad."

Maggie stared at the packet of advice for the lovelorn and tried to concentrate. "Ginny stole these?"

"Yes."

"Why?" Maggie stared at her daughter, hoping against all hope that Keeley wasn't going to say it.

"She was going to put them up on the bulletin board so everybody could see. She took them out of my back-pack, Mom! That's stealing. And she read them without asking. Mom? Mom!" But Maggie didn't hear her. All she could see were the words dancing in front of her.

"Your mother has to decide for herself if she loves Grady enough to marry him. You and your sister can't help her with that, so don't add pressure to this important decision by bugging her. I know you love him a lot. You can tell him that, of course. But your mother has to think of the future and whether or not Grady would be a good husband and a good father to you two. Once she's married, it's too late to change her mind."

She had to get out of there, Maggie decided. Before she screamed or tore up the sheets or stomped her feet. "I'm sorry Keeley struck Ginny, Miss Fortescue. And I will make sure she apologizes. I believe you said you'd asked her to stay in every day at lunchtime?" Janice hadn't but that didn't matter. Maggie stood briskly as the other woman nodded her head in agreement with Maggie's form of reprimand.

"I'll take Keeley home with me now and together we'll work out an appropriate punishment. Thank you for calling me. Keeley?" She lowered her brows at her daughter's stubborn look.

"I'm sorry, Miss Fortescue."

"All right, Keeley. You go home with your mother now. I'll see you tomorrow."

They walked down the empty hallway littered with bits of paper and erasers that the caretaker was sweeping into a pile. The door clanged shut behind them and Keeley jumped at the loud noise.

"Mom? Are you mad?"

"Yes!" Maggie responded vehemently, slamming the car door shut behind her. "And I would appreciate it if you did not speak to me until I tell you to."

They drove home in grim silence with Keeley's whitened face peering steadfastly ahead. At home, she climbed out of the car and walked stiffly into the house and up the stairs, her chin held high. Maggie ignored the sniffles she heard and went through to the kitchen to spread the papers on the table.

It was awful, far worse than anything she had expected. There it was in plain black and white, for anyone to see. The story of their lives for the past three and a half months. Every time the girls had seen Grady kiss Maggie, or put his arm around her waist was recorded. The discussions Katy and Keeley had held to find out Grady's preference.

Here were questions about what the girls would call Grady if he married their mother, and on another page, questions about Katy baby-sitting any children she and Grady might have.

It saddened Maggie to see that her daughters had addressed this woman named Debbie about things they should have been asking her. Why had she thought to hide their engagement? The girls' lives were at stake here, too. She should have kept them informed about Grady's role in their lives.

But as the thoughts rolled around in her mind, Maggie knew the reason she hadn't discussed her engagement with her daughters. Or anyone else, for that matter. The truth was that she was scared stiff to think about a future on this farm.

"Grady is a good man," she told herself. "But he can't guarantee the future any more than Roger could. I might spend the next thirty years grubbing in this land. By then I'll be too old to do anything else. I want to live a little before I die!"

Maggie studied the words on the paper one last time. This Debbie person certainly knew her stuff.

"Your mother has to be absolutely certain that Grady is the man for her. And she has to decide it for herself. You and Keeley have to back her up in whatever she decides. But she gets to pick the man she's going to marry herself. Just as you two will pick your own husbands one day."

"Okay, Lord," Maggie murmured, gathering up the white sheets and stacking them into a little pile. "Here comes another test. Please help me get through it."

Maggie walked slowly to the bottom of the stairs. "Katy and Keeley, I'd like you both to come down here, please."

They came at once, Katy first, with Keeley slowly following behind. Both sets of eyes were huge with worry as they studied her face.

"We need to talk," Maggie began. "I have some things to say and I want you both to listen carefully. If you have questions, you can ask them when I'm finished. Understood?" The girls nodded.

"Good. First, I want to say that I am very hurt that you would speak to someone I don't even know about my private and personal life. I would never talk about Keeley's crush on Jeremy Benstat or about Katy getting her braces caught on the bedspread because those are things that should stay in a family." Both heads lowered.

"Secondly, I am very ashamed that my daughter would dare to slap another human being. That is not the way we solve arguments in this family and you know that. Don't you?"

They nodded slowly.

"Third, you've both done something very dangerous by putting our name and address on the Internet. You both know that there are strangers all over the world who grab on to something like that. For that reason alone, neither of you will be allowed to get E-mail or go on the Internet for the next two months." Not a protest issued from either mouth.

"Now, since you wanted to know about Grady and me, I will tell you on the condition that this news is between you and I. No one else is to know. And I mean no one." Maggie slipped the chain out from beneath the high-buttoned neckline of her blouse and held up her ring. "This is from Grady. He asked me to marry him. I haven't told him for sure when I would, because I wanted a little time to think about things."

"You and Grady are getting married?" Katy burst out. "That is so cool!"

"Katy! We're not going to get married right away." Maggie hated seeing the look of disappointment cross her daughters' faces, but she labored on. "There are some things I have to think about."

"Like what?" Keeley peered up from beneath her lashes. "You love him, don't you?"

"Yes, I do." At least she was sure of that much.

"Well, then?"

"Keeley, it's not that simple. I don't know that I want to spend my life on the farm. I'd like to live in the city, get a real job, maybe send you guys to ballet lessons, or basketball, or swimming and gymnastics. There are a lot of opportunities in Calgary that Willow Bunch doesn't have."

"Would Grady move?" Katy's normally boisterous voice was quiet.

"I don't know. I want the very best life for my children," she added. "I have to make sure that I'm doing the right thing."

"What about what God says?" Keeley demanded. "I know He would want us to stay here."

"But *I* don't know that, honey. I'm not sure God hasn't given me this desire to move because that's the best thing for us. Do you see what I mean?"

"Yeah, I guess so." Katy screwed up her face in concentration. "You mean you're not sure what to do."

"Exactly. So I've been praying that the Lord would lead me wherever He wants me to be. And now I need to listen for His answer."

"You mean we don't have any say about it?" Keeley frowned. "We have to go along with whatever you decide?"

"Of course you have a say. But ultimately the responsibility to raise you girls rests on me. I have to provide for you as best I can and I'm just not sure it's the best thing for either of you to stay cooped up on this farm. It's been very hard to keep things going these last few years. You know that.''

"Boy, do we!" Katy rolled her eyes. "But Mom, Grady's got money. He could help us.''

Maggie narrowed her eyes and frowned. "And you think that would be fair—to marry someone because he has money that we just happen to need?''

"No.'' Katy pouted for a minute before her eyes lit up. "But you said you loved Grady!'' she crowed triumphantly.

"Yes, I do. And the money thing has nothing to do with that.''

"I'm very glad to hear it,'' a low husky voice murmured from behind her. "It would be a terrible thing to be married for my money twice in one lifetime.''

Maggie was startled by Grady's entrance, and his revelation.

"Is that what she did?'' When he winked Maggie blushed.

"Are you rich, Grady?'' Katy asked.

"Katy, me darlin'—'' Grady laughed as he chucked the girl under the chin and sank into the nearest chair ''—I'm as rich as a man can be. Your mother says she loves me.'' He winked at Maggie. "And I think you two beauties are the best thing since sliced bread. ''I'm richer than Croesus.''

"Who?'' Katy was frowning.

"The guy who had all the gold,'' Keeley told her. "I read it to you last week, remember?''

"You mean you've got buildings full of gold?'' Katy stared at him in disbelief. "And you're working as a farmhand?''

Grady stood and burst out laughing, the sound echoing around the room. "Katy, a man's wealth has very little to do with his bank balance. I have enough money to live on, but that's not important. Anybody can earn money." He hugged her close. "But not everybody," he whispered solemnly, "has the chance to have two lovely girls for his daughters."

"Is that what we'd be?" Keeley wanted to know. "Your daughters?"

"I'd like that very much," he murmured, glancing at Maggie. "But in here—" he tapped his chest "—you've been my daughters for a long time already."

"I love you, Grady," Katy burst out, hugging him tightly. He hugged her back, drawing Keeley into the embrace and then tugging Maggie nearer when she would have backed away.

"Group hug!" Katy called out.

Maggie good-naturedly let them maneuver her closer to Grady and returned the kiss he pressed against her lips, fully aware of two sets of very interested blue eyes.

"What are you doing here anyway?" Maggie demanded, pulling away. "I thought you were knee-deep in barley."

"Oh, I'd like to be! But that swather broke down. Again. Buster's gone to see if he can find a part." He tugged her close again, his eyes twinkling. "That leaves me with a little free time," he whispered loudly.

The girls cast each other knowing looks and moved toward the door. "We're going to do our chores," Keeley offered with a giggle. "So you guys can be alone for a while."

"Yeah, alone," Katy reiterated. They moved through the door jostling each other. A second later Katy's head poked back in. "Since you've got lots of money and we're going to be your daughters, do you think we could get a four-wheeler?'' she asked in wide-eyed innocence.

"Katy McCarthy!" Maggie pursed her lips.

"Well, I was just wondering. I know money isn't everything, but it sure must be nicer to have too much than too little," she retorted before closing the door behind her.

"She's got you there," Grady said with a snicker, drawing Maggie into his arms. "That's one very astute lady. She'll make a wonderful businesswoman one day. You ought to be proud."

"Right now I'm embarrassed," she told him. "They're so mercenary."

"No, they're not. They're just sweet little girls who know a good thing when they see it. I must say, I have to agree. Don't you want to go along with their plans?"

"Ha! Plans? I'll show you plans!" Maggie lifted the stack of papers from the table and shoved them under his nose. "Sit down, Grady."

"Why?" He frowned, trying to read the top sheet.

"Because if you don't, you might fall down. It seems that you and I have been the subject of an Internet-generated romance plot. Women around the world have been advising Katy and Keeley on how to get us together."

He sank into the chair. "You're joking!"

"Not hardly. Those two 'sweet little girls', as you so sweetly called them, gave a romance writer our name. She passed on their questions. These are the replies." She dropped the sheaf on the table.

To Maggie's surprise he looked not the least bit angry. Instead, his mouth curved in what looked like a proud smile. "Grady, have you any idea of what you'd be taking on here?" she asked.

"No, actually I didn't," he murmured, studying the

sheets more closely. "Not entirely. But you have to admit, at least it wouldn't be boring."

Maggie sagged back in her chair and closed her eyes. *Lord,* she prayed silently. *What's the plan here? Please, please, tell me Your plan.*

The only response to her plea was Grady's muffled laughter as he read through the sheets of advice from the matchmakers.

Chapter Thirteen

Grady was worried. Katy and Keeley had hunted him down in Marty Shane's garage ten minutes ago. He could tell from their tone over the phone that something was wrong.

"Grady, do you know where Mom is?" That was Keeley, her voice betraying just a tiny wobble.

"She's swathing." A prickle of fear niggling up his spine made Grady's arm tense. "Did you try her on the radio?"

"For the past half hour. She isn't answering." Katy gave the information clearly. "Should I go and look for her?"

"No." Grady knew that was precisely what Maggie didn't want. "I'm leaving now. I'll be home in half an hour. Less, I hope." He shook his head at Marty's offer of a coffee. "You guys call over to the McLeans' and ask Buster to look in the west field that adjoins his. Okay?"

"Y-yes, all right," Keeley whispered. "Please hurry, Grady."

"I'm coming, sweetheart. You just remember that God

is in control. Maybe you and Katy could say a few words while you're waiting. I'll be there soon."

He drove far faster than the speed limit, his powerful engine covering the miles easily. Precisely twenty-two minutes later he drove into the yard and squealed to a stop. Katy came racing out of the house, her little face white and pinched looking.

"Mr. McLean's away, Grady. Mrs. McLean said Timmy was sick so she couldn't help us. Keeley's trying some of the other neighbors." She threw her arms around him. "I wish she'd come home."

"So do I, honey," he murmured. "But right now I've got to go look for her. Run and tell Keeley we're going looking and ask her to stay by the phone."

Grady grabbed his tool kit from beside the combine and chucked it into the truck. Moments later Katy came racing back and they set off together.

"Do you think God wants my mom to go to heaven?" she asked in a hushed, frightened tone. "Maybe He needs her there."

"Nope. I think He knows that we need her here." Grady tightened his fingers around the steering wheel and drove faster than he'd ever done down the dusty rutted track. There in the distance he thought he could see the outline of the swather, but where was Maggie?

As they drew closer, Grady could see her bright red shirt on the ground. His heart sent up a quick prayer to heaven.

"She's on the ground, Grady. She's lying on the ground. What happened? Is she dead?" Katy rattled the questions off in a tense, tight voice.

"She's not dead." Grady surprised himself at his vehemence. "Stay here until I call you."

He raced across the furrows of perfectly cut barley, ignoring the chaff that flew up. As he went, he prayed.

"Please don't take her, Lord. We need her. The girls have already lost their father, God. They can't lose Maggie, too. I can't lose Maggie!"

As he got closer, Grady took note of her prone position. No bones at odd angles, no blood on her face. No marks. He did a quick, thorough study and was just breathing a sigh of relief when his fingers encountered the blood on the back of her head.

"Oh, no," he breathed, feeling the sticky red stuff ooze through his fingers. He moved her slightly to one side and gaped at the pool of red soaking into her hair. "She's lost so much blood. Help her, God. Katy!" He yelled across the furrows and saw Katy's little body jerk. "Bring the first-aid box behind the seat," he called, more in control now. "Your mom has hurt herself."

Maggie's big blue eyes fluttered halfway open just then and she stared up at Grady groggily. "Oh," she murmured softly, "I prayed and God brought you." Her mouth curved in a smile. "I hurt my head."

"I know you did, sweetie. Just lie still and we'll get you all fixed up. Katy's here and she's going to help me."

"Katy came? Hi, Katy." The thick golden lashes flopped down once, twice, before Maggie refocused on them. "Is Keeley here, too?"

"No, Mom. She's at the house waiting, in case someone calls. Are you all right?"

"I'm fine. Just a little woozy. I'll sit up in a minute." Her eyelids dropped down once more. Grady was grateful they stayed closed while he pressed a gauze pad on the injury and wound a ring of gauze around her head to hold the pad in place.

"Bring the kit, Katy," he murmured softly. "I'm going

to carry your mom to the truck. Then we'll put her in the back seat.''

"What's wrong with her?" Katy frowned as she followed him over and held open the truck door.

"I'm pretty sure she's got a concussion. We'll take her to the hospital.'' He closed the door and climbed into the driver's seat. The ignition had barely turned over when the thready voice from the rear objected.

"I'm not going to the hospital. I just hit my head. It's nothing serious. I have to finish the field.''

"Forget the field,'' Grady muttered brusquely. "It can wait. Your head can't. And yes, we are going to the hospital. Now be quiet!'' He hadn't meant to say it so harshly, but he was angry. How could this happen to Maggie?

Grady contented himself with praying silently all the way back to the farm where they picked up Keeley and then headed to town. Katy quickly explained the situation and both girls sat silent, casting worried glances at their mother from time to time. Maggie said nothing and Grady wondered if she'd blacked out again.

At the hospital, doctors and nurses brushed him aside. "You'll have to wait with her daughters,'' the nurse told him. "I'm sure the doctor will explain once he's examined Mrs. McCarthy. Are you a friend?''

"I'm her fiancé,'' he burst out, pleased to be able to finally say the words. He didn't care if the whole world knew; he wanted some tie to bind him and Maggie together.

"Oh.'' The nurse studied him thoroughly. "Congratulations!''

"Thanks,'' he said, glancing down the hall at the flurry of activity around Maggie's room. "Will you let us know when we can see her?''

"Of course." She nodded. "But don't worry. Maggie will be fine. She's a very strong woman, you know."

Grady clenched his hands to keep from telling her that he didn't want Maggie to be strong. He wanted her to depend on him and let down that protective barrier she carried so well. Anyway, Grady half suspected that underneath all that bravado, Maggie's stamina was slowly crumbling. He'd seen evidence of it once or twice himself.

"Is Mom going to be all right, Grady?" Keeley's hand slipped into his. "She's not going to die, is she?"

"No, sweetie." Grady squeezed the tiny hand in his own and held on. He wrapped his other arm around Katy and held them both. "Your mom's going to be just fine. She hurt her head and it was a pretty deep cut, but the doctors will stitch it up. She'll probably have to rest for a few days."

"But what about harvest?" Keeley whispered, staring up at him with her huge blue eyes. "We've just got to get the crops off this year. It's our last chance."

"What do you mean, 'our last chance'? Has something happened, Keeley?" Grady peered down into the white and worried face.

"Go on, tell him, Keeley." When her sister didn't speak up, Katy grabbed Grady's hand and tugged him toward the chairs in the waiting room. "Sit down," she ordered in a tone he'd heard Maggie use before.

"I'm only telling you because I'm worried about my mom. Okay?" She waited for his nod of agreement and then continued. "Mom got a call from the bank yesterday. If we miss the next payment, we have to move off the farm."

"Are you sure?" He stared at the nodding heads.

"I picked up the phone and she was talking on it. I didn't mean to listen in, but she sounded so...mad," Keeley whispered. "I knew she was scared, though. Her voice was all shaky."

Grady thought back. So that explained the frenetic activity of the past twenty-four hours. "I'll worry about the harvest," he told them finally. "Don't bother your mother with any of this right now. She needs to rest."

"Here comes the doctor." Keeley sounded scared and Grady couldn't help but hug her close.

"Are you friends of Mrs. McCarthy's?" The doctor glanced from one to the other.

"You must be new here," Grady muttered, shaking hands with the young man who looked little older than a teenager. He introduced the girls and then looked the doctor square in the eye. "How is she?"

"She has a rather long cut on the back of her head which will need stitches. The scan seems to show no other injury, and since she is conscious and speaking clearly, we are hopeful that the cut is her only problem. I'm keeping her overnight just to make sure. Do you happen to know just how long she was unconscious?"

Grady shook his head. "No idea. I left her just after noon and the girls came home close to four."

"Well, her color is good and she's quite responsive, so we'll take that as a positive sign." He brushed a hand over the girls' hair and bent down to their level. "I have to put some stitches in your mom's head so that the cut she has will heal nice and neat."

"Then will she be okay?" Katy scuffed her toe on the floor.

"I think so, but I'm going to have her stay here tonight just to make sure." He studied them solemnly. "Do you think you can manage alone, just for tonight?"

"Of course." Keeley straightened her shoulders.

"Grady will help us if we need it, and I can call Granny to come over. Just take care of our mother, Doctor."

"I'll do that." He stood and winked at them before drawing Grady aside. "Why don't you take them for some ice cream or something? It's going to be a while before they can see her."

So they did. Grady whipped the soiled seat cover off the back seat and stowed it carefully underneath so the girls wouldn't be reminded of their mother's injury. Then they ordered huge hot-fudge sundaes and took them to a nearby park to eat.

"Grady? Why does God let bad things happen to good people?" Katy stared up at him with her guileless blue eyes. "Our Sunday school teacher said God is all powerful and that He can do anything. So why didn't He stop the accident from happening to my mom?"

Grady groaned mentally under the difficulty of answering such a challenging question.

"Sometimes things happen that we can't explain, honey. Things like that cut on your mom's head. Maybe she didn't take enough care putting the hood down or something, and that was the natural result. I don't know." He drew a deep breath and continued. "But the important thing is that God is still there and He can see us through all the bad times. He is in charge and if something happened, there must be a reason. We just don't know what it is."

"I think we should pray for my mom," Katy murmured. "And I don't want to pray out loud. I want to pray by myself."

"She says God can hear her thoughts," Keeley advised him.

"Of course He can. Why don't we all find our own little places here in the park and say a few words to God about your mother?'' Grady watched as Keeley wandered away to find a tiny patch of sunlight hidden from the wind in the shelter of a big spruce tree. Katy found a crook in the arm of a huge maple and nestled herself against the rough bark before glancing toward heaven.

For himself, Grady preferred taking a slow stroll through the park. But he never let the girls out of his sight.

''I have to tell you, Lord,'' he began. ''I don't get it, either. She's worked so hard. She's been true to you, raised her kids properly and kept their lives going even though it's been a rough, rocky road. Why is this happening?''

He sat on the park bench and waited, wondering how God would explain it all to him. Would he hear a still, small voice? Would there be a rustling of leaves and then some great enlightenment in his mind as he at last understood the mysteries of life? Grady grinned at his own silliness. And just like that the old memory verse rolled softly through his mind.

''Be still and know that I am God.''

''I've got to hand it to You,'' he murmured. ''No pomp, no circumstance. Just cold hard reality. I'm supposed to realize that 'all things work together', aren't I?'' Grady grinned. ''And if I admitted the truth, that's the way I like it.'' He got up and ambled down the leaf-strewn path for several more yards, absently studying the brilliant autumn foliage.

''Okay, God. You're the boss. You lead and I'll follow as best I can. Just keep showing me the next step to take, okay?'' When a bird began singing from a perch high above his head, Grady took that as a sign of God's approval. ''Keep on keeping on,'' he told himself and walked back to the girls.

Chapter Fourteen

"Ugh!" Maggie stared at the side of her head in the hallway mirror and shuddered. "Why did they have to shave it?" she asked miserably. "I look ridiculous."

"You look beautiful," Grady murmured from behind. "In fact you look fantastic. And did I mention alive?" His lips brushed her neck as he turned her in his arm. "Gloria Stampford's on her way out here. I met her at Riley's. She said not to fuss."

"I'm not an invalid, Grady," Maggie complained sourly. "I can make coffee."

"Yes, you can do that. And that's all," he warned. "I'm going to see Garret Fraser. We have to get that wheat off, and that relic in the yard isn't going to make it back to life for the occasion." He gulped down his coffee and headed for the door. "Rest," he ordered, grinning from ear to ear.

"Grady. How can I afford to pay a custom combining outfit?"

"How can you not?" he volleyed back. "We have to

get the stuff into the bin somehow, darlin'. This will be the fastest. Bye.''

Maggie went to her bedroom to change out of the clothes she'd worn home from the hospital. When she came back into the main hallway, she found that Gloria had arrived.

''Maggie, honey, how are you?'' Gloria stood in the doorway, a small black suitcase tucked under her arm and a grin spread across her face. She moved to examine the shaved area on Maggie's head and let out a whistle. ''Those surgeons might stitch up a storm but they can't cut worth a whit.'' She giggled. ''Sit down, girl. It's time for some professional help.''

Giving Maggie no time to argue, Gloria took her hair scissors from her bag and began to cut away.

''Mom, you look beautiful!'' Katy was the first one to comment on her new look half an hour later. ''You can't even see where the stitches are.''

''Thank you, sweetie!'' Maggie hugged her daughter, her throat tight with emotion. ''Mrs. Stampford came up with the idea of leaving the top part a little longer and cutting the back very short. The stitches are hidden underneath. It feels strange,'' she added, shaking her head carefully. ''As though a weight's been lifted off my shoulders.''

''You look younger,'' Keeley added, her head tilted to one side. ''It makes your eyes look really big, too.''

''I loved your hair long,'' Grady added from the doorway. ''But you look beautiful this way, too. I must say, though, when you said you wanted a professional haircut, I didn't think you'd go to these extremes to get one.''

Maggie rolled her eyes at his droll look as the girls giggled in the background. ''Very funny,'' she muttered, marching over to turn off the oven and lift out a pan of rolls. "You should be in Hollywood!"

"Can't," he muttered, grabbing one of the still hot cinnamon rolls she'd put to cool on the counter. "More important stuff here. I thought I told you to relax." He glared at her but the effect was spoiled by the sticky sugar glaze that coated one cheek.

"Gloria mixed these up while I was resting," she told him cheekily. "She's gone home and they needed to come out."

He winked at the girls and lifted one hand to touch Maggie's forehead. "I don't think you're all well just yet." He grinned. "Who in their right mind would pick the hottest day of the year to bake?"

Maggie could feel the pink heat rising in her cheeks but she let his arm remain around her waist anyway. "It's going to cool off pretty soon," she murmured. "Fall evenings around here are always chilly. What about Fraser?"

"Starts in the morning," Grady told her, smiling at her sigh of relief.

"Wasn't he booked up?"

"Yeah, but the others agreed to wait until he was finished here. I think it's their way of helping out after the accident."

"I don't want charity," Maggie began, but Grady's fingers covered her mouth.

"It's not charity, Margaret Mary. It's an act of friendship by your neighbors. Treat it that way." His eyes were softly glinting in the warm kitchen and Maggie wondered if she would ever get used to having Grady there to lean on. "Why don't we have an early supper down by the creek, Maggie? The girls will help, won't you?" He tilted his head sideways as he glanced at the two.

Maggie saw wide grins split her daughters' mouths.

"With a fire and everything?" Katy asked. "All right!" She raced Keeley to the fridge and the two of them began pulling things out willy-nilly.

"We've got that jellied salad Mrs. Walton brought over. And Mrs. Enns-of-the—" She stopped upon seeing her mother's frown and reworded her sentence. "Mrs. Enns made these little sausage roll things. She said you just have to heat them in the oven."

"Gloria left some of her famous coleslaw," Maggie added, trying to relax and enjoy the moment. "And Henrietta came by with a chocolate cake this morning." It would be nice not to have to cook a meal in this heat.

"I can make lemonade," Keeley offered, and began lifting the lemons onto the counter. "I'll put it in that big jug."

"And your mother will sit down here and rest while we get everything ready. Won't you, Maggie?" Grady chided, pressing her into the nearest chair. "Won't you?" he repeated more quietly.

"Yes, all right. But I really do feel fine. I'm just concerned about that barley." She clasped his arm. "Is the swather working again?"

"It's running, if that's what you mean," Grady mumbled, placing different items carefully into the big, old-fashioned picnic basket. "I think, under the circumstances, that's the best we can hope for. I'll start cutting again tomorrow while they're combining. We should be well ahead of the game."

But some niggling doubt, some bit of worry nagged at the back of Maggie's mind, preventing her from completely relaxing later, after the girls gobbled down their food and then raced with the dog through the now-shallow river.

"They sure love this place," Grady mused, watching

Katy turn cartwheels on the sandy edge. He burst out laughing as Keeley tried and ended up toppling over onto her rump. His eyes moved and Maggie felt his intense scrutiny. "And regardless of what you say, I think you do, too."

"In the best of all possible worlds, I suppose I would like living here," Maggie murmured, fiddling with the hem of her shirt. "Given half a chance and a bit of modernizing, this farm could really be something."

"What was it like here when you were growing up?" Grady moved a little closer and slid his arm around her shoulders, hugging her against his solid warmth.

"I thought it was the best place in the world." Maggie let her mind slide back to those halcyon days when life had been carefree. "I had tons of animals. We all did. My dad had more land than I have now and we had two hired men who helped him out. We were never rich but there was always enough for everyone. At least, I thought there was." She wondered suddenly, if her parents had struggled to pay the bills. Somehow she didn't think so.

"What do you remember most clearly?"

Maggie closed her eyes and let herself relax. "Thanksgiving," she murmured. "I always loved the fall, but Thanksgiving was my favorite."

"Why?"

"I don't know. The bounty, I suppose. There was always the excitement of getting the crop off and the feeling of satisfaction when it was all done. We all helped get the grain in the bins, and dug and bagged the vegetables. We had to drag them into the root cellar. My mother always had shelves of fruit and jellies and jams. Dill pickles were usually ready by Thanksgiving." She got lost in those memories of the past.

"What else?"

"Well, there were the decorations at church, of course. My dad would haul in a couple of bales as the background for our display. We'd get donated pumpkins and potatoes—all kinds of stuff that would go to the Bible school in the city after the service. Beth and I always dried and pressed a pile of leaves and we'd lay them around. My mom saved a pot of flowers for the center of the display and sometimes Dad would have a sheaf of wheat there, too."

"Was that when the Thanksgiving quilt tradition got started?"

Maggie started, staring at him in surprise. "You know about that?"

"Of course. Your mother." He waited for her to explain and so Maggie did.

"Actually, the quilt was my grandmother's idea. She always had her Christmas shopping done long before anyone else, and when the fall came along, she said she got itchy fingers and needed to give one more thing. So she began making a quilt that was sold to raise money for a gift for the missionaries." Maggie grinned. "I loved helping her with that quilt, although I'm sure it caused her a whole lot more work."

"Why?"

"My stitches weren't exactly even, Grady! I think she pulled them out every night after I left and redid them so I'd start the next day after school. We'd talk the whole time and she'd always have tea in real china cups and biscuits with crab apple jelly. Then on the Saturday before Thanksgiving, we'd spread the quilt out over the edge of the bales."

"You have wonderful memories, Maggie. Just as your daughters will have."

"If we stay." She murmured the words softly, but they came out stark and bare.

"What else do you remember?" he asked, ignoring her remark.

"The food, of course. After church we'd have a little snack and then we girls would help Mom for a while. Once things were ready in the kitchen, we could go outside and play until we heard the magic word."

"Which was?" he asked, following her prompt.

"Dinner. And what a dinner. We'd all hold hands and say what we were thankful for and then my dad would say grace. Then he'd carve the turkey that we raised on our very own land. There were potatoes and yams, carrots, corn, pickled beets, salad, sliced tomatoes, gravy, fresh rolls and pumpkin pie. All from our own farm."

"And pickles?" Grady teased.

"Lots of pickles," Maggie affirmed. "Mom and Dad and our grandparents would go sit in the living room and my sisters and I would do the dishes. Then out came the crokinole board and we'd play Dad and the grandpas while the ladies knitted or crocheted." Maggie patted her stomach. "I'd usually sneak out to feed the horses a carrot treat and work off some of the calories, but I remember lying in my bed and listening to the house settling down, snug and warm and safe."

"Is that why you married Roger? For the security?"

Maggie laughed derisively. "No! Who thinks about that at eighteen? I married Roger because I was a starry-eyed teenager who thought her life would be like a fairy tale." She sat up, letting his arm fall behind her as she searched the gloom for the girls. They were cuddled together with the dog and Maggie had a hunch they were sleeping.

"Come on, Grady. We've been out here way too long." A rumble of thunder sounded in the west and Maggie cast a worried glance at the sky. To her amazement it was black, the stars obliterated. The wind was rising, too.

"We'll have to run for it," Grady called as they each grabbed a girl and helped her stand. "I think it's going to pour."

"Come on, kids." Maggie urged them up the steep incline, trying to ignore the dizziness that swam behind her eyes. Lightning split the sky in a terrific crack, lighting up the yard and the house. "Inside, quick." She hastened them through the door and dropped the blanket on a nearby chair. "You guys run up and get ready for bed. You should have been there half an hour ago at least."

"Are we going to be okay?" Keeley startled as another crack burst across the heavens. Her whitened face peered at the door as Grady stomped in, setting down the basket before shaking his wet head.

"We're going to be just fine, Keeley," he answered. "It's just electrical storm. Today was hot. The thunder and lightning are because a cool air mass has moved in." Keeley glanced out the window at the sheets of rain pouring down. "Go ahead, honey," he urged. "I'll come up with your mother and tuck you in after a bit. Okay?"

"Yes, okay," she whispered, moving toward the stairs.

"Oh, and Keeley?"

"Yes?" She turned quickly, her eyes huge in her small pinched face.

"Unplug the computer, would you? Electrical outages are hard on them." Keeley nodded and continued up the stairs.

Maggie sank into a nearby chair with relief, closing her eyes to stop the room from whirling around her.

"Maggie?" She opened her eyes to find Grady's warm brown gaze fixed on her intently. "Are you okay?" His hand brushed gently over her head.

"I'm fine," she murmured. "Just a little tired. I should have slowed down a bit, I guess."

"No, I shouldn't have taken you down there. I knew you weren't feeling up to par." As the rain poured down, Grady moved over to partially close the living room windows. He stood there staring out at the darkened landscape for a few minutes and Maggie felt prickles of awareness creep up her spine.

"Grady? What's wrong?" She got up and walked over to see the yard for herself. The dusk-to-dawn yard light gave only a faint glow through the torrents of rain the wind was dashing into the ground. She knew exactly what he was thinking. "All that heat caused enough stress on the crop but this wind has to be murder." She moved toward the screen door and stood staring out. "I don't know how much of it will stay standing in this."

"It'll be fine once it dries out," Grady murmured, but Maggie could feel the tension in his fingers when they wrapped around her shoulders and drew her against him. "We'll manage, Maggie. God's on our side." He hugged her. "Cooling off pretty fast, isn't it?"

They stood there, watching the rivulets form in the yard as the water took the path of least resistance to the ditches. Lightning crackled through the sky, momentarily illuminating the veranda and the rockers sitting there. Maggie would have liked to sit out in the air and watch, but now the girls had arrived and stood gaping at the sight, their mouths open in round O's of wonder. The rain slowed suddenly, rendering the night quiet.

"Is it over?" Katy asked, peering toward the barn. "Do you think my animals are all right?"

"They're fine, sweetie," Grady murmured, tucking her against his side. "It's just a little rain—" He stopped suddenly, and tipped his head to one side to listen.

And then it came, loud and almost deafening in its intensity as it hit the buildings with devastating accuracy.

Hail!

"No!" Maggie stared at the huge golf-ball-sized ice particles that drove themselves into the lawn. In a matter of moments the entire green expanse was covered in white balls. And it kept falling.

"It's like a snowstorm," Keeley breathed, staring at the whiteness that surrounded them. "You can't even see across the yard."

It was over in a matter of minutes. And before it had stopped completely, Maggie had tossed on her jacket and raced out the door. Her head ached with a viciousness that stung but she ignored it. The damage. She had to assess the damage.

She switched on all the outside lights she could find and then stood and stared at the mess. Her car was covered in pitted circles where the hail had dented the metal. The garden lay in ruins, sweet peas with flowers still clinging to their vines, now dashed into the black mud.

"Good thing I'd taken everything I wanted," she muttered, thinking of the pumpkins now hidden inside a corner of the barn. The barn! She hurried over, swinging open the door to study the damage.

"It's okay," Grady murmured from behind her. "That new roof can handle a little thing like a hailstorm. It's a good thing it's been replaced." And, in fact, the animals seemed perfectly comfortable nestled into the fragrant hay.

But now his words prodded her and all at once the full impact of a hailstorm penetrated Maggie's brain. "The crops," she gasped, staring at him. "What about the wheat?"

"Hail is usually localized to a specific area, Maggie. I

don't think we've lost much." He grabbed her arm as a wave of dizzying relief washed over her. "Come on, you're going inside. We can't tell anything tonight anyway. Morning is soon enough."

Maggie let him lead her back to the house and drank the hot, sweet tea he brewed. She obediently swallowed two of the aspirin he handed her and kissed the girls goodnight.

She was sitting in the living-room, when Grady came to speak with her. His eyes were shrewd and assessing.

"You overdid it, didn't you?" he muttered. "Maggie, you've got to slow down and start trusting God and His promises. You can't be everywhere and do everything. Whatever happens, we'll be fine. I have enough money for all of us to live on and I'm healthy enough. I can work."

"You're recuperating from a heart attack," she scoffed miserably.

"Which was caused by stress and tension, not hard work. You're going to be in the same boat if you don't let go and let God—" He brushed the strands out of her eyes.

"Let God what?" she queried grumpily, knowing he was right.

"Let God be God." Grady grinned. "Remember the verse from last Sunday? 'The Lord is near to all who call on Him.'" He winked. "That's what we should be doing instead of worrying. Don't you think God knows how much you need that crop?"

"Yes, I guess so." Maggie chewed on the tip of one fingernail. "But I guess I'm afraid He'll take away what I want the most."

"Oh, Maggie!" Grady enfolded her in his arms. "You break my heart. Don't you know that God never takes away without giving something so much better than we can even ask for."

"In my head I know," she whispered, holding him tightly. "But in my heart, I'm so afraid!"

"Because you're tired and in pain and just plain worn-out. Go up to bed, Margaret Mary." He kissed her softly and walked to the door. "Everything will look so much brighter in the morning. Good night, sweetheart."

"Good night." Maggie waited until he pulled the door closed behind him, before she went to bed and let the doubts and fears crawl through her mind once more. As she drifted off, Maggie tried to pray. Strangely, nothing would come.

By the time Maggie awoke in the morning, the girls were up, dressed and ready for the bus. Grady had fed them, they told her.

After Maggie showered, carefully keeping her head free of the water, she peeked out the window to see her yard in ruins. Her gladiolus were no more. The huge castor beans she'd planted were in tatters, bent over double. Tree branches and twigs lay scattered across the yard and a window was broken in the girls' playhouse.

She tied on her shoes and walked slowly downstairs, holding her shoulders stiffly erect. "What's the damage?" she asked once she'd reached the kitchen.

Grady's dark head jerked upward and he stared at her. She could tell from the drawn whiteness of his face that it was bad enough though his voice tried to deny it. "I'm not totally sure yet."

"It's pretty bad though, isn't it? I could tell from the size of those hailstones. I suppose Fraser can't start until tomorrow, when it's a bit drier." There was no response to this remark and from the corner of her eye, Maggie saw Grady's hand shake as he set down his coffee mug. "Grady? Tell me."

"Fraser's not coming."

"Not coming? Well, that's silly. You said he'd be over today. Surely he can wait one day. Can't he?" The last came out as a breathy whisper when she glimpsed the agony in Grady's eyes. "Can't he?" she repeated, begging for assurance.

Grady shook his head slowly. "It's gone, Maggie. It's all gone. The hail moved in a straight path across our land. It flattened everything. There's nothing to combine."

He didn't have to tell her. Maggie knew firsthand the damage hailstones of that size would cause. Still it didn't sink in. "But you said...you said we'd be okay. That it would be localized." She stared at him uncomprehendingly. "What about the Waltons? The Jeffers?"

"Waltons didn't get any hail," Grady murmured. "Jeffers lost part of a quarter of wheat that touched on to yours."

"So *I'm* the only one who got it all," Maggie demanded, fury strengthening her voice. "Good old Maggie takes the hit again! I have to see this for myself." She yanked on her jacket and stomped toward the door.

"Maggie, what's the point?" Grady's voice was full of tender concern and his hand brushed across her arm but she swiped it away.

"I want to see it," she grated, teeth clenched. "I want to see for myself how badly *my* crops are damaged." She stomped down the steps and toward her old truck. Grady's fingers closed around her arm.

"Fine. But we'd better go in my truck. That road is awful."

Maggie climbed into his truck, ignoring Grady's helping hand. She sat straight and tall as he drove out, but her eyes were taking in every inch of the desolation.

"You were right," she whispered, shocked at the lush landscape now flattened. "I can't see a blade of anything still standing."

Grady said nothing. His lips were clenched tightly closed as he drove past acre after acre of ruined crop. He glanced at her once or twice to make sure she was okay, but not a word cut the silence in the cab. When he stopped at the last field, the prime wheat field that had been so thick and heavy, Maggie climbed out and walked over to the edge, tears streaming down her cheeks.

"I'm wiped out," she murmured, picking up a few broken golden heads and letting the big ripe kernels fall through her fingers. "There's nothing left."

His arms came around her then as he turned her and let her cry all over his shirt. "Don't cry, sweetheart. We can start again. You'll have the insurance money. That'll cover things for a while."

Maggie tore herself out of his embrace, white-hot anger rising up inside. "Don't you get it," she yelled. "There was no insurance. I couldn't afford it. I had to cut corners to make ends meet and that's one corner I decided was too expensive." She sniffed. "Just another in a long line of errors I've made."

"It doesn't matter," he murmured, trying to console her. "We'll make this place a partnership and I'll buy you out in a fifty-fifty split. We can plant again, Maggie. We're together in this."

"No, Grady." She said the words firmly, the decision already made. "I'm finished here. I've scraped and begged and borrowed for the last time. If you want to buy the place, fine. I'll sell it for whatever I can get. And then

I'm leaving." She turned to stare at the mess that was her life.

"For where?" Grady was angry, too. She could hear it in the way he held his voice under control. "Are you going to run away when the going gets tough, Maggie? Refuse to find a solution to our problems? Are you going to dump me and ignore what you feel for me because it isn't convenient right now? Or were you lying when you said you loved me? Maybe you were just using me to help you out here?"

She swung around, furious that he would ask such a question. "I do love you," she said, her face heated with the emotions that whirled inside. "But I told you from the first that I had reservations about marrying you. I've tried, Grady. I've tried really hard. But God doesn't want me to be here. This is not where I belong."

"This is exactly where you and the girls belong. With me. Here, together, working side by side. So we don't have a crop this year. So what? We won't starve. I can give you designer clothes and a trip to Disneyland with the girls. We can redo the house and still have lots of money left over."

"It's not about the money."

"Sure it is. Poor little Maggie is destitute. She wants 'things' and can't get them. I've got money, Maggie. I can solve that problem without even feeling it. So why not marry me?"

"I don't want to marry someone for their money," she spat out, angry at his tone. "I've already had someone offer to *buy* me, and I turned him down! I want to go into a relationship knowing that I can hold my own. As an equal partner. Not like some kind of poor relation!" She stomped over to the truck and climbed in, slamming the door with a lot more force than necessary.

"But you would be my partner," Grady murmured placatingly as he got into the truck. "You own the farm. I would simply supply the capital to run it. When we earn some profits, we'd split them."

"I love that 'when' you threw in there," she scoffed. "Get this through your head, Grady. This place is a great big sinkhole when it comes to money. The more you put in, the more it demands. I just don't want to fight it anymore."

"But what about us?" The words were softly spoken as Grady shifted into gear and started across to the road. "What about me, Maggie?"

"I don't know." The tears started again and she let them fall. "I feel like I'm being torn apart, but in my heart I know that I have to leave here. This isn't where I should be anymore. Couldn't you come to Calgary, live there again?"

"And do what? I've sold everything, Maggie. I got out of my businesses because I wanted to farm. I feel like I've returned home when I come back here and look around. I don't want to run anymore."

"So I have to give up all my dreams because you've finally found this place? That doesn't seem fair," she complained.

"Maggie, I love you. If I really thought you would be happy living in Calgary or Timbuktu for that matter, I'd move there in a flash." He pulled into the yard and parked in front of the house. "But I think God brought us together here, for a reason. God promised to be with us all the time, not just during the good times. And I don't think He wants us to run away from our problems. He wants us to depend on Him."

"But that's just the problem!" Maggie stomped up the porch stairs and let the screen door slam behind her, knowing Grady was not far behind. "I've been depending so much, I haven't been facing the reality He's presented me with. Now it's time to deal with that reality, Grady. Head-on." She grabbed the telephone and dialed a number.

"Hi, this is Maggie McCarthy. I'd like an appraisal on my farm as soon as you can do it. No, just the land, buildings and machinery. There is no crop. Tomorrow would be fine. Thank you."

"Maggie, please don't rush into anything. Let's sit down and discuss this." He waited until she sank into a chair, his craggy face intent as he studied her. "I love you, Maggie. I love the girls. Please, let's make this our home and raise our family here."

"That was my dream once." She laughed harshly. "My children were going to have the same wonderful childhood that I once had. Well, you know what? It isn't wonderful. My kids aren't getting any great and noble life. They're getting a hand-to-mouth existence with a mother who can't even read the newspaper without bursting into tears." She saw the pain on his face and relented just a little, reaching out to touch his hand.

"I do love you, Grady. Very much, but I'm worn-out with trying to make a go of this place. I have to leave, to get a new perspective on things. I need a chance to prove to myself that I can be like other single mothers and support my family properly. I have to be worthy to myself before I can be worthy to you."

"And how long will that take? Six months, a year? What? I want to have a family, Maggie. And I want you there with me."

His disgruntled look made her smile. "Grady, I'm not going completely out of your life. Calgary isn't that far away. You can come and see us anytime. In fact, the girls would be upset if you didn't."

"They're going to be even more upset when they find out what you have planned."

Resolve straightened her backbone and Maggie got up from her chair. "I can't help that. I have to do what I think is best. For all of us. And with all that's happened, I think God is directing me away from the farm. I don't know what's in store, but I'm willing to find out. No, please—" she held up one hand "—I don't want to argue anymore. This is something that has to happen. If we're meant to be together, God will lead us that way. You just have to have faith."

He snorted, slamming his hat on his head. "That's rich, coming from you. You don't have the courage of your convictions, my dearest Maggie. God brought us together. He put the love in my heart for you. And He did the same for you, only you're too chicken to hang around and find out what could grow out of that." He stomped across the floor and out the door, only to reappear seconds later.

"I'm buying this farm, Maggie McCarthy. I don't care what the price is, I'll pay whatever you want. And you can go searching for greener grass in the place you think is the answer to all your problems. But when the day comes that you realize that this is where you belong, I'll be sitting right here." He pulled her into his arms and kissed her thoroughly.

"I'm not giving up on you, Margaret Mary. So go, run to the city. Try and find your perfect life. And when it's all said and done, I'll still be here. Waiting. Because I love you too much to just let you go."

His dark brown eyes were liquid as they slid over her face, his fingers gentle as they brushed over her hair. Then, lips tightened, he was gone.

Chapter Fifteen

Maggie glared at the store clock, desperately willing it to move. When had time ever dragged like this? She flipped through the swatches of fabric she'd chosen for tomorrow's appointment and mentally chastised herself. At least she had a job. What did it matter if the customers chose the patterns and combinations and all she got to do was stitch them up? The money from this little quilting shop was hard to beat for someone with no previous job experience. The hours were certainly regular.

It's boring, a voice in the back of her head announced, laughing. *There's no creativity in this stifling little room. You can't even step outside and breathe in some fresh air.* The smell of diesel penetrated the air vents, testament to the bus stop outside the door. *And Grady's not here.* Maggie shoved the thought away and stitched a little longer on the gaudy pink-and-purple squares that her last client had selected for her daughter's wedding quilt.

Eventually the clock hands reached five o'clock and Maggie gathered her purse and coat and locked up. Her

bus had just left, so she decided to walk a couple of blocks
and catch the next one at the station down the road.

"I know I'm living in dreamland again," she told herself, peering into the big show windows with their dis-
plays of gorgeous silks in vibrant autumn hues. They were
far beyond her price range, of course, and she couldn't
afford the fabric, even if she sewed them herself. But it
was fun to look, wasn't it?

"I'm doing all right," she'd said to Gloria Stampford
last night on the phone. "The girls are fairly settled in
their new schools and I've got a nine-to-five job." *Which
isn't the least bit glamorous,* she wanted to add, but
didn't.

The allure of the city had quickly lost its shine once
Maggie realized how expensive everything was going to
be. The rent on their tiny apartment took a huge bite out
of her paycheck. The car wasn't working properly, which
was probably good since parking near her work cost a
fortune. Instead, she took the bus and got home two and
a half hours after the girls. She had latchkey children,
Maggie suddenly realized with a pang.

But all of that was bearable, or would have been. If
only she didn't miss Grady so much. She wanted to talk
to him about Keeley's rebellious streak and Katy's pro-
pensity to talk to anyone she met. She wished she could
sit with him over a cup of coffee at the kitchen table, once
the girls had gone to bed, and discuss her rather eccentric
boss.

"You wanted to be independent," she muttered.
"Don't go mooning over everything now." The truth was,
she admitted privately, she missed his arm around her
shoulder, his kisses, his laugh.

"Lady, are you gonna get on this thing, or study it for
another half hour?"

Maggie came to and found the driver of the city bus glaring at her. "Sorry," she murmured, and climbed on, lugging up the steep stairs the few groceries she'd picked up at noon. She almost fell flat on her face when he jerked away from the curb and lurched into rush-hour traffic, but her fingers grasped the metal pole and she managed to stay upright The bus was full, of course, and there was no place to sit down. Weary beyond belief, arms aching from clinging to the strap, she climbed off at her stop aeons later and trudged up the street toward what was now home.

"Hi, Mom." Katy glanced up from the phone, greeting Maggie when she walked in. "I'm talking to Grady. Don't worry. He called me." Katy shook her head at her mother's warning look and turned back to the phone. "No, I can't go to the basketball practice when Mom's working and there's nobody to take me. I sure wish I could have my bike to ride around on, but there's no place to keep it at night, and people steal things. Mrs. Eversham in 108 got her lock picked."

Maggie stood upright in front of the fridge, tension racing through her. She hadn't heard of any break-in.

"Nah, they didn't even get it. Mrs. Eversham's got this really yappy dog, you see, and it set up a racket. She called the police." Katy stopped for a second, her forehead wrinkled. "Yeah, me and Keeley are real careful. Did you feed Laddie today? How is he?… Really?… You think they miss me?…I miss them, too."

A soft glow of happiness covered her daughter's generally sulky face and Maggie turned away as frustration overrode her. She wiped it away as Katy bellowed, "Mom! Grady wants to talk to you."

Maggie picked up the phone, every nerve in her body

waiting to hear that familiar deep tone rumbling over the line.

"Maggie, are you all right? You're late tonight." He stopped when he realized what this implied. "I phone the girls quite often," he said at last. "I guess I've gotten to know your schedule."

"That's very kind of you, Grady," she muttered stiffly, furious yet relieved that he was keeping such close track of the girls. "How is everything?" She could hear hammering in the background and wondered who else was there.

"Everything here is fine," he said brusquely. "I'm having a few things done before the snow flies." There was a gap in the conversation then—a long, drawn-out silence that Maggie had no desire to break. Grady, it seemed was not so hesitant.

"When are you coming home, Maggie?" he asked quietly. "I miss you and the girls. The house is so quiet, I'm back in the camper just so I don't feel so lonely." He waited, and when she didn't say anything, continued on a harsher tone. "You've been there almost a month. Haven't you proven your independence yet?" There was a sting in his voice that touched a nerve.

"Grady, we've barely settled in. We're managing, but it's been a change for all of us."

"Yeah, I know," he grated. "Keeley's been in the principal's office three times, and now she's sneaking out at lunchtime to meet a boy from the high school."

"What?" Maggie stared at her daughter's back where it sat hunched over the computer. "I, I, uh, I'm dealing with it," she mumbled at last.

"Sure you are. Like you're dealing with Katy's F in math?" His voice was full of frustration. "Why won't you come home? I love you, Maggie! Why is that so bad?''

''It's not bad at all,'' she whispered, fingering the ring he'd insisted she keep on the chain around her neck. So she wouldn't forget him, he'd said. As if she could! ''It's just that I have to do this, Grady. I have to stand on my own two feet here. I need to prove something to myself.''

''Well, you're hurting all of us while you *prove* it,'' he ground out bitterly.

Maggie bit her lip to keep from crying out at the unfairness of it all. *Why, God,* she prayed silently. *Why is it always so hard for me?*

''You are at least coming home tomorrow for Thanksgiving, aren't you? After work? Your mother told me she'd asked you.'' His voice was calmer now, resigned almost.

''I—I'm not sure,'' she stammered, thinking of the strange noise the car had made last week on an outing to the zoo.

''Maggie, your parents are expecting you. They want to see you and the girls. They've missed you!''

''I've missed them, too,'' she murmured.

''If you don't come, I'll come and get you,'' he warned angrily. His voice dropped as he spoke again. ''I'm sorry, honey. I didn't mean to yell. It's just that it's been so long and I miss you so much. And the girls. Please, say you'll come for Thanksgiving?''

''All right, if it means so much. But if you've missed us to that extent, why didn't you come for a visit? You know where we live, you moved our stuff here.''

''There's nothing I'd like better than to drive in and see you all. We could go out for dinner. Maybe see a movie.'' His voice fell, the enthusiasm draining away.

"But I can't get away. I've tried, believe me. But something always comes up."

Funny, Maggie frowned. He didn't sound very regretful.

"I know you'll think I'm nosey, but I'm still going to ask. Maggie, are you still standing on the promises of God?"

"I don't know what you mean," she lied, staring at her hands.

"I mean, are you certain that you're in the will of God? Have you really thought this out? Are you sure you're not making your own desires into your version of God's will?" His voice was soft, but the jab of guilt it dealt to her heart was not.

"What makes you qualified to judge me and my choices? Who are you to try and run my life, to make my decisions for me? Who are you to question me, Grady O'Toole?"

His voice was low and filled with sadness. "I'm the man who loves you, Maggie."

Tears formed in her eyes at the tenderness of those words, and she drew a shaky breath.

"I'm not trying to take over your life or tell you what to do. I'm not even asking you to come back—not if you don't want to."

Maggie pressed her fist into her mouth as if to staunch the pain. "Well, what are you trying to say then?"

"I'm just asking you to look into your heart and figure out if you really want to deny what God has given us— a second chance to love. I don't care about the past, Maggie. I don't care what could have or should have happened. I just want what's best for you and the girls. I want you to be happy. Are you happy, Maggie?"

On the other end of the line, Grady listened for an answer. When it didn't come, he quietly closed his cell phone. Behind him the hammers and saws resounded through the house as workmen tore out the old, water-ruined ceiling and installed a new dropped one. The aroma of freshly cut cedar permeated the house as the tongue-and-groove boards were fitted together in Maggie's studio. He'd had the skylights and east bank of windows specially installed so she could work in as much natural light as possible in her special room.

And it was Maggie's room. In fact, the whole house cried out for her presence. What did it matter that he changed the interior? She was still as much a part of this place as she'd always been. Would she ever come home?

"Lord, you know how much I miss her." Grady ambled down to the creek as he prayed, thrilled once more with the peace he'd found here. "And I do believe that it's Your plan for us to be together. So Lord, whatever it takes, that's what I'm prepared to do. If you want me to move to the city, I'll go." The word came out on a whoosh of desperation. "If you want me to go back to Shaughnessy's and restart the company, I'll do that. I've learned a lot here, Lord, and I could apply it to the markets."

He picked a cattail that had fallen over, its head top heavy and unwieldy, but his eyes were on the creek, remembering two small girls and their giggles of laughter.

"I don't understand Your ways, Lord." He stared at the serene sky and considered the vastness of it. "But you are God and it's not up to me to ask why. I'm nothing compared to Your majesty and power." Grady remembered the scripture he'd read that morning.

"Who gives intuition and instinct? Who is wise enough to number all the clouds? Who can tilt the water jars of heaven, when everything is dust and clouds?"

Another verse penetrated his brain. "God is not a man...nor a son of man, that He should change his mind."

"I'm like Job, God," Grady groaned, embarrassed at his lack of trust. "I have demanded answers too many times. You owe no one anything. Everything under heaven is Yours. This situation with Maggie is beyond my understanding and yet, You can use even this. Show me what to do and I'll do it."

The words came as if someone had spoken them in his ear. *Finish the work. What I have planned, that will I do.*

As Grady got up and strode back up the hill, he felt rejuvenated, renewed. Somehow God would handle this. And nothing any woman could do, even one as determined as Maggie, would stop God from completing His work.

Maggie shut off the alarm with a groan, reminding herself to speak to the super about the incessant parties next door. It had been well after three before she'd fallen asleep last night, and she had to get up before seven to get to work on time.

"Katy! Keeley!" She rumpled their sleepy heads and pressed a kiss to each cheek. "Time to get up and get ready for school." The girls groaned and rolled over, and Maggie took the opportunity to slip in and out of the shower. "Come on, girls. It's getting late."

Maggie sipped her coffee as she scanned the newspaper. The headlines didn't catch her eye, but the photo did. It was an old one of Grady. He looked younger in it, but not happier. Quickly she scanned the write-up and gasped.

Local entrepreneur Gradin O'Toole may lose everything in his bid to outfox his lovely ex-wife, Fiona

Spenser, who has announced her intention to file another suit. This time the claim is against O'Toole's
trust fund, gifted to him by the late oil tycoon, Har-
rison Fellows. Mr. Fellows claimed in his will that
Grady O'Toole was the most honest broker he'd ever
known and insisted on bequeathing his fortune to the
Calgary businessman. The money has been tied up
in litigation and now Ms. Spenser claims that the
fund was improperly obtained when Mr. O'Toole
prevailed upon the ailing magnate to adjust his will.
Mr. O'Toole could not be reached for comment, but
his legal counsel has issued a statement denying all
claims.

Maggie couldn't believe her eyes. She'd let him buy
the farm, glibly accepted that Grady was able to take over
her mortgage and other debts! She'd let him blow his
precious resources on that farm when she knew the place
would only cost more money. And now he was going to
lose whatever security he had—and all because of her and
her determination to get away.

Why hadn't he told her about it?

The answer was clear. Grady's love was selfless. He
wanted her to be happy. And was she?

Maggie glanced around the dinky apartment and grimaced. Yes she had a job that freed her at a set time each
day, and they were near all the amenities. The little bit of
money left after the farm debt was paid off she'd squir-
reled away for the girls' future educations. She was free
of the farm.

And yet she had lost much more than she gained, Maggie realized. Gone was the relaxing cup of coffee in the
sunshine whenever you needed a break. Fifteen-minute
coffee breaks didn't allow for lazing in the sun and dream-

ing of the future. The people she'd met at the neighborhood church were friendly, but Maggie missed her lifelong chums and the knowledge that her friends would drop in whenever they got a free moment.

Her children came home to an empty apartment now and although she insisted they call her the minute they came in, there never seemed to be a second to lazily discuss their day while they played outside. The rules for surviving the massive city school terrified Maggie—knives, guns, drugs. It was all so much closer now.

But most of all, Maggie missed Grady. She missed knowing he was there to talk to, share her day with and discuss the girls. She missed his reassuring hugs and warm kisses. This terrible loneliness in a city full of people was the worst thing of all. Maggie picked up her Bible and let it fall open to Matthew, staring down at the words.

"If you, then, though you are evil, know how to give good gifts to your children, how much more will your Father in heaven give good gifts to those who ask him!"

"Mom? Aren't we having breakfast? And you're going to miss your bus if you don't hurry."

Maggie glanced up into Keeley's worried face, the words ringing through her head with bright clarity. This was her child and she wanted the very best for her. But what if she was wrong? What if moving the children away from Grady and the farm wasn't the best?

"Mom?"

"Yes, honey. Go ahead and eat. I'm leaving in a minute." She stared at Keeley's blond head for a long time, studying the gamine features closely. "Keeley?"

"What?" The sullen look was still on her daughter's face.

"Can I ask you something?" Keeley's eyes widened, but she slowly nodded. "Do you miss Grady?"

All at once the harshness fell away as tears rolled down the child's pale cheeks. Maggie gathered her up in her arms and rocked back and forth, holding the girl tightly against her. And she let her own tears fall.

"Oh, Mom," Keeley wailed. "I miss him so much. I wish I had him as my father."

"You do?" Maggie knew the girls adored Grady but apparently she hadn't realized how much they needed a father in their lives. "I didn't know you missed your dad so much, sweetie."

"It's not just that," Keeley mumbled, wiping her eyes. "It's because we were like a real family when Grady was there. Everything was fun and happy. You laughed a lot, Mom. And…" She stopped, glancing up through her lashes at her mother with a strange look on her face.

"Go on, sweetheart. Say the rest of it. You can tell me anything."

"Why won't you marry Grady? Is it because you really don't love him? Or is it because you're scared he'll go away like our father did?"

Maggie stared. "Why would you say that, Keeley?"

"Because that's how I feel. Sometimes it seems like everything is going really well and then all of a sudden, bang! Something goes wrong and you've got to start worrying all over again. And then I wonder if God even cares about what's happening."

"God always cares, sweetie. Of that I am very sure." Katy walked up slowly and Maggie held out her other arm. "I was just reading my Bible and I came across this verse." She read it to them. "Do you know what it means?"

"It means that if people can give good gifts, then God can give even more," Katy told them.

"That's right. And if He's in control, there's no need for us to worry about anything."

"You mean nothing bad will happen?" Keeley asked doubtfully.

"No, silly. She means that even *when* bad things happen, God is still there, watching out for us. And worrying about that guy downstairs doesn't make it any better or worse," Katy told her sister firmly. "Grady taught me that a long time ago."

"What guy downstairs?" Maggie studied her daughter anew. "What's bothering you, Keeley?" She watched the girl struggle to keep her face from showing her true emotions. "You have to tell me, honey. Otherwise I can't help you."

"I'm afraid, Mommy." Keeley buried her face in her mother's shoulder and sobbed her heart out. "I'm always afraid. At home there was Granny or Grady or even the Waltons to call if I got in trouble. But here there's nobody. At school the kids think I'm a geek because I get all A's. One of them stopped me in the bathroom and said if I answered the teacher's questions again and got them more homework, they were going to beat me up after school."

Help me, Lord, she prayed silently. *Give me the right answers.*

"Girls, God didn't give us a spirit of fear. It says in here—" she quickly turned the pages in her Bible to Second Timothy "—'God has given us a spirit of power and love and of a sound mind. We don't have to be afraid.'"

"But you are, Mom," Keeley protested softly. "You're always afraid that we won't have enough money. And when we were on the farm, you worried that the crops wouldn't get off or that they wouldn't sell or that the rain wouldn't come or that the snow would come too early. Isn't worry like fear?"

From the top of her head to the soles of her feet, Maggie felt a deep profound sense of shame. Were these the values she had imparted to her children? Fear and worry?

"You're afraid to marry Grady, too," Katy accused "He told me that you didn't trust him enough."

It was true. It was all true. God help her, she'd been running because she was too afraid to stand still and let God handle it all. Grady was right. God had filled His side of the bargain. He'd sent Grady to help them through the tough times, to love her and the girls, to shore them up when they most needed it.

And because she wouldn't believe or trust in what was in her own heart, Maggie had thrown it all away for the foolish dream of security.

Well, she asked herself. *Are you secure now?*

"Mother, you've missed your bus!" Keeley was back to her usual responsible self and Maggie realized that it was something her child did to protect her, the mother.

"Don't you worry about me, sweetheart," Maggie murmured, hugging the little girl tightly. "I'm the mother here and I know when I've missed my bus. It so happens I don't care." She glanced from one surprised face to the other. "And you two aren't going anywhere, either."

"We aren't?" Katy frowned suspiciously. "Why? Did the teacher call you?"

"No, it's me," Keeley groaned. "I probably got suspended."

"Neither of the above." Maggie grinned. "Today this is one time you girls and I are going to have a day on the town. We'll go to the Devonian Gardens this morning and drop out to Calaway Park this afternoon. And in between we're having lunch at McDonald's."

"We are?" The twins looked at each other and shrugged.

"Yes, we are. And then we're coming straight home to pack." Maggie watched the hope light up their eyes.

"You mean, we can go to Granny's for Thanksgiving?" Keeley's face shone one minute and then dimmed the next. "But what about the money?"

"For once, I think I'll depend on God to take care of things for me." Maggie grinned. "'...My Father will give you whatever you ask in my name. Until now you have not asked. Ask and you will receive, and your joy will be complete.'" She hugged each one. "Let's just spend a few minutes thanking our Father for the wonderful things He's given us."

She listened first to Katy's little prayer and then Keeley's, and then Maggie whispered her own. As the girls scurried out of the room to gather their jackets, Maggie closed her eyes.

"I believe You have a way planned for me," she said silently. "I don't know what it is and I don't know how I'll handle it, but I'm giving it all over to You. Forgive me for not believing when I should have and help me trust You more."

As they pulled out of the parking lot, Maggie found herself wondering how Grady would greet their homecoming. She could hardly imagine he would welcome them back now, with this new disaster looming on his own horizon.

Chapter Sixteen

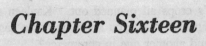

"Sweetheart, your father and I would have come and picked you up. You didn't have to drive out here." Kayleen was frowning as she helped the sleepy girls out of the car.

"Believe me, if I'd known I'd have car trouble, I would have called you." Maggie stretched. "As it is, I'm dead beat. The traffic was awful. The girls conked out a while ago." She stared up at her parents' house and absorbed all the familiar details. It would be nice to sleep without the thudding of bass drums against her ear, Maggie decided.

Katy and Keeley were content to snuggle down in their grandfather's study, their eyes drooping closed almost immediately. Maggie smiled as she snapped off the light and gently closed the door.

"Now, dear, I've made a fresh pot of tea. Come and tell us all about Calgary."

Maggie fielded the questions as best she could, but just the same, Kayleen managed to acquire quite a bit of information. It was time to turn the tables.

"Mom, how's Grady?" Maggie tried to say it nonchalantly, keeping her eyes downcast.

"Why, he seems fine, dear." Her mother's bright eyes were narrowed knowingly. "We've been out several times, your father and I, and the changes around the old place are amazing. Grady's been getting Elmer Hawkins to inquire into some different types of seed, and he's got next year's crops all planned out." Kayleen sipped her tea thoughtfully. "Did you know he has a degree in agriculture and another one in commerce?"

"No, I didn't," Maggie whispered, ashamed at the little she really knew about the man she'd fallen in love with.

"I can't imagine how a smart man like that got involved with a woman like her!" Kayleen flicked a finger at the open newspaper. "She's created such an awful ruckus around here that poor Grady's been afraid to leave the farm."

And it was all her fault! Maggie knew it as surely as if someone had screamed the words out. "I'm going for a walk, Mom. I'm just too wound-up to sleep right now. You and Dad go ahead if you want. I'll lock up when I come in." She slipped on her denim jacket and moved toward the door.

"Why don't you go through the park?" Kayleen murmured helpfully. "The leaves are a wonderful color right now, and this is perfect Thanksgiving weather."

Maggie walked out the door, barely catching her father's puzzled voice.

"There's not much to see in the park when it's this dark, Kayleen. And you sure can't tell the color of the leaves when it's almost midnight!"

Maggie smiled as she pulled the door closed and made her way to the street. Good old Willow Bunch, where you could still go for a walk in the park and no one would bother you.

"Maggie?" The voice was soft behind her left shoulder but she would have known it anywhere. Wheeling around, she came face-to-face with Grady's twinkling brown eyes. "Hi."

"Hi," she whispered, drinking in the sight of his wonderful craggy good looks and crooked smile. "How are you?"

"Lonely." His hands enfolded hers. "How are you?"

"Lonely," she murmured back, curling her fingers around his. Seconds later she was in his arms and his mouth crushed hers in a kiss that was long overdue.

"Maggie, I came as soon as your mother called. I couldn't stay away." They reached the park and found a bench by the playground. "When are you going to marry me? If Calgary's where you want to live, that's fine with me. I'll start a new company, find a new job. I don't care. As long as I'm with you."

"You're certainly not leaving the farm now?" Maggie gasped, turning to stare at him. She saw the love glowing in his eyes and almost forgot what she wanted to say. Almost. "I know how much you spent to buy the farm, Grady. You can't just dump that investment. Especially not now."

"Why not now?" he asked, puzzled. But Maggie was continuing.

"It's my fault you're in this mess in the first place," she stated firmly, although there was a little quaver in her voice. "I realize that now."

"Maggie, darling. What are you talking about?"

"I'm talking about me not seeing God's hand in things. About not trusting and believing that the God I serve is big enough to handle mortgage payments and broken ma-

chinery and hailstorms. Don't you get it?'' Maggie
frowned. When he shook his head from side to side she
began again.

''I've been a fool,'' she stated baldly. ''I got so caught
up in my 'poor me' syndrome, that I couldn't see the
bigger picture. You were right, Grady. I *was* running. As
fast as I could. Nothing was going the way I planned and
I lost my perspective on things. Somehow I figured if I
could just get away from the farm, get that millstone off
my neck, I'd find such greener pastures on the other side.

''So I refused to stick it out and discover what God had
in store for me. I figured if He wouldn't even save that
wheat crop, I needed to take matters into my own hands.
Maybe that would stop the fear.''

''What are you afraid of, sweetheart?'' His arm slid
across her shoulders and Maggie snuggled into his
warmth.

''The girls helped me see that I was afraid of everything,'' she told him. ''Frantically worrying about the
money and the bills and what was going to happen in the
future made me crazy with fear.'' She glanced up at him.
''I think I was afraid God would leave me to stand on my
own two feet and face the mess I'd made of things. And
now I've gotten you in trouble.''

He frowned. ''You have?''

''Of course, I know you'll deny it, but sinking all your
money into the farm was the worst thing you could have
done.''

''It was?''

''Naturally! You're going to need that cash freed up to
help settle the claim on your inheritance.'' She tugged a
check out of her pocket. ''I know it isn't much, but it's
what was left from the farm.'' Maggie held it out toward

him. "I'll pay you back as much as I possibly can each month, Grady."

"When are you going to get it into your head that I don't care about money?" His voice was harsh but a hint of pain shone from his brown eyes. "I didn't buy the farm so I'd have some hold on you. I bought it because I wanted us to live there and I thought once you had a chance to live out your dreams of fancy clothes and a nine-to-five job, you'd see that happiness—real happiness—doesn't have anything to do with money. It's a state of mind we choose when we depend on God.

"Don't you get it, Maggie? I love you. For richer or poorer. In sickness and in health. Until death do us part. And money or some silly legal case isn't going to change that. I love you. Period."

"I love you, too," she breathed, afraid to look away from those compelling eyes. "And it's not because of the money or anything else."

"Then why won't you marry me?" His voice was curt.

"I will." She grinned. "If you'll ask me. I don't care where we live, Grady. I finally realized that places and things don't matter a whit if you don't have someone to share them with. The girls taught me that. I think I was happier on that run-down, derelict old farm with you there, than I have been for a long, long time."

"Hey," he teased, pulling her close, "that's my home you're maligning." Slowly and carefully he lifted the shiny sapphire from the neck of her blouse and unfastening the chain, slid the ring free. "Maggie McCarthy, will you please, please marry me? Soon?"

"Yes," she cried, holding her hand out as he finally slid the ring into its rightful place. "As soon as you want."

"Tonight," he whispered before his mouth covered hers in a promise of a lifetime of love.

"Not tonight." She giggled. "I want to have my family around when I finally get to call you 'husband.' How about tomorrow?"

"Nope," he told her. "Tomorrow we're having a real Thanksgiving dinner. And it's going to be at my place. With my new family right beside me. Kayleen and I have it all planned. You and I are going to have Thanksgiving Monday all to ourselves."

Tears formed at the corners of her eyes. "You had that much faith in me?" She hugged him tightly.

"That and a whole lot more," he whispered. "'With God, all things are possible.' Didn't I tell you to stand on the promises? He will never let us down."

"Yes, you did," she murmured, tilting her head back for his kiss. "Thank you."

"You're very welcome. Now about a date for this wedding?"

It was a long time before Maggie heard the town clock chime one o'clock. Regretfully, she leaned back and closed her eyes.

"I've got to get going, handsome." She chuckled, when he tried to kiss her again. A new thought hit her. "Grady, what about Fiona and the money?"

"Nothing about Fiona and the money. She has no claim. I'm not destitute, if that's what you're worried about." His face mirrored his uneasiness at her grin. "Does it matter, Maggie?"

"Not to me. Not in the least! But maybe if you gave her some of it, she'd realize that true happiness doesn't come from money and things. We could do that, couldn't we, Grady? After all, we've got each other now and she hasn't got anyone."

Familiar and harsh, the bitterness rose in his face. "She lost my child, Maggie. She was pregnant and deliberately ignored the doctor's orders to take it easy. She wouldn't let me take care of her either. And she ended up losing the baby. My baby." His fingers clenched. "I don't owe her a thing."

"I'm sorry, Grady. So sorry." She slipped her hand in his, tears welling in her eyes as she felt the pain of it grab hold of him. She waited, long interminable minutes, for the grief to ebb. "I know how much you love children. It must have been terribly hard to lose that precious baby."

He nodded, mouth tight with emotion.

"But don't you see, darling? Giving away that money wouldn't be for her. Not really. It would be for you, to free you." She cupped his chin in her hand and forced his head up. "God can use even that sad thing to bring glory to His name. But to do it, you need to let go of the bitterness and hate. Let God worry about it."

She waited breathlessly as he sat there, staring at her, his body tense. Finally Grady closed his eyes and let out a whoosh of air, loosening his fingers as he did.

"When did you get so smart?"

"Just recently, as a matter of fact. I'm a quick study. I love you, Grady O'Toole."

"I love you, Maggie McCarthy."

Tomorrow came quickly and everyone rushed around the tiny bungalow to get ready for church. Grady showed up just as they were about to leave, and after thoroughly kissing her, to the delight of her family, helped Maggie transfer her Thanksgiving quilt to his truck. His fingers meshed with hers as they drove to the church.

"You finished it," he said as they spread it behind the

jars of preserves and sacks of potatoes and carrots. "It's beautiful."

"Of course I finished it," she sputtered, half-indignantly. "It's a tradition around here."

"I love tradition," he whispered in her ear as the church began filling with old friends and neighbors eager to welcome her back. "Especially wedding traditions."

Maggie felt her heart fill as so many people greeted her. Then the service began and she couldn't help but pour her feelings of thanksgiving into the lovely old hymns and several new choruses. Pastor Jim gave each one something to think about as he spoke of God's faithfulness to His children, and Maggie dwelt on the verse he'd recited.

"'Though the mountains be shaken and the hills be removed, yet my unfailing love for you will not be shaken, nor my covenant of peace be removed,' says the Lord, who has compassion on you."

When they finally left the church with hearty congratulations ringing in their ears, Maggie's heart was full. She rode quietly down the old familiar road toward the farm, content with her life at last.

"Where are the girls?" she asked finally. "They love riding in this truck."

"They're coming with your parents in a while," he told her. "I wanted to have you to myself for a bit."

"That's nice." She snuggled against his shoulder with a sigh and then sat straight up. "Oh, my! This place looks wonderful."

The farm did look wonderful. The grass was lush and freshly cut, the fences were standing erect, the land was tilled as it waited for the spring. Her flowers still bloomed in the garden and a big pot now sat next to the front door. The screen porch had been repaired, with new corner posts, and everything bore a fresh coat of paint. Nothing had changed, and yet, Maggie realized, everything had changed. She was home.

"Oh, Grady," she whispered, stepping out of the truck into his arms. "You've done so much work. Everything looks cared for, loved."

"I do love it here," he murmured. "But I love you more." He kissed her quickly. "Come on, I've got to go check on the turkey."

Maggie would have liked to look around a little more, but he seemed impatient to go inside, so she went along. Nothing creaked or sagged when she stepped up and the brand-new door opened soundlessly.

"Welcome home, Maggie," Grady murmured, ushering her inside.

Maggie stared.

Everything gleamed and glistened, from the hardwood floors under her feet to the sparkling light overhead. It was the same and yet it was wonderfully different.

"Grady, what have you done?" she gasped, wandering into the living room. Under her feet the plush beige carpet absorbed all sound. The room was an exact replica of a picture she'd once cut from a magazine, all neutral tones with an accent of plum and palest pink and touches of silky smooth oak here and there.

"I made a few changes," he murmured, stepping across to the gleaming fireplace. "The TV and VCR are in here." Panels slid open at the touch of his finger, revealing stereo equipment of every possible kind. Her plants still grew, lush and cared for, now along the window ledges.

"I have to check that turkey," he reminded her, crossing the hall toward the kitchen. "Come on."

Maggie did, staring at the burnished wood of the staircase as she passed. "It smells deli—" Her voice choked up. "Oh, Grady!"

"I wasn't sure about this room," he told her, his voice hesitant. "The others I took from pictures I found in your room, but you never had a kitchen picture. Is it okay?"

Maggie slid her fingertips along the smooth countertop and glossy oak cabinets. A wall oven was tucked into one corner and in another, a huge refrigerator. In the center of the kitchen was an island with a cooktop on one end and seating at the other. Six comfy chairs sat nestled there, waiting for occupants. Maggie could see beyond the kitchen to the dining room. A long, covered table sat glistening with linen, crystal, china and silver settings. In the middle lay a horn of plenty with fruits and vegetables pouring out.

"Maggie, you're crying! It wasn't supposed to make you cry." Grady wrapped his arms around her. "I thought you'd like it," he murmured, soothing her.

"I do like it," she said, hiccuping and sniffling inelegantly. "But you shouldn't have done it. It's too much. I don't need all this if I have you."

"Maybe you don't need it, but I wanted to give it to you. I just want you to be happy, sweetheart."

"I'm very happy," she whispered and burst out bawling when she sighted two clay figurines on the shelf above the sink. "Those are the girls'!"

"Yes, and they belong in our home, don't they?" He patted her back awkwardly when the words sent Maggie into fresh tears.

Grady didn't say anything but pulled Maggie into her workroom. Stopping just inside, she couldn't help but gasp. A huge ribbon was strung across the wall and the little gold letters on it spelled out Welcome Home Maggie.

Her fabrics lay on specially built shelves in a corner so that each color was displayed. The big tables had been refurbished so no fabric would snag or tear on that surface. There was a gigantic wall-to-wall mirror on one end of the room and a quilting frame that folded down from the wall. And everywhere there was that wonderful cedar smell. And there, propped against the wall stood a brandnew fishing rod and reel with a red-and-white striped lure attached. She picked up the tag and read "To my dearest love. Grady."

"Oh, Grady," she cried, "please say there isn't any more."

"Well, there's a Jacuzzi upstairs in the master bedroom," he told her, frowning when more tears formed. "And I put a—Maggie, will you please stop bawling!"

Maggie threw herself into his arms and clung for dear life. "I'm sorry," she murmured at last, swallowing the last sob. "I love it, really I do. It's wonderful. But it's far more than I ever needed or wanted, Grady. All I want is you."

"Well," he asserted, slightly disgruntled that his surprise had caused such a downpour, "you've got me. And this house. If you don't like it, we can change it."

Maggie burst out laughing and stood on tiptoe to kiss him. "We're not changing one thing, Grady O'Toole," she told him firmly. "Not one thing. I love it and you." She danced around the tables, laughing.

"God knew all this back when you first showed up in your snakeskin boots, looking for a place to crash for the night. He had it in mind all along. 'My unfailing love for you will not be shaken,'" she quoted. "Isn't God wonderful?"

"Awesome, as Katy says," he agreed, kissing her once more.

* * *

"They're kissing again." Katy giggled, entering her sister's bedroom. "I saw them in the kitchen."

Keeley switched off the computer and joined her sister, who'd stretched out on the brand-new blue carpet. "They'll probably do that lots now," she told her younger sister importantly. "Adults do that when they're in love."

"I guess that means we're moving back home," Katy whispered, rolling over to stare at the glossy white ceiling. "I'm glad."

"Me, too." They high-fived each other before Keeley poked her sister in the ribs. "After the wedding, it might be a good time to have another talk with Mom about babies. There's lots of room and I'd kind of like to have a baby brother."

"Yeah." Katy thought about that. "It's pretty cool how God worked all that out, isn't it?"

"It sure is." Keeley closed her eyes. "Thanks, God," she whispered. They lay for a few minutes, storing up memories.

"Do you think it's a sin to ask God for a four-wheeler?" Katy studied her sibling curiously.

"No, probably not a sin. But He's already given us all this." She waved a hand around. "Maybe you should wait a little bit. Like until after Thanksgiving anyway."

"Okay." Katy nodded. "But then you and I better get serious about it. Granny always says two heads are better than one." They grinned at each other, remembering how well it had worked in the past. "Besides, it's not that long till Christmas, you know!"

Epilogue

"Well, Mr. O'Toole, it looks like you've got yourself the son you wanted so badly." Maggie smiled, lifting their two-day-old baby up for Grady to lay in the nearby bassinet. "It's wonderful to be home again." She smiled at him. "I hope you're happy."

"I'm ecstatic," he told her, returning to press a kiss against her lips that only hinted at the fullness in his heart. "I have a gorgeous wife, two heartbreaker daughters and a new baby to make our joy complete. And I didn't care if he was a boy or a girl—you know that! God has given me everything I've ever dreamed of. What more could anyone want?" Grady sat down beside her on the sofa and pulled her against him, sighing with contentment.

"Mmm." Maggie relaxed against his shoulder, breathing in that strong, spicy scent that was pure Grady. "God *is* good," she agreed. "Although I think we might have some disagreement from Katy."

"Katy?" Grady sat up straight. "I thought she loved Jordan?"

"Oh, she does." Maggie smiled as she tugged him back to her. "I heard her thanking God for him tonight."

"But? There is a but, isn't there?" He looked worried, his forehead pleated in a frown. "What's wrong?"

"She really does love Jordan. They both do. But, actually, what Katy really hoped for was a four-wheeler."

Grady laughed appreciatively and then kissed his wife. "Our daughter has a lot to learn about the best things in life."

* * * * *

Dear Reader,

Okay, I admit it! I've often looked at someone else's life, home or job and wished I had it! Are we *ever* satisfied with our portion? Greener grass always beckons, and sometimes I have to remind myself to stop wasting time envying what I don't have and, truthfully, don't even need, and concentrate on the blessings I enjoy right now. When we do need something, isn't it so easy to complain and fuss instead of trusting God to supply all our needs?

There's a danger in worrying too much. We lose sight of the big picture and get bogged down in the little stuff. Stuff that we'll forget or maybe laugh over ten years down the road when our perspective has changed. Perspective means seeing the big picture, and the big picture is what most people remember after we've gone. So really, the only thing of significance is what we've done that lasts on in people's memories. When I was a child at Vacation Bible School, we carved out a verse on wood. It said "Only one life, 'twill soon be past. Only what's done for Christ will last." That's focusing on the present!

May we create memories of joy, love and gladness today in the lives of everyone we meet.

Blessings to you and yours.

Lois
Richer